A Distant Summer

A Distant Summer

Mike McNair

Edmond, OK

Acknowledgements

I wrote *A Distant Summer* because I had a story floating around in my mind that insisted upon being told. When I began writing it, I did so for my own satisfaction with no thoughts of publication. It's published because of the efforts of many people, and I'd like to thank them.

To Nancy, my wife and an avid reader. Thanks for convincing me *A Distant Summer* should be published and for your patience, encouragement, and help along the way.

To Don, my brother. Thanks for your brotherly advice, professional input, and superb editing skills. You've made me a better writer.

To Dundee, my son. Thanks for your proofreading and constructive criticism.

To Brooke, my daughter. Thanks for your enthusiasm.

To Vivian Zabel, 4RV Publishing president. Thanks for your faith in *A Distant Summer*.

To everyone else who encouraged my writing along the way. Thanks for your support.

Chapter 1

RETURN TO POTTER

W*here is that sign?*

Mike Long slowed his car and glanced across Highway 41's dual lanes. The huge Morrison Packing Company billboard that had stood at Potter's Kemp Avenue intersection fifty years ago had been replaced by a small strip mall. Only two streets remained before cornfields took over again. He braked hard, yanked the steering wheel right, and screeched onto Oak Street.

He looked about. At least some things in the little southern Indiana town that straddled the Gibson-Vanderburgh county line had stayed the same. Oak was narrow, like most Potter streets, in sharp contrast to the familiar Madison, Wisconsin multilane thoroughfares. Telephone pole posters advertising the Button Brothers' Circus Friday and Saturday, June 6 and 7 flashed by, their large red capital letters shouting, "THREE RINGS! FIVE ELEPHANTS!" Smaller, blue letters at the bottom whispered, "Special matinee for kids of all ages on Saturday."

Ahead on his right, vehicles packed a parking lot next to the Oak Street Baptist Church he'd attended as a child. He slowed, then again pressed the accelerator. The church was third on his mental agenda of sites to visit in the town of fifteen-hundred residents, behind his old elementary school and his boyhood home. Seeing them out of order would be giving in to a whim. Besides, he didn't have time to dawdle. He had only today to visit childhood sites. Tomorrow he'd pay his respects to The Commander and then rush back to Madison on Tuesday before the whole government project he was overseeing crashed down around his ears.

He'd expected to see the old two-story Potter Elementary School

1

building from several blocks away. He didn't. The tall, red-brick building had been replaced by a squat, one-story structure. A large, wooden sign next to its handicap-accessible entrance declared, "Potter Community Center built 1993," and a flagpole to the left flew both the United States and the Indiana flags. He climbed from his car and snapped a picture.

The playground matched nothing in his memory. The giant strides that used to fly him and his classmates in breathtaking circles were gone. Even the border of huge maples that once framed the schoolyard had disappeared, to be replaced by smaller trees and newer equipment. A soccer field had somehow bullied its way onto the spot where he'd played basketball. A soccer field!

His mind saw what the place looked like before the bully chased the hoops away. Boys playing basketball ran to get into the open. His own voice shouted from behind the free throw line. *I'm open! Throw me the ball!* The basketball hit his hands, and his arm stretched toward the hoop. The ball arched and scraped through the metal net at the exact instant the bell rang to end recess. *Two points! We win! We win!* Half-century-old pats landed on his back, and his legs twitched in response to the long-ago triumphant jog back to class.

An attractive woman, about his age, parked her car next to his and walked toward the spot where the old school had once stood. Her light blonde hair blew in the gentle breeze, and she brushed it back. She looked in his direction, and he quickly glanced back at the soccer field.

"Mike?"

He turned toward her.

"Mike Long?" A smile spread across her face. "It is you. I'm Mary Carpenter."

His brain cells tried to process the unfamiliar information. "Mary Carpenter?"

"Murphy. You knew me as Mary Murphy."

He smiled and walked to her. "Mary. Look at you. You haven't changed at all."

She touched his arm. "That's not like you, Mike."

"What do you mean?"

"To lie like that."

They both laughed. She opened her arms and hugged him.

Mike fidgeted with his glasses. "Good to see you. Why, I haven't seen you since—"

"Since high school." Her voice softened. "I attended all the reunions, but you never came. Why not?"

He shrugged. "I just got busy."

"I always thought it was because of that coal mine thing in fifth grade." She slapped a hand over her mouth. "I'm so sorry. I shouldn't have said that."

"That's okay. I manage." He gestured toward a park bench. "Would you like to sit?"

"Love to." She sat next to him and smoothed her slacks with her hands. "You here for The Commander's funeral?"

Mike nodded.

"Me, too. I knew his wife was trying desperately to find you. She obviously did."

"Yeah. About three weeks ago. She said she had no idea where I lived. I guess she didn't even think about Googling me." He wiped moisture from his forehead with his sleeve. "I planned to visit him in June. Susan thought he had several more months."

Mary made a face. "Cancer's a terrible thing."

"Had you seen him recently?"

"We met by chance three summers ago," she said. "We happened by Wendy's at the same time."

"How'd he look?" Mike held his hand up. "I'm sorry. I didn't mean to interrogate you. It's just that ... well, when The Commander died, I got this overwhelming feeling something was missing in my life. There've always been memory gaps about growing up here, like the eighteen missing minutes in that Watergate tape. I allowed myself this one day to see if I can find what's missing by retracing childhood steps. I figured after half a century, I owed it that much. This is my first stop."

"I don't feel interrogated. Mike, he looked great. He looked just like The Commander you knew, only older, of course. Husky. Muscular. Had a dark tan. White hair in a crew cut. He'd just retired a year earlier. He made general, you know."

Mike's eyebrows shot up. "General? I didn't know. He seemed more interested in finding out about me than discussing his accomplishments."

"He was a general in the Iraq War. Earned a ton of medals over the years. But all the while he was still The Commander. You know, down to earth. Genuine. Sincere."

"Susan seemed nice on the phone."

3

"Very. You'd really like her." Mary frowned. "What about you, Mike? What have you been up to?"

He shrugged. "There's not much to tell. I teach physics at the University of Wisconsin."

"That doesn't surprise me. You always were good at math and science."

"Well, I still can't spell," he said. "I consider the computer's spell checker to be one of man's greatest inventions."

"A physics professor." She leaned back against the bench's armrest. "Wow. I guess that means you have a Ph.D."

"Yeah. They give you one if you stay in college long enough."

She laughed. "When I got my master's in business, I swore I'd never take another college class. A Ph.D. And in physics yet. Why, that practically makes you a rocket scientist." She laughed again. It sounded just like her laugh from years ago. "I feel special. How many people can say two of their best friends became a general and a rocket scientist? Not many, I'll bet."

Mike stood and took her hands, pulling her up. "Mary, it's been special seeing you again. I hope we can visit more before I go back."

"Me, too." She glanced at his hand. "I don't see a wedding ring. Not married?"

"No. Not married."

"Never?"

"Never."

She crossed her arms and studied him. "I'm surprised. I'll never forget how caring you were when we were kids. I always pictured you becoming a loving husband and a doting father. I can't see you as a bachelor."

"Well, I almost got married once. We'd even set the date."

"What happened?"

Mike adjusted his glasses. "I don't know. It just didn't seem right somehow. What about you? Your name's Carpenter now. That must mean you're married."

"Happily. It's like a fairytale. I married a knight in shining armor and am living happily ever after. Four kids. Eight grandkids."

"That's great."

A wind gust swirled her hair, and she brushed it back. "We live in Foley, Alabama, down by Gulf Shores. My husband's a building contractor. He's pretty busy, but we usually come here every other year or so to visit or attend class reunions." She looked back at the playground. "I always come here. Guess I'm sentimental. Even with the old school building gone, there are so many memories."

He looked back at the soccer field. "Yeah, I was just remembering a few of my own."

She squeezed his hand and leaned in. "She's still here, Mike."

His gaze remained on the soccer field. "Who is?"

"Heidi Beck. She still lives here. Lives by herself in the same house she grew up in."

A heat flash scorched his face, and he tried unsuccessfully to force words from his mouth. The awkwardness that always grabbed him when someone mentioned Heidi's name when he was a kid gripped him again.

"Why, Mike Long. Are you blushing? That's sweet."

"I'm ... I'm not blushing." He swiped his sleeve across his forehead again. "It's the sun. The Indiana sun's a lot hotter than the Wisconsin sun, you know." He cleared his throat. "I guess she's married now."

"She married her junior year at Indiana University. They had a little girl, Jane. She looks a lot like Heidi."

"What about her husband?" His bluntness surprised him.

"Her marriage lasted three years. She moved back to teach fifth grade about the time Jane started school."

Mike cocked his head. "Heidi taught fifth grade here in Potter?"

"Still does. I keep telling her it's way past time to retire, but an invisible force keeps her in that fifth grade classroom. Why don't you go see her, Mike? I'm sure she'd love that."

He checked his watch. "I ... I don't know if I'll have time. I have quite a few gaps that I need to fill in, and just so much time to do it. I have this big government grant that—"

She gripped his arm. "Promise you'll think about it."

"I'll think about it."

"Promise?"

"Promise."

They hugged again, and Mike watched her drive away until she turned toward the highway and disappeared.

***

Mike rested his hand on his car's open door and stared at his birthplace. It had undergone an extreme makeover. The weathered, left-leaning garage that once protected Grandpa's 1949 Ford had disappeared, as had the gravel drive that led to it. What were those little white rocks that covered the driveway called? He smiled. Chat. That's right, chat. Back then, everyone had chat driveways.

The two huge maples that once flanked the driveway and welcomed hundreds of cackling starlings with open branches on hot, summer evenings were also missing. Now a shrub-lined asphalt drive led to a sturdy, two-car garage with beige vinyl siding and attached lights that resembled nineteenth century lanterns. A shiny, black Toyota Tundra hogged the driveway. Mike wiped his eyes with his sleeve, only this time it wasn't sweat he blotted.

The house that stood by the detached garage had a light-brown metal roof, beige siding that matched the garage, and energy-efficient windows. A marigold-lined concrete sidewalk had replaced the brick walk that once led to the screened-in porch.

Porch? The walk now ended at a deck with a large grill and a round glass table complete with umbrella. A barefooted woman in her twenties stood a few feet to its right where the peonies used to be, spraying water from a hose at her three- or four-year-old son. He squealed when the cold water splashed him and ran away to muster courage for another run-by.

The woman looked up. "Can I help you?"

Mike grabbed his camera from the passenger seat and walked toward her. "Maybe. You live here?"

She nodded, squinting to keep the morning sun from her eyes. "Are you looking for someone?"

"Well—I lived here as a child. Okay if I take pictures?"

She studied him. "Sure. I guess that'll be okay."

He snapped pictures of the house and walked toward the back. She and the little boy followed. He took a picture of one of Morrison's large barns that stood beyond the cyclone fence at the yard's back edge and pointed. "My dad used to work there." The camera found the red-brick main building, and he snapped another picture.

"That so?"

"Yeah. He started right after high school and worked there until he died."

Mike gestured down the street. "It took him three minutes to walk the two blocks to the main gate. When I was about your boy's age, I thought that was too far so I dug a shortcut under the fence to use when I grew up. Every day when my mom wasn't looking I dug with my toy shovel. One day she caught me standing by that barn petting a cow."

The woman laughed. "Don't give Kameron any ideas."

Mike adjusted a camera setting and took another picture. "She spanked me and made me fill in the hole."

"That sounds like reasonable punishment." The woman looked at her son. "He got a spanking, Kameron, so don't you try it."

Mike leaned against the cyclone fence. "My toy shovel disappeared the next day. I found it in the attic when I was a teenager, next to a set of toy drums that disappeared the following year."

He took a picture of another barn. "I assume you've gotten used to the smell."

"What smell?"

"The plant's smell." He shut off his camera. "I can still smell it. If the wind was just right when they shook hides, it was nearly impossible to breathe." He sniffed. "Smells pretty good today, though."

Kameron snuggled up to his mother, and she put her hand on his shoulder. "It always smells good."

"Really?"

"Well, it's been shut down for years."

Mike stepped back. "Wow! That's hard to believe. There must have been over fifty people working there when I was a kid. That's a big loss to a small town like this. I'll bet everyone's upset it closed."

"Not really. No one cares anymore."

"How could they not care? People need jobs."

The boy stepped away from his mother and did a somersault. He lay on his back and smiled up at her. "Very good, Kameron," she said. "That's your best one yet." She turned back to Mike. "Mister, it just got old. The owners said it got too expensive to keep it running. Did you see the new Toyota plant near Princeton?" She motioned toward where the plant stood thirteen miles to the north.

"I drove by it," he said. "It's huge."

"It's new, and they hire twenty times more people than Morrison's ever did. That's why no one cares."

"Well, it's still a shame." He surveyed the vacant plant, looking for signs of life. "So much has changed. It's hard putting everything together."

The woman pulled Kameron up from the ground after his second somersault attempt and brushed grass from his shirt. "That's okay. I understand."

He walked to the front yard and paused by his car. "Thanks for letting me take pictures. It was nice meeting you and Kameron."

"Nice meeting you, too," she said. "I enjoyed your story about the toy shovel."

He tossed the camera onto the passenger seat and drove away slowly, watching the old house, the barefooted lady, and the little boy become smaller and smaller in his rearview mirror.

***

Mike walked toward the Oak Street Baptist Church in slow motion. For years he'd recalled it in generalities, but each measured step refreshed his memory—stained glass windows, five red concrete steps leading up to the heavy oak door, and parading pigeons on the roof cooing blessings to passersby. He detected some changes. White vinyl siding had replaced the wood weatherboarding, and a simple sign in the front lawn read, "Beemer Baptist Church Thrift Store." A banner above the door announced:

Annual Clothe Thyself Day Sale
Sunday May 11
75% OFF ALL CLOTHING
Open 9:00 to 5:00

Someone had scribbled at the bottom of the banner, "Jesus saves and so can you at the Beemer Baptist Church Thrift Store."

Mike snapped three pictures of the old church from different angles as several people entered and exited it. He climbed the red steps slowly, as if to delay entering the building. Nothing, he knew, would be as it used to be. Three elderly women leaving as he entered chattered loudly about their bargains.

The morning sun highlighted figures of Christ and other religious icons in the stained glass windows, but the pews had been replaced by racks of clothing and tables of items for sale. Used appliances stood in line on the right, and television sets sat on shelves behind them. But mainly there were clothes—racks and racks of clothes. Mike's shoulders fell. He stood motionless as he watched the crowd.

"May I help you?"

A petite lady in her mid-fifties, wearing black jeans and white Nikes, approached him. Auburn hair accented an attractive face. Like the other workers, she sported a cranberry-colored shirt with *Beemer Baptist Church* embroidered in white above the front pocket.

Mike smiled. "No, thanks. Just looking."

"Let me know if you need help." She turned to leave.

"Wait. Maybe you can help me."

"Yes?"

"I attended church here when—well, when it was a church. Whatever happened to the Beemers? And the church? Is there a new one somewhere?"

"Yes, it's in the Beemer Hills addition by Lake Stella," she said. "But I wouldn't call it new, Mister ... "

"Long. Mike Long."

"Mike Long," she repeated, frowning. A large lady elbowed him as she yanked a bargain sweater from another shopper, and he almost lost his balance.

"Listen, I know you're busy. I'll just look around."

"Don't worry about the crowd. The others will take care of them. At Beemer Baptist we put individuals ahead of the multitude. It's good to meet you, Mike. My name's Louise Cruthers-Wallace."

"Pleased to meet you." He shook her hand.

"Do you still have family around here?"

"No. My parents were killed in a car accident my senior year in high school."

"Oh ... I'm sorry," she said. "When did you leave?"

"In 1961, when I graduated from Potter High."

Preacher Louise let out a short, high-pitched whistle. "That was a long time ago. Do you visit often?"

"No. This is the first time. I'm here for a funeral tomorrow."

"I'm sorry something sad brings you back. You must be here for the military officer's funeral."

"That's right. He was a friend."

She stepped back as several women approached. "You asked about the church," she said after the last woman passed by. "It's called the

9

Beemer Baptist Church now. It was built in 1969, but I think of it as always being there."

"And the Beemers?"

"They're both dead. They reached out to sinners until the day they died, and the congregation finally got too large for this building. I was fifteen when they built the new church, and I knew just what I wanted to do with my life—preach at that church. They helped me through college and gave me my first call in 1981. My only call. My husband preaches there, too."

Mike watched the activity. "This place looks successful."

"Oh, it is. This is one of the Beemers' innovations. It's all about self-esteem, helping others, sharing, volunteering, and spreading the good word about our Lord. All the workers are volunteers from our church." She pointed to the front of the thrift store. "You wanted to know what happened to the Beemers. That display tells all about them."

Mike peered over the clothes racks. "Over there?"

"That's right. And don't hesitate to ask other questions. Remember—individuals ahead of the multitude."

That motto echoed in his mind as he approached the display. He slowed and then stopped altogether as he remembered something that happened here sixty some years earlier. He was a five-year-old, wearing blue slacks and a white and blue Polo shirt, talking with another kid with curly blond hair and prominent freckles. What was his name? The boy had lived in Potter for less than a year before his dad was transferred out of state. Timmy? No, Tommy. Tommy Simons. His family was rich, and Tommy had everything a five-year-old kid could want. He delighted in flaunting his wealth by parading his all-white pony through the town's streets, its silver saddle bells jingling with each step.

***

Sunday school had just ended. While the other kids ran upstairs to show their parents their crayon-scribbled renditions of Jesus and his disciples, Mike and Tommy talked in the hallway by their classroom door.

"I'm going to ride Trotter after church." Tommy adjusted his tie and brushed his pants. "You don't have a pony, do you?"

What would riding a real pony be like? Mike had ridden a pony once at the county fair, but that didn't count. A fat man in a straw hat led

10

the pony around in a small circle. Trotter, on the other hand, moved as fast as his name implied and followed the rider's commands, not the monotonous commands of a slow-footed man. Maybe Tommy planned to invite him over to ride Trotter after dinner.

"No, I don't," Mike said. He waited for the invitation.

"I know why you don't have a pony."

"Why?"

"Because your family can't afford one. My parents are rich."

Tommy's remark stung, like the tightly-packed snowball that exploded unexpectedly against his cheekbone during last winter's neighborhood snowball fight. Mike considered his options for responding to the insult and selected the "I couldn't care less" approach.

"I don't have a pony because I don't like them. They're dumb."

"You don't have a pony because your parents are poor."

The "I couldn't care less" approach wasn't working. Mike stomped his foot. "My parents are rich. They're millionaires. I could have a hundred ponies if I wanted. Dad wanted to buy me a pony again today, but I told him I didn't want one because they're dumb. And smelly. And people who ride them smell, too. Dad's going to build a ranch next week and buy a thousand horses. He's going to put up a sign that says 'No ponies allowed' because he doesn't want the ranch to smell. Then you'll see."

Something made Mike look up. A thin man in a blue suit and white shirt walked briskly toward them. Preacher Beemer! Silence replaced Mike's claims of wealth.

Preacher Beemer looked at the other boy. "You'd better go upstairs now, Tommy. I'm sure your parents are wondering where you are." Tommy quickly disappeared.

As Mike attempted to follow, Preacher Beemer stuck out his arm and snagged him. "Whoa, young man. Why don't you stay and talk with me for a while?"

Mike stared at the floor. "What about?"

"Oh, I don't know. How about ... ponies? You don't hate ponies, do you, Mike?"

Just as he'd feared, Preacher Beemer had overheard their conversation. Mike shook his head.

"You lied when you said that, didn't you?"

Mike nodded.

"In fact, you'd like to own a pony, wouldn't you?"

He nodded again.

"Mike, look at me. You also lied when you said your parents are millionaires and your dad is going to build a ranch, didn't you?"

Tears snaked down Mike's face. He refused to look at the preacher, but managed to nod once more. He heard footsteps and saw Mrs. Beemer walking toward them. "Jacob," she said in a whispered shout, "you're late. It's past time to start the service."

Mike felt relieved. Being caught in a lie was bad enough, but having to talk about it with the preacher was even worse. Now at least Preacher Beemer would leave, and he wouldn't have to talk about the lie anymore.

The preacher turned to his wife. "I'll be there as soon as I can. An individual needs me now. You take care of the multitude, and if I'm not there in time for the sermon, bless the congregation with your singing."

"Good luck." She walked back up the stairs, and her footsteps became fainter and fainter.

Preacher Beemer continued God's work. "You're embarrassed because I caught you in a lie, aren't you?"

"Yes." Mike wiped tears from his eyes.

You thought you and Tommy were the only two here. There were three of you here, son—the two of you and God. God is everywhere. He hears every truth and every lie you tell. Did you know that?"

"Yes, sir."

"Mike, I'm always upstairs getting things ready long before Sunday school lets out. I never leave until I finish the service. Today I left and came here. I didn't know why then, but I now know God sent me. He knew one of his fine little boys was in trouble—telling lies—and he wanted me to talk with that boy."

"I'm sorry I lied. I won't do it again. I promise."

Preacher Beemer pointed toward the heavens. "Don't promise me, son. Promise God."

Mike looked at the ceiling. "I promise I won't lie again, God."

The Preacher took the hanky from his lapel pocket and wiped Mike's tears. "There, there. No more crying. God forgives you. In John chapter eight verses thirty-one and thirty-two Jesus says, 'If ye continue in my word ... ye shall know the truth, and the truth shall make you free.'"

Mike wasn't sure what that meant. But if it meant he didn't have to talk about the lie anymore, it sounded pretty good to him.

Mrs. Beemer was singing when they joined the church service. She sounded like an angel must sound. Preacher Beemer took his usual chair by the pulpit, and Mike slid in between his parents. His mother leaned toward him and whispered, "Where were you?"

Mike fidgeted. "The preacher stopped by—"

"Well, that explains it." She lowered her voice even more. "He can certainly get long-winded. You haven't missed anything here. His wife's been showing off her voice for the last ten minutes. Too bad she can't sing half as well as she thinks she can."

The preacher smiled. Mike was sure he smiled just at him, and he liked the idea of being set free by the truth. It was like having a special secret only he, Preacher Beemer, and God knew. Mike smiled back.

At the end of the service the Long family joined the large crowd to shake hands with Preacher and Mrs. Beemer. His mom hugged the preacher's wife. "Mrs. Beemer, thank you so much for singing those extra songs. I always look forward to hearing you sing. Your beautiful voice just fills my heart with love."

"Thank you, Mrs. Long. You always say the nicest things."

She shook the preacher's hand. "Preacher Beemer, you did it again. I look so forward to church because I always learn something when you preach. And you make it so interesting, too."

"Why, thank you, Mrs. Long." He turned to Mike. "What about you, young man? Did you learn anything today?"

"Yes, sir." Mike had learned a very important lesson. God could be in the room even if you don't see Him, and He isn't above informing someone in charge if He catches you lying.

"Good. Glad to hear it, and that's no lie." He winked and shook hands with the people behind them.

***

"Do you have any more children's coats?" a heavyset woman yelled at one of the thrift shop workers.

"No, that's all we have," the worker yelled back.

Mike chuckled over the long-forgotten memory and continued on to the Beemer display, a very professional-looking mini museum. Pictures of the preacher and his wife with various congregation members lined the wall under the words THE BEEMER YEARS. One showed Preacher Beemer baptizing converts at Lake Dundee. Seeing it brought back to

13

Mike the feeling of helplessness that overtook him when fully submerged, and the euphoria that greeted him when the preacher pulled him safely back up, cleansed of all sins. Another picture captured Preacher Beemer speaking from the pulpit. Mike could almost hear his voice and sense his humor. Still another showed Stella Beemer playing the organ and singing. She was indeed one of God's angels. A final picture froze in time the Little Christian Soldiers Youth Group on a hayride, probably one he was on. The laughing boy toward the wagon's front reminded him how he looked in those days.

Artifacts in a glass case included Preacher Beemer's Bible opened to a page showing detailed handwritten notes, his watch and fob, collection plates, old hymnbooks, programs from the early days, and a cardboard fan that sported a Popsicle-stick-like handle and featured a picture of the old Weber Funeral Home.

Two white marble pedestals supported bronze busts of the Beemers, evidently made in their later years but resembling the younger Beemers he knew. Inscribed on a gold plaque at the bottom of the busts was:

Jacob Michael Beemer
Servant of God
March 2, 1913 – June 18, 1991

Stella Mae Beemer
Servant of God
August 21, 1913 – October 10, 1996

Mike stood between the busts and placed his arms around them. "Thanks for all the lessons. I appreciate everything you did for me." He winked at Preacher Beemer's likeness. "And that's no lie." He took pictures of the exhibit. It wasn't yet noon, and he had already made the first three stops.

Mike went outside. As he opened his car door to leave, he heard a fluttering sound. A pigeon flew from the church roof, landed ten feet in front of him, and strutted in semicircles. He stared at the cooing pigeon's white, black, and purple markings.

"Squall Baby?" he said aloud.

Like a catalyst beginning an abrupt reaction in a scientist's lab, the pigeon sighting replaced the present with memories of Squall Baby and his own 1954 fifth grade world.

Chapter 2

THE ENTIRE CLASS

M ike's flu bug yesterday spoiled his fifth-grade perfect attendance record, an accomplishment that would have pleased
his teacher. She hadn't missed a teaching day in over fifteen years. Since
she forced herself to come to school whether sick or not, she expected the
same from her students. "If you're not dead or in the hospital," she often
told them, "I expect you in this room working hard on your schoolwork."

Mike finished his Cheerios and walked the block to Jim Mackey's
house. Jim's yard was a menagerie. He had nursed Quackers, a male mal-
lard duck, back to health after finding it with a broken wing last summer
at Jeb Johnson's farm pond. Jeb was so impressed with how Jim took care
of Quackers, he gave him an old horse trough he had laying around for
the duck to use as a swimming pool. Jim built a large platform on one side
of the trough from lumber salvaged from the town dump for Quackers
to relax on when not swimming. He nailed an eight-foot long, twelve inch
wide board to the platform—Jim called it "the waddle way"—for easy
access from the ground.

The duck always swaggered up to Mike, quacking and wagging his
tail like a dog. Doodles, a big green-tailed red rooster that just showed up
one day and decided to stay, was subtler. He pecked invisible but apparently
delicious morsels off the ground, following a trail that usually ended within
a foot of where Mike was petting Quackers, and Mike would pet him, too.

Jim also had about a dozen barn pigeons. Squall Baby, one of those
pigeons, was the Dale Evans of barn pigeons. Queen of the Cowgirls at
the local theater's Saturday movie matinee, Dale teamed with her King of
the Cowboys husband Roy Rogers to bring bad men to justice. While the
others behaved like the birds they were, Squall Baby acted almost human.

Why, she should have her own television show like Lassie did.

Mike often pictured the show's opening. Jim walks into the yard, places his hands around his mouth, and yells, "Squall Baby! Squall Baby!" The camera pans skyward, focusing on a dot that gets bigger and bigger until the viewer can tell it's a bird, then a pigeon, and finally a white, black, and purple pigeon, the special markings that distinguish Squall Baby from all the other pigeons. She lands on his shoulder. She has answered her master's call and is ready for another adventure.

Squall Baby could do everything Lassie could do. She could find lost children, bring criminals to justice, and reunite long-lost relatives. Her ability to fly gave her a special view of the world Lassie could only dream of. It would make a fantastic television program.

"Hey, Mike. Come on over. I just have to finish feeding and watering the birds."

Mike joined Jim and watched him dump the old water and add fresh. "You should've seen Squall Baby last night." Jim placed the fresh water in her cage. "I laughed until my stomach hurt. Even my ears hurt."

Squall Baby was always doing something funny, brave, or mysterious. "What did she do this time?" He smiled in anticipation.

"Well, when I fed the pigeons, she danced and cooed for them. It was like she thought she was Patti Page. The other birds watched as they ate, like they had their own dinner theater. After they finished eating, she bowed and ate her own food. My stomach still hurts just thinking about it."

The pigeons pecked at the fresh wheat and crushed corn. Last evening's performance must have tired Squall Baby because this time she ate with the rest of them. "I wish I had a pigeon," Mike said.

"No problem." Jim dried his hands on his jeans. "You can have one from the next batch."

Jim got his birds by climbing into barn lofts in the middle of the night and grabbing them while he blinded them with his flashlight. He stuffed them into a burlap bag for safekeeping until he got home.

"Thanks, but you know my mom. No way will she allow a filthy animal near our house." He watched Jim continue his pigeon chores. "You about ready? It's getting late."

"Yeah, I'm done. Let's go." Jim turned toward the house and shouted, "Bye, Mom. Bye, Betsy. Bye, Grandma. Don't forget—I'll be home late tonight." Jim's mother, grandma, and his four-year-old sister waved from the living room picture window.

"I didn't know your grandma was here," Mike said as the boys began the ten-block walk to school.

"Yeah. She came on the train yesterday. She wants us to live with her in Louisville. She says it's too much for Mom to support Betsy and me by herself."

"Do you want to go?"

"Are you kidding?" Jim said. "She lives in an apartment. No room for ducks or chickens or pigeons. Or adventures. And what would become of Squall Baby?"

"I'd take her."

"Right. You just said your mom wouldn't let you have a pigeon."

"She might if it were Squall Baby."

"I don't think so. Until she understands Squall Baby's special, she'll never let you keep her."

Two robins hopped in the neighbor's yard. Mike had first sighted a flock of fifteen or so a couple weeks earlier, in mid-February, and now they were all over the place. They must have brought summer with them because the warm weather that arrived that day never left.

"Why are you going to be home late?"

"That's right," Jim said. "You missed the whole thing. Miss Schneider's keeping the entire class after school for punishment."

"The entire class? Why would she do that?"

"She walked into class as Skip was imitating her. He sounds just like her, you know. Walks like her, too. Well, he was by her desk going through all these motions, and everyone was laughing, when she walked in. She's punishing us by making us sit without talking for a full hour after school."

"A full hour? Boy, I'm glad I was sick yesterday. We're going to Princeton after school. Grandpa and I will sip strawberry sodas at Castle Drugstore while Mom shops. He always gives me a dime to buy a comic."

"That sounds like fun."

"I'll think about you while I drink my soda and read my comic."

Jim made a face. "Thanks. You're a real pal."

When the two reached Potter Elementary School, a full bike rack showed most of the kids were already inside. The bell had not yet rung when Mike and Jim entered the room. Miss Schneider wasn't there, but the students sat quietly, either staring straight ahead or working on schoolwork.

Each year Miss Schneider divided her students into three work

18

groups based upon intelligence. After checking their handwriting for neatness, she had them read a paragraph aloud, answer ten geography questions, spell twenty hard words, and solve ten math problems. Within a week she knew exactly how smart each student was and seated them in descending order of intelligence. She arranged five rows of student desks five desks deep and placed the smartest students in the row closest to the door and the dumbest ones in the row way over by the windows. No boy had ever made it into the smart row, and no girl had ever been placed in the dumb row. That's just the way life was in her fifth grade classroom.

Each work group had a name. Miss Schneider's sister, Margie Culpepper, who lived in Carbondale, Illinois, painted pictures that showed the type of students sitting in each row. According to Miss Schneider, her sister was married to a chemical engineer and had the most handsome, intelligent, and talented child in the world. He was a fifth grader, just like they were, only much smarter.

One thing was for sure. Her sister was a very good artist. Miss Schneider placed the pictures on each of the front desks. The smart row of five students was named the Busy Bees, and their picture showed a beehive, flowers, and five very busy bees working hard on a beautiful summer day. Two flew away from the hive, two flew toward the hive with legs covered with pollen, and one gathered nectar from a flower's bloom. The bees were working hard to prepare for their future.

She referred to the five students who made up the dumb row as the Lazy Grasshoppers. That row's picture showed five grasshoppers being lazy on a late autumn day. Three slept on the colorful leaf-covered grass, another lay on the ground, its head resting on one of its hands, and the last one reclined in a hammock, watching leaves float from a tree. Those grasshoppers did nothing to prepare for a future that would soon become the present.

She placed everyone else in descending rank of intelligence in the middle three rows. Miss Schneider called this group the Happy Butterflies. The three front desk paintings depicted butterflies flitting from flower to flower on a sunny summer day. To Mike, their fate seemed no better than that of the grasshoppers. Both species would be dead by winter when the bees would be relaxing in their hive, sipping honey.

Although there were always five students in the Busy Bee and Lazy Grasshopper rows, the number of students in the Happy Butterfly section varied depending upon the class size. If someone from the smart row moved away, the girl closest to that row in the Happy Butterfly section moved up to make it complete. If someone from the dumb row moved away, the Happy Butterfly boy closest to it moved down. Mike sat in the middle seat of the middle row of the butterfly section, while Jim occupied the last seat of that row.

The bell rang to begin class. Miss Schneider was still not there, yet no one spoke. Mike scanned the room.

Heidi Beck sat in the Busy Bee row's first seat. She was much more than just the smartest person in the class. Petite with short black wavy hair, sparkling black eyes, and a deep tan, she was the prettiest girl, too. And the sweetest. She was perfect. Mike knew that ever since first grade.

Their eyes met. Mike turned quickly, knocking a book from his desktop. It landed on the wooden floor with a bang, forcing a sudden rush of heat to his face.

Just behind Heidi sat Mary Murphy, her best friend. With long blonde hair and blue eyes, she was arguably the class's second best looking girl. Heidi whispered to Mary, and both smiled before looking straight ahead again as they waited for their teacher.

Mike's mind continued to wander. His brown hair, brown eyes, and glasses made him look ordinary. If he looked like some of the other boys in his class, there'd be a better chance that Heidi would like him as much as he liked her. Jim Mackey's curly black hair, for example, made him stand out.

Tony James, who sat in the first seat in Mike's row, had brown hair and eyes, too, but he wore his hair in a nifty crew cut, was very good looking, towered half a head over the rest of the boys, and was athletic. All the girls followed him around at recess and practically swooned if he looked in their direction.

Even Skip Gander, who sat in the Lazy Grasshopper row's next-to-last seat, had more going for him in the looks department than Mike did. His red hair, green eyes, and freckles made him look like a cute Howdy Doody. On the other hand, he was embedded deep into Lazy Grasshopper territory, not exactly a selling point to the opposite sex. At least he was smart enough to avoid imitating Miss Schneider today. He sat with his hands folded, staring at something through the window.

Jerry Harders sat behind him in the Lazy Grasshopper's caboose seat. He had failed two times and was thirteen years old. His dishwater blond hair always needed washing and cutting, and the overlong hair on the back of his neck curled and looked wormlike. He was big boned and heavyset, and his belly often tested his faded shirts' strength and his buttons' willpower. He loved to call kids names, trip them, and elbow them in the stomach. And he was clumsy. Almost every week he came to school with a bruise somewhere from falling down or walking into something.

Miss Schneider entered the classroom, and all the students sat a little straighter. She walked briskly to her desk and stood with her hands on her hips.

Shirley Schneider stood nearly six feet tall and was just about that big around. She forced her coal black hair into a perpetual bun and always wore a white blouse and a dark skirt that touched her black shoes. She was at least forty years old and maybe even as ancient as fifty or more.

"That's better," she said. "That's how you should act when I am out of the room." She paced in front of her desk a couple of times with her head down as if trying to gather her thoughts.

She looked up. "Children, the principal will be here soon to see how you are progressing. He's happy when students answer questions correctly because that means they're learning. You want Mr. Jackson to be happy, don't you?"

"Yes, Miss Schneider," the class answered in unison.

"Good. When he comes in, you'll be working on your math. He has some school rules to talk about first. Then I'll ask you some math questions. Raise your hand if you want to show Mr. Jackson how much you know."

All the students raised their hands.

"Very good. Okay now, to show Mr. Jackson you are learning, I want all of you to raise your hand each time I ask a math question. If you are one hundred percent sure you know the answer, raise your right hand. If you are less than one hundred percent sure, raise your left hand. I will call on you only if you raise your right hand. Is that clear?"

"Yes, Miss Schneider," the class said.

"Lazy Grasshoppers, which hand should you raise if you don't know the answer?"

"Our left hand," the five said together.

"Good. Now, grasshoppers, when I say 'three' I want each of you to raise your left hand. Ready? One. Two. Three."

Everyone in the dumb row raised his left hand at the same time.

"Good. Good. I see our practice last week paid off. Now, everyone take out your math book, a piece of paper, and a pencil. Turn to page 193 and work on problems one through fifteen."

Eldon Jackson, the principal, was in his early forties and a slender six foot three. A distinguished-looking man with wavy blond hair and blue eyes, he had an old war injury that caused him to limp. The kids respected him, and it was no secret the hearts of many women fluttered when he was near.

Perhaps because of his military background, he believed strongly in a no-nonsense approach to discipline. He did his best to help students make the right choices, or at least avoid making the same wrong ones twice. To that end, the Board of Education, as he called it, hung prominently on his office wall. All the students knew if they made bad choices, they'd likely be called to his office to meet with the Board of Education.

They also knew Mr. Jackson paddled students until they cried and continued until they stopped crying. He usually had to take only two swats, since most kids started crying the instant the Board of Education hit its target the first time and stopped the instant it landed the second time. Very few wrongdoers could say if it hurt or not because they were too busy calculating the crying cycle's beginning and ending to notice.

Mr. Jackson entered the room, stood by the door for several seconds, and jotted something in a notebook.

"Children," Miss Schneider said, "Mr. Jackson has come to visit us. Aren't we all happy to see him?"

"Yes, Miss Schneider," the class said.

Mr. Jackson set his notebook on Miss Schneider's desk. "It's good to see you all so hard at work. I have just a couple of things to say, and then I'll let you get back to your studies.

"First, now that March is almost here, more of you are riding bicycles to school. I want to remind you not to ride them on Main because that street's just too busy. If you do, you'll receive a paddling, no questions asked. Does everyone understand?"

The class answered with a murmur of yeses.

"Good. Now, one more thing. Someone is stealing items, including money, from classrooms. This must stop. I'll deal harshly with anyone caught stealing. If you know of anyone who is stealing, tell me right away so I can deal with it. Knowing someone is doing something terribly wrong and not informing proper authorities is also terribly wrong. Stealing is just plain wrong, and we must do everything we can to stop it."

Mr. Jackson picked up his notebook, walked to the back of the room, and sat in a chair Miss Schneider had provided for him. He opened the book and took out a pen. Miss Schneider picked up a piece of chalk from the tray behind her desk.

"Children, it's time to review our math." She wrote the number 495,784 on the blackboard and turned to the class. Skip's right hand waved frantically. She ignored him and looked at the Busy Bee row.

Skip emitted noises. "Ooooh. Ooooh." Miss Schneider folded her arms and stared at him. He continued waving his hand.

"Skip," she said, finally. "You want to tell us what this number is?"

He lowered his hand. "No, ma'am."

"Then what in the world do you want?"

"I have a question."

"What?"

"How do you know where to put it?"

Miss Schneider frowned. "Put what, Skip?"

"The comma. How do you know where to put the comma? Do you just guess?"

"No, you don't just guess. Three, Skip."

He scratched his head. "Three what?"

"You always put the comma exactly three places to the left." She touched the 4, 8, and 7 with the chalk and counted. "One, two, three, comma. If you'd pay attention when I teach these concepts, you'd know how to do the work."

"I do pay attention. I just forget sometimes. Three places. The comma always goes exactly three places to the left."

"Now that we've established where the comma goes, who knows what this number is?"

All hands shot up.

"Heidi?"

"Four hundred ninety-five thousand, seven hundred eighty-four."

"That's correct, Heidi. Very good." Miss Schneider wrote more six-digit numbers on the board—with the comma inserted exactly three places to the left—and students provided the correct answers.

She wrote one last number, 212,123, and eyed the grasshoppers. All of them had their hands in the air, but only Skip had his right hand up. She stood silent for a long time. "Skip, what is the answer?"

The other students lowered their hands. Skip looked around the

23

room. His entire body trembled.

"The ... the number is ... "

Skip stared blankly at the blackboard.

"The number is ... "

Now he looked Miss Schneider straight in the eye.

"The number is two hundred twelve thousand, one hundred twenty-three. And the comma goes exactly three places to the left."

Every student in Miss Schneider's class applauded. A few butterflies stood, and before long every student in the classroom was part of a standing ovation, the likes of which Mike was sure had never before been seen in a Potter classroom.

Gradually the students sat, and the clapping ended. Skip sat back, and the tenseness left his body. This may have been the only time in his life he had been acknowledged in a positive way for something academic. Miss Schneider sighed, "Very good."

She placed the chalk on the tray and moved toward the class. "Children, it's time to review for our upcoming geometrical figures test. If there's something you don't understand, now's the time to ask about it. Who wants to ask the first question?"

Don't fall for this. It's a trap! Miss Schneider doesn't like students to ask questions. If you ask a question she'll just say you should have paid attention when she taught it. Don't raise your hand.

No one moved.

"Come, come now, children. Surely someone has a question. Remember, there are no dumb questions."

Her saying "there are no dumb questions" apparently gave Tony the courage to raise his hand.

"Yes, Tony. What is your question?"

Tony lowered his hand slowly and talked in a soft, hesitant voice. "I don't quite understand the difference between finding the area of a square and the area of a rectangle."

Mike closed his eyes to block out the massacre about to take place. Tony was going to catch it big time for asking about something she'd already taught the class. She'd certainly consider that a dumb question. *They're the same. There is no difference. A square is a rectangle.*

Miss Schneider walked to the board and picked up a piece of chalk. "That is a very good question, Tony. Let me explain it by beginning with the rectangle. You find its area by multiplying the base times the height."

24

She presented several examples on the board. "The base and height of a square are the same. Therefore, if you know either one, you simply multiply it by itself." Again, she showed examples on the board.

"Do you understand how to do these problems now?"

"Yes, ma'am."

She eyed the class with one eyebrow slightly raised. "Are there any other questions?"

Student after student developed enough courage to ask a question. Each time, Miss Schneider answered it. Never before had she seemed so patient, so understanding, so ... humanlike. Even when Skip asked about the difference between a circle and an oval, she explained it patiently without raising her voice or telling him to pay attention next time.

Mike was so wrapped up in the unbelievable experience of watching Miss Schneider answer students' questions, and with a smile no less, he barely noticed Mr. Jackson leave. Something he thought would never happen was about to become a reality. He was going to ask Miss Schneider a question about something he didn't understand. He raised his hand.

"Yes, Mike?"

"I have a question. I know you find a circle's circumference by multiplying the diameter by pi. And I know pi is 3.14. What I don't understand is why. Why is pi 3.14 and how was it discovered if you multiplied 3.14 times the diameter, you'd end up with the circumference? Why does it work?"

Mike grasped his pencil in preparation to record her answer.

Miss Schneider's right hand found her hip. "What difference does it make why it works and how it was discovered? All you need to know is it works and how to use it."

She closed her book and laid it on her desk. "Okay class. That's it. When you start asking dumb questions, it's time to go on to something else." The smile was gone.

Mike slumped in his seat. She had answered everyone's question but his. His question must have really been dumb for her not to even want to answer it. Maybe he hadn't paid as much attention as he should have when she explained how pi worked, but he wasn't trying to ask dumb questions. It was just that everything relating to finding the areas and perimeters of squares, rectangles, and triangles was logical. But with this circumference thing, pi just seemed to come from nowhere and make no sense.

He couldn't keep the tears back. He blotted them with the back of his hands and hoped no one noticed. She'd never again trick him into asking a question. She could beg and plead with him to ask a question, but he wouldn't. Why, he'd become as dumb as Skip before he'd ask her another question.

At recess, Mike sat in the grass by himself. He didn't feel like playing softball or basketball. He didn't even feel like talking. He was so angry and embarrassed he didn't notice Heidi walking toward him until she sat in the grass in front of him.

"Hi, Mike. Are you okay?"

Seeing her made him feel even more embarrassed. "Aren't you ashamed to be seen talking to someone as dumb as I am?"

"You're not dumb. You're one of the best math students in our class. I'm proud to be seen talking to someone brave enough to ask Miss Schneider a good math question."

"Yeah, right. How can it be a good question if Miss Schneider said it was dumb? She answered everyone's question but mine." He pulled out pieces of grass and threw them back at the ground, repeating the process several times.

"All I know is I came over here to thank you for asking that question. I always wondered the same thing. Why does pi work? I was disappointed Miss Schneider didn't answer your question."

"Really? You don't know either?" If she doesn't know, and she's the smartest person in class, most of the others probably don't know, either. Maybe it wasn't such a dumb question.

"Want to swing with me?" Heidi stood and offered her hand.

He reached out—then hesitated. She probably did know how pi worked and was just saying she didn't to make him feel better. Maybe he was the only one in the room except for Skip who didn't understand how it worked. Maybe he was dumb. He pulled his hand back and placed it on the grass. "No. You go ahead. I think I'll just sit here for a while."

She walked to the swings. Tony took the swing next to her, and they talked and laughed as Mike sat on the ground and watched. The more fun they had, the worse he felt. He never realized before that it was possible to feel both anger and loneliness at the same time. Someday he'd do something to make her proud. At the moment, however, that day seemed far away.

***

Mike looked at the clock for the tenth time since the class came in from afternoon recess. It was thirteen minutes after three. Two more minutes and the bell would ring to end the school day, and what a confusing day it had been. Miss Schneider said his question was dumb, and Heidi called him brave. At least he didn't have to stay after school like everyone else. He'd soon be on his way to Princeton to sip strawberry sodas with Grandpa.

The bell rang, and the rest of the class remained in their seats where they would stay for the next hour as punishment for their terrible behavior yesterday. Mike took his math and English books and a couple of makeup worksheets from his desk and walked toward the coatroom.

"Mike, where are you going?"

He paused and faced Miss Schneider. "I'm going home." He assumed she'd say, "Have a good evening," or maybe even "Sorry I said your question was dumb. It was really a very good question. You are a brave young man."

"Home? You can't go home. Have you forgotten? The entire class is to stay after school for acting so terrible yesterday." She folded her arms and tapped her left foot.

He stammered. "But ... but I didn't act terrible yesterday. I wasn't even in school. I was home sick." Heidi sat less than two feet from where he stood. Her face was expressionless. He fidgeted with his glasses. "No one said anything to me about staying after school."

Miss Schneider didn't say anything, and Mike stepped toward the coatroom.

"Mike, you're being punished along with the rest of the class."

He turned. "What? Why am I being punished?" The loudness of his voice startled him.

"I said I am punishing the entire class, and you are a member of this class, are you not?"

"Well, I ... I ... "

"Mike. Answer my question. Are you a member of this class?"

He hung his head. "Yes."

"Had you been here yesterday, you would have acted up like everyone else. Don't try to tell me you wouldn't have. That's why you're being punished. You are being punished for the way you would have acted had you been here." She pointed to his desk. "Sit."

"But—"

"Don't 'but' me, young man." She still pointed to his desk.

It was all over. Once she called a boy "young man" or a girl "young lady," it was useless to try to reason with her. That was her way of saying she had made up her mind, and God Himself wouldn't be able to change it.

"I'll have to call my mom to tell her I'll be late," Mike said.

"You are not going to call home now. You should have made arrangements earlier like everyone else."

"I couldn't let her know earlier. I just now found out about it."

"I'm sorry, Mike. It's time for the entire class to sit for one hour without talking, and it would be selfish of you to make them wait while you made a personal telephone call. I'm sure they want to get their punishment over with as soon as possible."

Mike sat. *This isn't fair; this isn't fair; this isn't fair.* He was being punished for something he didn't do. He couldn't go to Princeton. Mom and Grandpa would worry about him. His mom had told him to come home right after school. He'd get into trouble again at home for something he didn't even do. *This isn't fair; this isn't fair; this isn't fair.*

Miss Schneider dismissed the class at fourteen minutes after four. Mike walked as quickly as he could through the hallways, down the stairs, and out the door. He ran the ten blocks home where his mom and his grandpa waited for him on the front porch. Martha Long was dressed up, ready for her shopping trip to the county seat. A small white hat perched on her newly permed black hair, which appeared even darker than usual. Beads, a white belt, and white gloves accented her outfit. Her right hand clutched a small, finely-beaded purse.

As usual, Grandpa wore overalls.

She stared at him. "Well, it's about time you got home. Didn't I tell you to come right home?"

Mike dropped his books and bent over with his hands on his knees, trying to catch his breath. He started to say something, but instead waved his left hand and continued to breathe deeply. Finally, he managed, "Miss Schneider kept everyone after school. She wouldn't let me call."

His mom sniffed. "I know all about it. I called the school to see why you weren't home, and talked with her. She said the entire class acted up yesterday, and had you been there, you would have behaved just like the rest of them. How do you think that makes me feel? Here I am—the vice president of the PTA—and the only thing that keeps you from causing trouble in school is being home sick."

"Martha, don't." Grandpa stood from the swing and took her arm.

She pushed his hand aside. "You stay out of this, Grandpa. Mike is my son, and I'll raise him right. It's time he showed some respect. I don't know if he would have acted up in class yesterday or not, but his very own teacher who has had him in class all year thinks he would have. That's what concerns me. She wouldn't think that if he'd behaved perfectly all year."

Grandpa thrust his arms in the air.

"Sometimes I think you hang out with that Jim Mackey and his filthy animals too much. He doesn't have a father, and his mother just lets him run wild."

"But Mom, I didn't do anything wrong."

"Maybe not. But Miss Schneider, who knows you better than any-one else outside of your family, thinks you would have. You need to start acting in a manner that makes her think you're going to behave. Grandpa and I are going to Princeton as planned. When your father gets home, you tell him how badly your teacher thinks you would have acted yesterday."

"Let's go," she said to Grandpa, and they walked to the car. Soon they were out of sight.

This isn't fair. I wasn't even in school yesterday. I'm being punished twice for something I didn't even do once.

Chapter 3

THE SECRET MISSION

"Agent Ekim, are you ready to begin the mission?"

Mike stood taller. "I'm ready, Agent Mij. I have the box."

Mike and Jim turned to the third member of the secret trio, the only female taking part in today's dangerous mission. "Are you ready, Agent Ysteb?"

"I'm ready, Agent Mij. I'll wait here for the message."

"Then we're off." Agent Mij took the box from Agent Ekim, and the two left on their secret mission.

Mike and Jim loved being secret agents, and Betsy usually pretended along with them. Although not yet five, she made a good secret agent. She was smart and funny, and her blonde hair formed little curls that reminded Mike of Shirley Temple. The old Buster Brown shoebox Jim carried contained Squall Baby. The top, which was secured by string, had about a dozen holes punched in it.

Jim held the box high. "Listen to her coo. She's ready for the mission."

The boys' destination was the schoolyard. They could choose from two routes—the normal way, which consisted of ten blocks of sidewalks, and the secret woods way. They usually took the normal way. But if they weren't in a hurry or if they were on a mission, they usually went through the secret woods, which had winding trails and a small creek that was home to minnows, crawdads, leeches, and other exotic wildlife. A small peninsula provided a place for two boys to rest and talk—three if one didn't mind getting a foot wet.

They walked two blocks to Waterworks Road and turned right. A hundred yards later they turned left, trotted across a rocky field, and entered the secret woods. The groundcover was just leafing out, making it difficult for communists to find decent hiding places. Still, Mike and Jim walked slowly with darting eyes.

A noise! Mike thrust his arm against Jim's chest and pressed a finger to his lips. He slowly pointed at a big basswood tree fifty yards ahead. Mike kicked loose a baseball-size rock from the path's edge and threw it at the basswood. It hit with an echoing thud. Something jumped and climbed up the tree. A squirrel. The boys sighed with relief and continued their careful walk through the woods. They saw several birds and a rabbit, but not a single communist.

Thick briars lined the woods' edge next to the railroad tracks. Mike moved two branches that hid an opening and slipped through. He held the branches until Jim crawled through, carrying Squall Baby in the shoebox. He let go, and the opening disappeared.

They climbed up the rocky bank to the railroad tracks and surveyed the Potter Elementary School playground a block away. "There must be a thousand of them," Mike whispered.

"A thousand and one," Jim said. "You missed the communist soldier leaning against that maple. We'll have to let Agent Ysteb know so she can send help."

They slid down the train track bank and crossed Main to the playground. Jim took a piece of paper from his pocket and wrote, "1,001 communist soldiers here. Send help. Agent Mij." Mike took Squall Baby from the box and held her while Jim tied the note to her left leg.

"Now?"

"Now."

Mike threw her into the air, and both boys shouted, "Fly home, Squall Baby! Fly home!" Squall Baby flew higher and higher. She made a complete circle, something she always did, and flew toward Jim's house.

The boys returned a quick wave to Mr. Jackson, who was walking toward his car, and took off running. They'd never beaten Squall Baby home. When they reached Jim's house, panting and out of breath, Agent Ysteb waved the message. "Mij. Ekim, I have the note. Would you read what it says?"

***

Grandpa had told the young agents to see him after they finished their secret mission. When they entered Mike's backyard, the old man sat in the swing under the big oak tree smoking his pipe. Ted Barton was Mike's grandpa on his mom's side. In his mid-seventies, he had a strip of white hair around the sides and back of his head, but was completely bald on top. He sported a full white beard. And, of course, he perpetually wore overalls.

He looked up as they approached. "How'd the mission go?"

Jim smiled. "Like a charm, Grandpa."

"Did she beat you home again?"

"Yeah. Betsy already had the note. Squall Baby's just too fast."

"Already had the note, huh, Betsy?" Grandpa poked her tummy with his finger, and she giggled.

Mike watched Grandpa puff out small smoke clouds that disappeared into the air. "Why don't you come next time? You could be a secret agent just like us. It'd be fun."

"No, I'm too old. You have to be young to be a secret agent."

Betsy squinted. "Were you ever young, Grandpa?"

He took a couple more puffs. "Once upon a time, Betsy. I had adventures just like you guys. My friends and I used to do all kinds of things—like going to the ol' swimming hole on hot, sunny days."

"When was that?"

"When was what, Betsy?"

"When were you young? Was it last summer?"

He puffed his pipe and leaned back in the swing. "No. It was a long time ago."

"Summer before last?"

"Long before that. It wasn't even three summers ago. It was a distant summer." He paused. "I'm living on borrowed time now."

"What does that mean?"

"What? To live on borrowed time?"

"Yeah. What does 'borrowed time' mean? Do you have to give it back when you're done with it?"

Mike's mom hated it when Grandpa talked about living on borrowed time. She yelled at him whenever she heard him say it, especially if kids were around.

Grandpa looked up into the oak tree. "Well, let's see now. How can I explain that? It means I've been around so long, God has forgotten where I am. It's like He misplaced me. I'm okay as long as He doesn't remember. That's why I can't run around with you playing secret agent. If I did that, God might see me and say to Himself, 'Is that old goat still there? I thought I called him home years ago.' Then He'd holler out to me, 'Old man, you're too old to be on earth. Come on up here to heaven where you belong. All your old friends are already up here swimming in the ol' swimming hole.' Then I'll go to heaven and spend eternity swimming with my friends, and we'll all be young again forever."

Betsy grinned. "That sounds nice. Don't you want to go to heaven and be young? And go swimming with your old friends again?"

Grandpa took another puff. "Sure I do, Betsy. In fact, I'm looking forward to it. But not just yet. I figure I have eternity to enjoy that heavenly swimming hole, but just a very short time to enjoy you." He looked at the boys. "And you ... and you. That's why I spend so much time sitting here. It doesn't draw God's attention to me. I just enjoy watching you have fun." He picked up a cardboard box from the ground next to him. "Oh, here. I made this for you, Jim."

Jim took it. "What's in it?"

"Open it." Betsy jumped up and down. "Open it."

Jim opened the flaps and lifted out a wooden object. "A little cage!" he shouted. Mike got closer and peered at it. It was a little larger than the Buster Brown shoebox. It had wooden bars on all sides as well as on the top and bottom, attached by thin leather strips. It sported a metal handle on the top and a small door on the front. Grandpa had used cherry stain.

"It's swell, Grandpa." Jim threw his arms around him. "Thanks."

Grandpa pointed to the object. "It's a portable cage, Jim. You can use it instead of a shoebox to carry Squall Baby on your secret missions. I never did think secret agents should have to use shoeboxes, especially in this day and age. There's just too much at stake. Why, do you know what I heard on the Philco today?"

"No. What?" Jim turned the cage to admire the workmanship.

"The United States tested a hydrogen bomb in the Pacific Ocean yesterday."

Mike peered at him. "A hydrogen bomb? What's that?"

"I don't know. I assume it's more powerful than the atomic bomb. Otherwise, why would they invent it? Anyway, we now have a choice. We can blow up the world with either the atomic bomb or the hydrogen bomb."

Grandpa sucked on his pipe, but nothing came out. He searched his pockets, pulled out a kitchen match, and scraped his thumbnail over it.

On the second try it flared brightly and then dimmed to a normal flame. He took a couple of puffs.

"I bought a new whittling knife at Sears and Roebuck in Princeton yesterday. You'll never guess what they're selling there now. Any guesses?"

Jim and Mike shook their heads. Betsy sat in deep thought.

"Well, I'll tell you. They are now selling—"

"I know. I know." Betsy jumped up and down. "They're selling hydrogen bombs."

The two boys turned from Betsy to Grandpa. They'd soon find out if she had guessed correctly.

Grandpa laughed. "No Betsy. They aren't selling hydrogen bombs."

"No, Betsy. That would be silly," Jim said in his big brother voice.

She crossed her arms and stared at the grass.

"They aren't selling hydrogen bombs ... yet. But that was a very good guess."

She uncrossed her arms. "It was, Grandpa?"

"Yep. It sure was. What they're selling is bomb shelters."

"Bomb shelters?" Mike made a face. Would Sears and Roebuck really sell those?

"Bomb shelters. They have one with glass walls so you can see what it looks like inside. A disc jockey from the Princeton radio station is going to broadcast from inside it all day Saturday and Sunday, and anyone ordering one this weekend gets ten percent off and a free ten-cent mug of root beer at Mason's Drive-in."

"Can we go see it?"

"Maybe. Know what else I heard on the Philco? Some Puerto Ricans attacked the Capitol Building and injured five Representatives. These are trying times."

He struck his shoe heel with his pipe several times to knock the burning tobacco out, looked inside the bowl, and blew into the stem three or four times, making a gurgling sound. "Gonna have to get more pipe cleaners. Anyway, that's why I made the portable cage. With all the problems in the world, we can't have you secret agents using a beat-up Buster Brown shoebox to carry Squall Baby on your missions. Call it my gift to the peace effort."

Jim held the cage up and admired it again. "I'm going to show this to Mom and Squall Baby. Come on, Betsy. Thanks again, Grandpa."

Mike watched Grandpa creak back and forth in the old swing

hanging from the huge oak tree, which he said was even older than he was. He noticed the old man's attention was drifting, perhaps to the heavenly swimming hole or the earthly one he'd frequented as a young boy. He didn't want to disturb Grandpa's thoughts, so he lay in the grass with his chin on his hands and enjoyed the warm spring sun. It was getting lower in the sky, and the air was cooler now than during their mission.

Mike heard his mom talking and realized his dad was home. He must have forgotten to wipe his feet or pick up something at the grocery store or committed some other criminal act. Her voice boomed in an unpleasant tone she used sometimes when talking with family. But he'd never heard her use it in public.

"You're awfully quiet, Mike," Grandpa said. "Thinking about another secret mission?"

"No. I was just thinking about ... nothing."

"About nothing, huh?" He glanced toward the house.

Mike couldn't hear everything his mom said, but he understood some of it. *"I'll tell you another thing. If it weren't for me, nothing would ever get done around here. I work my fingers to the bone. This house doesn't clean itself."*

As quickly as it had started, the talking ended. The only sound now was the steady squeaking of Grandpa's swing.

"A circus is coming to town."

The abruptness of Grandpa's statement made it seem out of place. Perhaps he hadn't heard right.

"A circus?"

"A circus. I saw the signs on the telephone poles downtown. It's gonna be at Kiwanis Park in mid-April for two glorious days."

"With elephants and everything?"

"Yep. Tons of them."

"That sounds like fun."

The swing's creaking continued. "Circuses are more than fun, Mike. They're magical."

Mike shifted from his stomach to his side and studied his grandpa. "What do you mean 'magical?'"

"If it hadn't been for a circus, your parents may never have married. A circus cast a magical spell over them and *caused* them to get married."

"No."

"Yeah."

Mike frowned. "I didn't know that."

"It's true." Grandpa continued his methodical swinging. "Your parents were friends, just like you and that little Heidi girl you're sweet on. Your mom wanted to marry your dad long before he suspected anything was amiss. She had to somehow convince him he wanted to marry her, too, but nothing worked until she came up with the perfect plan."

"What was the plan?"

Grandpa stopped swinging, and silence engulfed the backyard. "She took him to a circus."

Mike made a face. "I don't get it."

"Well, your mom bought two circus tickets and invited your dad to go with her. They had a great time. I guess your dad thought being married to her would be fun like that circus with its clowns and cotton candy and animals that do tricks, so he proposed. I thought about warning him, but I never did. I think he's kind of happy in his own way. Well, anyway, never underestimate the magic of a circus."

Chapter 4

THE PORCH

Spring came early in 1954. Unlike most years, when the warm and cold air play tag until summer, the weather stayed unseasonably warm. The early March warmth invited the Long family to the screened-in front porch after supper, their favorite place to relax when the weather was nice.

Just as Grandpa enjoyed listening to the Philco, Mike's dad enjoyed reading the paper. Charles Long was a quiet man—henpecked, Grandpa said—of average height and build with thin, brown hair and a receding hairline. He leaned back in his wicker rocker, put on his wire-rimmed glasses, and picked up *The Evansville Courier*.

Grandpa entertained himself by whittling on his latest creation, a donkey with an old man that looked like a gold prospector on its back. He liked the front porch swing as much as he did the backyard swing, except for the fact Martha had banned him from smoking on the porch. He occasionally took a couple of smokeless puffs, but he could do no more. Martha took out her knitting, and Mike sat by the men.

The neighborhood stretched before them between the two porch posts like a movie screen. A rabbit nibbled the grass ten feet beyond the red-brick sidewalk that led to the recently tarred street. Judy Brown, a big woman perhaps forty-five years old who his mom often called "that huge spinster," worked in her flowers several houses down the street. After a few minutes she walked toward the Long house.

"Look at her," Martha said in a loud whisper. "I swear she gets fatter every day. She doesn't go for a walk—she goes for a lumber. And look at her hair. You'd think she'd at least wash it once in a while. I swear she combs it with a pork chop."

Judy neared the porch. "Hi, Judy," Martha said. "Going for a walk?"

The woman stopped, panting. "Oh, hi, everyone. Yeah. I try to make it around the block once a day. Someday I hope to go farther than that. Maybe even to town and back."

"Well, your walks must be working," Grandpa said. "You're looking good. You've lost quite a bit of weight, haven't you?"

"Oh, how nice of you to notice, Grandpa. Almost three pounds this month. I didn't think it would show."

"Well, keep up the good work."

"I will. Bye now." Judy waved and continued on her way.

Martha went back to her knitting. "She didn't lose that weight, you know. It's following her. If she doesn't watch out, it'll attack her and swallow her whole."

"Martha, you shouldn't say things like that."

She adjusted the yarn. "Don't worry about it, Grandpa. As long as she doesn't hear me, it's the same as my not saying it."

Grandpa studied his wooden statue. "Speaking of hearing, guess who had a baby yesterday."

"I don't know, who?"

"Ben and Jane Cruthers."

"You mean the goofy guy and his homely wife who farm the river bottoms?"

Grandpa whittled around the donkey's ears and held the statue to the light. "Well, they are farmers. They named their little girl Louise."

"That poor girl doesn't have a chance. She'll probably end up both goofy and homely."

Mike looked back to the street. Bertha Kramer was trimming her hedge at the end of the block. A short, hunched-over old woman, she wore her gray hair in a bun like Miss Schneider's. She spent hours every day standing on a ladder clipping the huge hedge that surrounded her house and rarely acknowledged anyone who greeted her.

Martha made a flurry of knitting stitches. "She's as crazy as a loon, you know."

Mike looked up at her. "Who?"

"That Bertha Kramer. The leaves haven't even sprouted yet, but just because it's warm, she thinks it's time to start clipping."

Charles spoke for the first time since he began reading the paper. "You're not going to believe this."

"What's that?" Martha asked.

"Someone came up with a magazine called *TV Guide*. It lists the programs on television each night."

"So?"

"So how long can that magazine last? Can you imagine how boring it would be to read a list of television shows week after week?"

"Oh, I don't know, Charles. Maybe people who actually own television sets would find it very interesting."

Charles didn't say anything. He'd been saving for a television for two years, but after paying each month's bills there was little left over. Some months he even had to borrow from the television fund.

"Well, maybe if ... " Charles stopped in mid-sentence and went back to reading his paper.

Again, Martha stopped knitting. "Maybe if what, Charles? Maybe if I didn't buy any decent clothes, we'd have money to buy a television? I'm the vice president of the PTA. I have to look presentable. What do you want me to do, wear old overalls like Grandpa?" Charles turned the newspaper page, snapping it in the process. Everything got quiet.

"Oh, Mike," Grandpa said, finally, "did you see anyone at the schoolyard on your mission today?"

Mike shook his head. "No, not really. Just Mr. Jackson."

"You know, you should get him involved in your secret missions."

"Why's that, Grandpa?"

"He's a war hero."

"I knew he was in the war. A hero? Really?"

Grandpa sucked on his cold pipe. "He saved a dozen men from sure death. Pulled them to safety while killing seven enemy soldiers even though he was seriously injured. He took care of the men until help arrived. Spent weeks in the hospital. Almost lost a leg. He got all kinds of medals."

"And he is divorced," Martha said. She made the word *divorced* sound terrible, like polio or cancer.

"A *TV Guide*," Charles said in a barely audible voice. "It won't last another year."

Chapter 5

A RIDE ON THE WILD SIDE

On Monday and Tuesday, Jim had a mild sore throat. By Wednesday he could hardly swallow, and his temperature shot up to a hundred and one. Mike rode his bike past Jim's house on the way to school and waved to Jim's mother, who was feeding and watering the pigeons. Two blocks later Tony motioned for Mike to catch up to him, and the two talked as they peddled toward school. When they reached Main, Mike crossed it and kept on going. Tony veered right onto the forbidden street. Both boys screeched to a stop.

Mike jammed his left foot to the pavement and gripped his handlebars tight with both hands. "What are you doing?"

"Going to school. Come on. Let's go."

Mike shook his head. "We can't ride on Main. Have you forgotten what Mr. Jackson said? He'll paddle us."

"Come on, Mike. We're going to be late."

"But the rule. The paddling."

"Mr. Jackson will never know." The tone of Tony's voice suggested he'd become impatient with the standoff. Then he said the four magic words that force eleven-year-old boys to do things they know they shouldn't. "What are you, chicken?"

Well, sure he was, but he didn't want Tony to know it. He slowly turned his bike around, and soon the two rode down the forbidden street. Each time he pushed the pedal with his left foot, the words "Bend over" echoed in his mind. When he pushed it with his right foot he heard, "Swat." All the way down Main Street he heard it. *Bend over. Swat. Bend over. Swat. Bend over. Swat. Bend over. Swat.*

A sour fluid erupted into Mike's mouth when he eased his bike into the nearly-full rack, and he swallowed it back down. He put his hands on his knees and took deep breaths, all the while surveying the schoolyard to see if Mr. Jackson had seen him. The principal was nowhere in sight. Tony was right—he'd never know.

Mike overcame the nauseous feeling, but he couldn't shake the overwhelming emotion that he'd done something terribly wrong. He sat at his desk in the exact center of Miss Schneider's world and stared at the wall. After a while he removed his glasses, placed his elbows on his desk, and pressed the heels of his hands against his eyes, pushing hard to make the feeling leave. It didn't.

A hand rested on his shoulder. "Are you okay?" Heidi!

"Yeah, I'm fine." He didn't look up, and moments later the hand lifted, and she walked away.

Miss Schneider started math class, but Mike couldn't concentrate. He simply opened the book and pretended to follow along. Finally, after she told the class to work math problems on their own, he could stand it no more. It made no difference if Mr. Jackson knew or not. He'd broken a rule, and God saw him do it. Doing something wrong and then not owning up to it was like telling a lie, and God must be disappointed that he lied. He had only one option. He had to confess to Mr. Jackson. That would be the right thing to do, and it would make God smile.

Miss Schneider was grading papers when Mike found himself standing at attention by her desk, waiting for her to acknowledge him. She finished one paper, grabbed another, and looked up. "What's the matter?" She continued grading papers. "Don't you understand the work?"

"Yes, ma'am."

She marked three answers in a row wrong and shook her head. "Well, you should have gone to the bathroom before class started. Now, you'll just have to wait." She marked two more wrong and made clicking sounds with her tongue.

"I don't have to go to the bathroom, either."

She laid the red pencil on top of the stack of papers and folded her arms. "If you understand your work and you don't need to go to the bathroom, why in the world are you standing by my desk instead of sitting at yours, working on your lesson?"

"Well, I uh, I need to see Mr. Jackson."

She stared at him. He remained at attention and didn't retreat to his desk. Finally, she picked up the red pencil and pulled another paper from the stack. "If you must see Mr. Jackson, go ahead. When you get back I expect you to work twice as hard on your work to get caught up. Understand?"

Mike left the room before she could change her mind.

Mr. Jackson's office door stood open, and his side of a phone conversation overflowed into the hallway. He saw Mike and motioned for him to enter and take the seat just inside the door.

The office was neat and uncluttered. A George Washington picture hung on the wall to his right. George certainly had a thick nose, and with his lips pursed together, he seemed humorless. Being the father of his country was a big responsibility that probably didn't allow much time for smiling or being frivolous. Besides, if he smiled, everyone would see his wooden teeth and poke fun at him. In spite of his greatness, it was a wonder he ever attracted a woman. Then again, Martha Washington was no raving beauty herself.

The paddle hung behind Mr. Jackson in the wall's exact center with the words *Board of Education* forming a semicircle above it. Only about a quarter-of-an-inch thick, but a good foot-and-a-half long and six inches wide, it sported six eighth-inch drilled holes, rumored to make it fly faster. The worn handle testified to the many paddlings he had invested in students over the years.

Mike studied the paddle, trying to anticipate how it would feel. He'd heard it used on others and knew it made a loud noise when it hit its destination. *WHAM!* Everyone on the second floor could hear it. He'd have to be sure to start crying the instant it hit the first time and stop as soon as the second swing began its downward movement.

Mr. Jackson hung up and raised his left eyebrow slightly. "What can I do for you, Mike?"

Mike bit his lower lip and looked at the floor. "I rode my bike on Main Street this morning."

Mr. Jackson tented his hands. "Why are you telling me this? You do realize I'll have to paddle you, don't you?"

"Yes sir."

"Do you want to be paddled?"

Mike continued looking at his shoes. "No."

"And you are telling me this because ... "

"Because I broke a rule. Breaking rules is like telling lies, and 'fessing up is the only way to make it right." He eyed the paddle. He was ready.

42

Mr. Jackson didn't say anything for a long time. Finally, he stood. "Okay, Mike, I have a few things to take care of first. You go back to class, and I'll get you later for your paddling."

Mike trudged back to Miss Schneider's room. He didn't feel better yet, but he would once he'd received his punishment and didn't have to worry about it anymore. He felt Heidi's gaze follow him to his seat, and when he looked up after he sat down, she smiled. He looked away.

The day dragged by. Noon came and went with no paddling. *He must be busy. He'll get me this afternoon.* The school day ended without a paddling.

After school, he jumped on his bike and rode home as fast as he could. Trees, children, and even houses blurred. When he arrived home, he waved to Grandpa, who was weeding the flower garden by the birdbath. "Your mom's not home. She's gone shopping downtown."

Mike ran to his room and slammed the door. He lay across his bed, placed his glasses on the pillow, and pressed his eyes hard against the two fists he made on the mattress. Soon red and gray geometrical designs formed in the blackness between his brain and his eyeballs, and for a moment they chased thoughts of the illegal ride and the impending punishment from his mind.

Chapter 6

THE PARTNERS

A bell rang above Martha Long's head when she opened the door to the Chic Shoppe, Potter's only clothing store. Owner Ida Jennings stood behind the counter talking with a customer who had tried on a blouse with bluebirds on it, and two other women looked at a rack of skirts to the left. The final customer stood in the back by a mirror, holding a dress against herself. She stuck her right leg out and studied the image.

"Can I help you, Martha?"

Martha smiled at Mrs. Jennings. "No, thanks. Just looking."

She moved from display to display, finding little to her liking. She reached a rack of white spring dresses with little flowers, grasped the hem of one, and stepped back to fan it out for a better look. She backed into someone and her automatic apology reflex kicked in. "Excuse me," she said. "I didn't realize you were there."

She turned to see whom she had nudged. A mannequin, dressed in a light green skirt and a white blouse with yellow spring flowers, stared back at her.

She flushed, and her automatic apology reflex responded again. "I'm sorry. I thought you were a person." Mrs. Jennings and the bluebird blouse lady stopped talking and looked in her direction.

Martha tucked her purse under her arm. "Don't look at me like that! I don't have to come in here and take this from you. You never have anything good, anyway. All your clothes have ugly little flowers or stupid-looking bluebirds."

She opened the door and set off the bell that startled her so, she dropped her purse. She picked it up, walked out, and heaved the door shut with a slam and a ring. "Hope I knocked that stupid little bell off the wall!"

She took long strides down the sidewalk. Two blocks later she stopped to watch Trashman and Burly Thompson load an old washing machine into Trashman's green horse-drawn wagon. Burly stood in the wagon waving his arms and carrying on an animated, one-sided conversation. Trashman jumped up onto the seat. He grabbed the reins, reached under the seat, and brought up a half empty whiskey bottle. He swigged from it, cleaned the bottle's neck and mouth with his shirt, and held it out to Burly, who cleaned it more by twisting the bottle's neck several times under his arm.

Martha made a face. "Disgusting men." She continued her brisk walk home.

***

Trashman's real name was Seth Harders, but almost everyone called him Trashman behind his back. He was Jerry's father, the boy who occupied the last seat in Miss Schneider's dumb row. He and his wife Connie lived in a dilapidated shack next to the railroad tracks a block from the Potter Elementary School playground, not far from the secret woods' briar-protected opening. Unlike his son, Trashman was thin—wiry, actually. He stood six feet tall and his hair consisted of a few wisps of brown and gray that stuck out here and there. He always wore a two-day growth of mostly white beard.

An independent businessman, he offered the town's citizens two services. For two bits a week, he'd dispose of their trash. All they had to do was set it by the streets and alleys, and he'd haul it to the dump. His old horse, Cinders, had only one good eye, but still managed to clop, clop, clop the trash wagon through the town's streets at speeds well below the posted limits.

Trashman also supplied the grunt work to move heavy objects. When a store sold a big item, they'd have him haul it to the new owner's house. If he needed help, he'd contact his best friend and drinking buddy, Burly Thompson. Though only five-foot seven, Burly was heavy and strong. His low center of gravity allowed him to move heavy objects with relative ease.

People feared Burly. Rumor had it he'd killed two people. According to one story, at age ten he killed his younger brother in an argument over a Clark Bar. He beat him with his fists until he went down, and the boy never got up again. Another story had him murdering a man in Tennessee over a working woman.

No one knew if the stories were true or not, but everyone played it safe by avoiding him. When drinking in a bar Burly might, for no apparent reason, point to another patron and say, "Dance." The selected person never tried to reason with him. He'd simply set his drink down and dance until Burly ordered him to sit. It was common knowledge that if you frequented Potter bars long enough, you'd end up dancing a jig for Burly Thompson.

He had worked at the Kaden Coal Mine five miles from Potter for ten years until it closed eight years ago. He had even worked his way up to foreman before the owners barricaded the mine, put up *No Trespassing, Closed,* and *Danger* signs, and sneaked away in the middle of the night. Mothers warned their children to never go near the place because dangerous tunnels honeycombed the area, and if the ground ever gave way, the hidden tunnels would gobble them alive and swallow them whole.

As far as anyone knows, except for the time the county hauled away the dynamite left behind, no one has set foot on the land since the day it closed. Trucks laden with coal used to rumble down Kaden Mine Road. Potholes now decorate it, and brush has narrowed it, turning it into little more than a seldom-used animal path.

After the mine closed, Burly's lack of people skills and questionable reputation made it almost impossible for him to find a job. He became Trashman's partner and took up residence in the Red Dog Pool Hall's basement, where he stayed rent-free in exchange for cleaning the place each night. Both Burly and Nate Sampson, the owner, benefited from the deal. After a long day, Nate could simply lock up and go home. Burly later cleaned the grill, swept the floor, and replenished all the items needed the next day.

Nate reaped another huge benefit by having Burly in the basement. Before he lived there, burglars looted the establishment four or five times a year, and Nate found it impossible to buy insurance. After making the deal with Burly he hooked up an intercom system that consisted of a microphone placed by the cash register and a speaker mounted next to Burly's bed. The slightest noise in the pool hall sounded like Notre Dame's marching band at halftime when it reached Burly's ears.

It was a simple but effective system. Only one burglary was attempted at the Red Dog in the eight years since Burly moved in. On Christmas Eve a few weeks after he came, two burglars smashed the glass door with a brick and entered the pool hall. Burly heard the noise and hid behind the counter before they reached the cash register. He'd already called Slim Smart, the town marshal, and gotten him out of bed.

When Slim arrived, he found two bleeding men on the floor hovering just above the unconscious state. Burly stood over them groaning and holding his right hand. Ambulances rushed all three to the hospital. The doctors soon patched Burly's broken hand, but the more seriously injured intruders remained in the hospital for several days. The burglary attempt made headline news, and word of the Christmas Eve Massacre, as the media called it, spread. Soon, most people in Gibson, Vanderburgh, and surrounding counties knew Burly lived at the Red Dog and slept with an intercom speaker inches from his ears.

Nate bought some paint and brushes and wrote PREMISES PROTECTED BY BURLY THOMPSON on the window and took out weekly ads in the local paper with a similar message. He even taped the front-page article about the incident on the pool hall door. He had free nightly cleanup and insurance, and Burly had a free place to stay and fifty percent off all the hamburgers and fries he could eat. Nate regularly slipped him a sawbuck or two just to make sure he remained happy with the arrangement.

The Trashman-Burly team was quite a sight. The nearly bald, tall, and thin Trashman was a stark contrast to the short and heavy Burly with his unruly black hair. Yet, no one ever heard a cross word between them.

Trashman liked to drink. When he enjoyed the hobby too much, he'd become belligerent, mellow, or pass out. Once he started drinking in earnest, no one knew which Trashman would be around when the drinking ended.

When he passed out from drinking, men placed him in the trash wagon and yelled, "Take him home, Cinders." An old, brown horse pulling a driverless wagon through Potter streets late at night and making a sizable deposit in front of the First Federal Bank was a common sight.

Very little had gone right for Trashman the day Martha Long saw him. He twisted his ankle that morning and had to work the rest of the day in pain. He drank more and more whiskey to ease the pain, with little success. After he dropped Burly off at the pool hall, he tossed the empty fifth into the back of the wagon and headed home.

***

Jerry was catching crawdads in the ditch that paralleled the tracks in front of the shack when he heard Cinder's clop, clop, clop. He lay motionless. Trashman yanked the reins. The wagon stopped in the driveway, and he looked around.

"Jerry! Come put Cinders away." He missed a step climbing from the wagon and fell hard to the ground, shoulder first. "Jerry! Where is that boy?"

Jerry held his breath.

Trashman's wife Connie, a slight woman, ran from the house. She wrapped an arm around his waist and pulled his left arm over her shoulders, and they limped to the shack. Trashman's gaze darted about.

"Where is that boy?"

"He's playing by the tracks." Connie's voice remained calm in contrast to her husband's shouting.

"I want him to come when I call him." Trashman grimaced and rubbed his shoulder. Connie hesitated, watching him.

"He'll be here shortly."

"I don't want him here shortly. I want him here now! When I call him, I want him to come. He needs to take care of Cinders."

Jerry watched his parents enter the shack and stayed hidden for several minutes. Finally, holding a Folgers coffee can against his belly, he inched the shack's door open. Trashman rose from his chair by the kitchen table and, shaking a finger at the boy, walked toward him.

"Come when I call you!" He swung and knocked the can from Jerry's hand, and it slammed hard against the wall, spewing water and small crawdads. He pointed at Jerry and moved his entire hand to accent each word. "You come when I call you, you hear?"

Jerry fixed his stare on the floor. "Yeah."

"Speak up. Do you hear me?" Trashman stepped toward him.

"Yeah. I hear you." His response matched his father's loudness.

"Then come when I call you." He swung again, and his open hand caught Jerry's left eye, knocking him against the wall. Jerry crossed his arms in front of his face.

"I'll teach you to come when I call, you fat elephant."

Connie grabbed his arm. "Don't hurt him again, Seth. Don't."

Trashman jerked his arm back, hitting Connie with his elbow. She fell back, holding her chest. He staggered to the bedroom and collapsed onto the bed.

Jerry leaned against the wall with his hands over his eyes. Connie hugged him, and he swung his arms up, knocking hers away. "Don't you touch me! Don't you ever touch me! I hate him, and I hate you!" He ran out of the house, slamming the door behind him.

Chapter 7

THE PUNISHMENT

Mike was still in bed when his mother tapped on his door. "Mike, you get up this instant. This is the last time I'm going to call you."

He stretched and opened his eyes. "I'll be right out." She was right. He'd better hurry because Miss Schneider doesn't like students being late. He couldn't sleep most of the night, thinking about the paddling he'd get. Twice, after he finally did fall asleep, he woke with a start, all clammy and sweaty after reading nightmare headlines from the Kiln, Potter's weekly newspaper. The first one read *Mike Long to receive well-deserved paddling.* The second, even more terrifying headline, read *Mike Long unable to cry; paddling lasts forever.*

He dressed, ate breakfast, and met Jim by the pigeon coops. Jim had recovered from his illness and chattered all the way to school about an amazing trick Squall Baby did the previous evening, but Mike heard very little. For the first time in his life he didn't care what Squall Baby did. Thinking about the paddling was too overwhelming for him to care.

When he entered the classroom, Heidi greeted him from her Busy Bee seat with a perky "Hi, Mike." He returned a curt greeting that resembled more of a grunt than an actual word. He marched past her and collapsed in his seat.

Miss Schneider, busy at her own desk with a stack of papers, looked up when Jerry entered the room. She studied his face. "Jerry, stop. Look at me. Come closer."

He stepped hesitantly toward her and stood next to her desk.

She squinted at him. "Did you bump into something again, Jerry?"

He looked away. "Yeah."

50

"What was it this time? Another tree limb?"

He continued looking away. "No, ma'am. I tripped on a tree root and hit my eye on a rock."

She grasped his chin and angled his face toward the light. "It must have been a big rock."

Jerry pulled his head back and stepped away from her desk. "It was, Miss Schneider. Big and ugly."

She sighed. "I worry about you, Jerry. I really do. You've got to be more careful, or one of these days you'll really hurt yourself."

Jerry looked away again. "I'll be more careful. Can I go now?"

"Yes, Jerry. You *may* go." She went back to the paper she was grading and marked two wrong, clicking her tongue.

Recess came and went with no sign of Mr. Jackson. At lunch, Mike picked at his food. When it was time for noon recess, his plate was still full. He'd just moved the franks and sauerkraut to different locations.

Several kids asked him to play with them, but he refused them all. He entertained himself by pulling white parachutes from dandelions and watching the wind carry them to faraway lands where paddlings were forbidden. Miss Schneider approached and stopped two feet from him. "Are you okay, Mike?"

He looked up. "I'm fine, ma'am. Just didn't get much sleep."

She bent over and felt his forehead. "Maybe I should take your temperature. You might be coming down with something."

"No, really. I'm fine. I just—"

"Miss Schneider! Miss Schneider!" Tony ran toward them.

She straightened. "What is it, Tony?"

"Two grasshoppers are fighting." He pointed toward a circle of kids forming at the playground's edge, by the big maples. "One is clobbering the other."

The circle grew as Miss Schneider walked briskly toward it. Skip lay on his back with his arms crossed over his face. Jerry's closed fists hit him again and again. "I'll knock your stupid block off, you stinking crybaby!" Blood covered Skip's nose and mouth, and the area around his eyes was fire red.

Miss Schneider approached Jerry from behind, lifted him high in the air, and set him on the ground away from Skip. "You stay there, young man," she said. "Now, what's going on here?"

Jerry pointed at the bleeding boy. "He started it. He stared at me. I

51

told him to stop staring, but he didn't. He should've stopped when I told him to. He started it."

Skip continued crying as blood rushed from his nose and mouth. Miss Schneider snatched a handkerchief from her pocket and wiped his face and then held it against his nose. She pulled him up and glared at Jerry. "As for you, young man, sit in the red chair—immediately." She helped Skip walk back to the schoolhouse with his head at a forty-five degree tilt and the handkerchief pressed firmly against his nose. Jerry followed with his head down and his hands stuffed in his pockets.

When the students returned to class after the noon recess, Jerry sat slouched in the red chair Miss Schneider kept by her hall door for students who acted up. His scowl and tightly crossed arms showed he was not in a good mood.

Mike sat and looked around. Three people were missing: Jerry, who was in the hall, Skip, whose injuries were being tended to, and Miss Schneider. The rest waited quietly for her return.

Five minutes into the period, hallway voices overflowed into the room. "You will sit in this chair, young man. As soon as Skip's parents pick him up, Mr. Jackson will get you for your paddling. Do you understand?"

"Yeah."

"Jerry, you can't go around hurting people. When will you understand that?"

"Skip started it. He stared at me. He should be the one getting the paddling."

Miss Schneider sighed. "I don't know what more I can say. Maybe Mr. Jackson can help you understand."

She entered the classroom, grabbed a stack of mimeographed worksheets from her desk, and passed them out. "Skip's okay," she said when the final worksheet reached the last person remaining in the dumb row. "He'll rest at home the remainder of the day. Jerry will sit in the hall this afternoon. As I put together work for him, you are to complete the geography worksheet I just passed out. I believe the instructions to be self-explanatory."

Mike stared at the worksheet. Was there anything more boring than geography? Why would he ever care what Norway's major exports or Sweden's major imports were? He took the geography book from his desk and found the Norway and Sweden section. Ten minutes later he had just rediscovered that Oslo was Norway's largest city and capital and was ready to record the information on the worksheet when Miss Schneider carried two books and several sheets of paper into the hall.

The exciting Gander-Harders fight had taken Mike's thoughts off his own troubles. But now that things had quieted down and Jerry sat in the hall waiting to meet with the Board of Education, thoughts of his own paddling returned. His mouth became so dry he could hardly swallow.

When Miss Schneider returned, he walked to her desk before she had a chance to begin grading papers and stood at attention. She grabbed the top paper, laid it in front of her, and sighed. "I assume you're standing here for a very important reason."

"Yes, ma'am." He made his throat sound raspy to show how very important it was. "My throat is very dry. I need a drink of water ... desperately."

"Desperately, huh?" She leaned back and studied him. "Mike, what is Norway's capital?"

"Oslo, ma'am. It's also Norway's largest city."

"Okay," she said, looking at the paper, "you may get a drink of water. But don't dawdle."

Mike stepped into the hallway and noticed Jerry's chair was empty. The principal's office door was shut. He walked closer to the office and listened. Mr. Jackson was saying something he couldn't quite make out.

Then, *Whack*. It resounded in the hallway. No crying. *Whack*. Still no crying. *Whack*. *Whack*. *Whack*. *Whack*. The sounds of six distinct swats came from the office. Was that a whimper? The paddling stopped. How could a paddling last longer than two whacks? Maybe Jerry was as dumb as his placement in the last seat in the grasshopper row suggested. Or maybe, he was just that tough.

Mike drank for a long time, and his throat felt better. He stood by the fountain, staring at the principal's office when the door opened, and Jerry came out. He'd never before wished he were Jerry Harders, but at that moment he wished he were because then his own paddling would be over. He took reluctant steps back to class, and the school day ended without a paddling.

He'd get it tomorrow. Tomorrow was the last day of the school week, and there would be no way Mr. Jackson would let it go until Monday.

***

Martha looked up from her front porch knitting. "What's wrong with you, Mike? You've moped around for two days now."

He turned from watching Bertha Kramer snip, snip, snip her hedge. "Nothing."

"You know what you need? A good enema. Your insides need to be cleaned out good. I'll go find that enema bottle."

Grandpa stopped whittling the first stage of an African elephant statue that currently resembled a wooden block more than an elephant. "Sit down, Martha, and leave the poor boy alone. He's just worn out from school, that's all."

"If he needs an enema, he's getting one." She walked toward the living room door.

"Fine." Grandpa went back to his whittling. "You know, I've been feeling a mite poorly myself lately. I think I need a spring tonic. Yes sir, that's exactly what I need. I believe I'll walk to Brown's Drugstore and buy me a bottle of Hadacol."

Martha paused and placed her hands on her hips. "I will not allow Hadacol in this house. It's almost all alcohol. You may as well just drink straight whiskey."

"I wouldn't do that. I know how you hate it when I drink whiskey. However, like I said, I've been feeling a mite poorly. A bottle or two of Hadacol may be just what the doctor ordered. They claim it cures almost everything."

Martha returned to her chair. "Okay, I won't give him an enema. But if he's still moping around tomorrow, he's sure getting one."

"He'll feel better soon." Grandpa held his wooden statue to the light. "I'm starting to feel a little better myself. Guess I won't need any Hadacol after all." Grandpa spoke after a long silence. "Oh, Mike, do you know why they call Hadacol 'Hadacol?'"

He had heard Grandpa tell this joke many times. But since he seemed to enjoy telling it so much, Mike always pretended he'd never heard it before. "No. Why?"

"Well ... " Grandpa tried unsuccessfully to keep from laughing ... "they Hadacol it something!"

***

Friday morning greeted Mike with a headache, sore throat,

backache, stomachache, and several pains he couldn't quite identify, but his mom made him go to school anyhow. The day dragged on. After lunch he knew it wouldn't be much longer. Then, at 3:10, just five minutes before school would let out for the weekend, Mr. Jackson walked into the room.

Miss Schneider stood. "Good afternoon, Mr. Jackson. What can we do for you?"

"Well, I stopped by for two reasons. First, to see how your class is doing." He walked up and down the aisles looking at each child's work. When he got to Mike's desk he stopped and put his hand on his shoulder. "And second, to wish you and your class a nice weekend."

Miss Schneider smiled. "Why, thank you, Mr. Jackson. You have a good weekend, too."

"Thank you. I will." He patted Mike's back. When he got to the door, he waved. Everyone, including Miss Schneider, waved back.

"Well, class, wasn't that nice of Mr. Jackson? I, too, want to wish you a nice weekend. I have a surprise when you return to school Monday." The bell rang, and everyone gathered books to take home for the weekend.

Mike had walked only a few blocks when it hit him. Mr. Jackson never had any intentions of paddling him. He had simply used an alternate punishment to the Board of Education, a plan that involved Mike's worrying three days about a paddling he'd never get. The alternate punishment proved to be far more effective than a paddling. It would have been *Whack. Cry. Whack. Silence.* A paddling can't be stretched out over three days, but worry can. Mike ran to catch up with Jim to find out what Squall Baby had been up to.

Chapter 8

THE BULLY

Tires squealed against the warm pavement and brought the rusty blue pickup truck to an abrupt stop. The driver honked his horn and stuck his head through the open window. "Watch where you're going, kids. Want to get killed?" Four or five young offenders reached the sidewalk, talking and laughing. The driver continued honking as he drove slowly through town.

Every Saturday afternoon, downtown Potter endured an infestation of kids that swarmed to the Star Theater to watch the Saturday matinee. Today, as usual, Mike and Jim were a part of that swarm. "One." Mike held up his index finger to the teenage ticket booth girl, and she took his dime and gave him a red ticket passport to an afternoon of adventure and fun.

Kids jammed the theater to watch the latest Bowery Boys movie. They sat in the seats, stood in the aisles, and ran to and from the lobby. Periodic popcorn kernels flew great distances, occasionally bouncing off heads and chests. Each kid talked as loud as possible to be heard over all the other kids, who also talked as loud as possible to be heard.

A friendly voice broke through the confusion. "Hi, Mike. Hi, Jim."

Heidi! Panic placed Mike in a hammerlock and held on tight. He always got nervous around Heidi, but seeing her now made him more anxious than usual. At school he expected to see her and could plan— even mentally rehearse—what he wanted to say. But today she came from nowhere and stood next to him with a zillion kids yelling and shouting around them.

Mike flinched when a popcorn kernel bounced off his cheek and shouted to be heard above the din. "Hi, Heidi. Come to see the Bowery

Boys movie, did you?" He bit his tongue. Of course she came to see the Bowery Boys movie. Why else would she be here, to climb a mountain?

"Yes. I like them, don't you?" She didn't comment about his question's stupidity. He breathed a sigh of relief.

"Yeah, I do, and this one is supposed to be very funny."

A tall, blond, somewhat husky kid in the aisle a few rows up yelled at and shoved kids around him. The obnoxious bully wasn't from Potter. His parents probably dumped him in front of the theater like irresponsible people dump unwanted kittens near a farmhouse. Almost certainly his parents' car squealed out of sight before he could see which way they headed.

The lights dimmed, and everyone found seats. Jim sat to his left and Heidi to his right, next to the aisle. Of all the places she could choose to sit, she chose to sit next to him.

Previews came on first. Next week's matinee would be a Roy Rogers movie. Mike glanced at Heidi a couple of times during the funny parts in the Popeye cartoon. She sure looked cute when she laughed. The feature started, and he eased back to enjoy what could be the most memorable afternoon of his life.

Then he felt it.

Something was on his head. It didn't weight much, but it was definitely there. What in the world was it? He picked it off and examined it in the theater's dimness. A popcorn kernel.

Maybe one of his friends had played a little joke on him. Probably Tony. He looked behind him. The bully. Somehow, in the rush to get seats when the lights dimmed, they sat directly in front of the out-of-town bully. Mike tossed the kernel to the floor and sat back to enjoy the movie.

The bully placed another kernel on his head. He flicked it off. Another. He flicked it off. Another. He hit it hard with his hand. He continued swatting corn from his hair, a little harder each time to show his displeasure, until he realized that was just what the bully wanted. He changed tactics. The next time the bully placed a popcorn kernel in his hair—one that felt even bigger and heavier than the others—he let it lay undisturbed. It worked. The bully stopped putting popcorn in his hair, and Mike again settled back to enjoy the movie.

However, after sitting with the huge popcorn specimen protruding from his head for about ten minutes, he felt ridiculous. What would Heidi think if she knew he had a gigantic popcorn kernel on his head? Maybe she'd never find out about it, but he knew it was there, and so did the bully and the kids sitting around him. The popcorn had to go. But if he just knocked it off again, the bully would simply put another in its place. He'd have to remove it without the bully knowing it.

He came up with a plan. During a very funny part in the movie he'd act as if he were laughing hard and snap his head back to propel the popcorn to the floor unseen by the bully, who would also be laughing at the movie. It just might work.

Sach, the most comical of the Bowery Boys, said something funny, and every kid in the theater laughed. Mike feigned loud laughter, snapped his head back, and the popcorn kernel fell from his head. Had the bully seen it? Would he put more corn on his head to replace it?

A minute passed. Then two. Then three. His head remained popcorn-free. His plan had worked. He turned back to the movie, and for the next hour basked in his good fortune. Heidi had chosen to sit next to him.

Credits rolled, and the lights came up. Heidi laughed. "That was a funny movie, don't you think?"

Mike smiled in agreement. "Bowery Boys movies are always funny, but this was the funniest one yet."

They started toward the exit when suddenly the bully blocked Mike's way. He shouted several incoherent words. The only thing Mike understood was, "You're paying for these pants."

Mike stepped to his left, and the bully countered by moving to his right. Mike quickly moved back to his original position, and the bully moved back to his. The blond-haired kid repeated his demand a little louder. "You're paying for these pants."

Mike threw his hands in the air. "What in the world are you talking about? Why should I pay for your pants?"

The kid narrowed his eyes. "Because you ruined them—that's why. Just look at what you did." He turned to expose a huge gob of bubble gum stuck to his posterior like a glued-on orange omelet. "It'll cost a good fifty cents to clean these pants, and you're not leaving this theater until you give me the money." He puffed his chest out.

Mike puffed his out as a countermove, but doubted if the maneuver was noticeable. "I didn't do that. I don't even have gum."

"You did, too. I put it in your hair, and you put it in my seat. And now you're going to pay to get these pants cleaned."

So that's what happened. That last kernel wasn't a kernel after all. It was a huge wad of chewed-up gum full of spit the bully had removed from his germ-infested mouth and placed on his head. That's why it seemed so huge. And when he flipped his head back, it evidently didn't float to the floor. The bully must have been in the lobby getting more popcorn, and it landed in his seat. When he returned, he sat in it. Sure. And he didn't realize what happened until he found getting up from his seat again more difficult than he'd expected.

Mike usually had a hard time finding the right words when around Heidi. But in spite of standing next to her and being yelled at by the bully, he thought of the perfect comeback. When the bully shouted again that he was going to pay for the pants, Mike shouted back, "Oh yeah?"

The bully evidently hadn't expected such a glib reply. He ran toward the exit, pushing kids out of his way, and disappeared.

Bright sunlight greeted them when they stepped outside the theater. Mike shielded his eyes from the glare. "Beautiful day, isn't it?"

"It certainly is," Jim said. "But you know what my mom says about Indiana weather?"

"What does she say?"

"Just wait a few minutes. It'll change."

Chapter 9

MISS SCHNEIDER'S SURPRISE

Heidi was already at her desk when Mike entered the classroom Monday morning, and memory of Saturday's glorious events convinced him to do something he'd never done before. He walked right up to her, cleared his throat to find the most natural-sounding voice possible, and started a conversation.

"Hi, Heidi."

"Hi, Mike." She closed her math book.

"That was a funny movie, wasn't it?"

"It was very funny, but I was frightened by that bully." She changed her expression just enough to form two of the most beautiful dimples in the history of the world. "You didn't seem scared at all."

Mike flipped his hand to indicate what he'd done was of little significance. "You can't be scared of bullies. You've got to stand up to them and put them in their place. I don't think he'll bother us again."

"No, I don't think he will either," she said.

Miss Schneider marched into the classroom. "Well, uh, see you later," Mike stammered. He took his seat in the middle of the room.

Miss Schneider's march stopped at her desk. She performed an about-face and beamed at the class. "I told you Friday I had a surprise for you. We have a new student—not just any student, but my nephew. His parents are—well, experiencing some difficulties, and until they resolve them, he will stay with me. He is with Mr. Jackson right now. Before he comes in we'll need to rearrange the room."

She put her finger to her chin. "Okay, let's see now. Mike, would you and Jim bring the empty desk in the back of the room to the Busy Bee row? Bring it up here." She pointed to the spot Heidi's desk occupied. "Be

60

careful not to hit anyone with the desk, boys. While they are bringing the desk, I would like for everyone in the Busy Bee row to stand and push your desk back to make room."

Jim and Mike placed the empty desk where Heidi's desk had always been. "It's rather late in the year to move someone out of the Busy Bee row, so for the remainder of the year we will have six bees. My nephew will sit here." She patted the empty desk.

Mr. Jackson stood just outside the room with Miss Schneider's nephew, and Mike stretched to get a good look at him. *What would a boy smarter than Heidi look like? Heidi was beautiful. If he's smarter than she is, he must be very handsome.*

Miss Schneider talked with Mr. Jackson in the hall and then came in with her arm around the boy's shoulders. She led him to the front of the room, and they faced the class. "I would like for everyone to welcome Steven Culpepper. I am sure you will all make him feel at home."

Mike's mouth froze open. Miss Schneider's nephew was the boy who sat behind him at Saturday's matinee. The popcorn bully took his place as king of the bee row.

***

Jim paused on their walk from school and pointed at two figures in front of his house, two blocks up the street. "What's going on up there?"

Mike squinted. "It looks like Betsy's crying. Isn't that the bully with her?" They took off running, and in moments reached the pair. Jim knelt next to Betsy.

"What's going on here?"

The bully crossed his arms. "Nothing's going on. I was just walking by, and she started crying."

Mike inspected her face, arms, and legs to see if the bully had inflicted wounds. "What happened, Betsy?" She continued crying. He looked up at the new kid. "What did you do to her?"

"I didn't do anything." He uncrossed his arms and pointed at her. "She's just a crybaby—that's all."

Jim stood and stepped toward him. "She is not a crybaby. You take that back."

"I'm going to die, Jim," Betsy said between sobs.

Jim knelt by her again and put his arm on her shoulder. "Die?

How are you going to die?"

She pointed a shaking finger at the bush by the sidewalk. "It's going to kill me."

She tried to catch her breath, but it came in big, uncontrollable sobs. Mike and Jim looked at the bully and then back at the bush.

"How's that bush going to hurt you, Betsy?" Jim asked.

She tried to answer several times, but couldn't. Finally, she paused and took a deep breath. "Not the bush—the spider."

Mike inspected the bush. A huge yellow and black garden spider sat motionless on an enormous web. Sure. That's what she's talking about. Some of the web's strands were much thicker than others and looked like handwriting, especially to kids who don't know how to read. He'd forgotten about the garden spider legend he'd learned when he was Betsy's age. His society of four-year-olds believed the garden spider was a killer. According to that legend, the huge spider crawls from the web at night while everyone sleeps, sneaks into a child's bedroom, tiptoes across the floor, climbs the covers to the child's neck, and bites and bites until the child dies. It then gallops back to its web as fast as its eight legs can carry it and acts nonchalant, as if nothing happened.

Just as the rattlesnake gives a warning by shaking its rattles before it strikes, the garden spider, according to the legend, also gives a warning by writing the intended victim's name in its web the day before the kill. To protect himself from the spider, Mike learned how to spell his name. Each night he'd check all of the webs near his house to see if a garden spider had scribbled his name in one of them. His name never appeared, and each night he went to bed knowing he'd live to see a new day.

Jim found his big-brother voice. "Betsy, that spider won't hurt you. Don't be so dumb."

Mike motioned for him to be quiet. "Why do you think that spider will hurt you?"

"Because it wrote my name in there."

"Betsy, that's not your—"

Mike again motioned for Jim to be quiet. "Betsy, you can't read. How do you know that's your name?"

"'Cause that big kid there asked me my name. I told him, and he said the spider had written it in the web and is going to bite me to death tonight in my sleep."

Mike gave the bully a dirty look. He walked up to him, bent down, and picked up something by his foot. "Why, look at this. Hey, Betsy. That spider isn't going to hurt you."

"It's not?" Her crying lessened. "Why not?"

"Because of this." He held a rock about the size of a large marble high above his head. "I can't believe our luck. You know what this is? It's a magic rock. It won't let that mean ol' spider anywhere near your room. Here, put this magic rock in your room. As long as it's there, you'll be safe. Isn't that right, Jim?"

"That's right, Betsy," her brother said, pretending to admire the rock. "Nothing can protect you better than a magic rock."

Betsy took the rock and smiled. "Thanks, Mike. I'll put it under my bed. Maybe it'll protect me from the monsters that live there, too." She ran to the house, prepared to defend her room from deadly spider intrusions and occasional stray under-the-bed monster attacks.

Jim walked up to the bully until he stood a foot from him. "What are you doing, telling my sister that stuff about the spider?"

The new kid moved his hands to his hips and raised his voice. "I'm just going to my aunt's. I didn't know she was your sister. Anyway, what are you going to do about it?"

Jim considered the question. "I'm not going to do anything about it," he said, finally. "Just stay away from my sister, or I'll tell Mom, and she'll call the marshal on you." He turned to Mike. "Let's go get Squall Baby."

The new kid followed them to the pigeon cages. "Who's Squall Baby? Is that another sister?"

Mike swung around and faced the bully. "That just shows how much you know. Squall Baby is the world's greatest pigeon. She's braver than Lassie, funnier than Charlie McCarthy, and smarter than you. I don't care if you do sit in the front of the bee row with the girls. Only sissies sit in the bee row, anyhow."

The boy eyed the pigeon. "Oh, yeah? If she's so great, name just one thing she can do."

Jim took Squall Baby from her coop and petted her. "Well, it's hard to name just one thing. Right now we're taking her to the school-yard on a secret mission and having her fly back home with a message tied to her leg."

The bully gave an exaggerated yawn. "What's so great about that?"

"Can you do it?" Jim asked.

He ignored the question. "What else can she do?"

Jim's face took on a serious look. "She loves going on these secret missions because she's good at spotting the enemy."

The bully frowned. "How does she do that?"

"It's impossible to explain. It's something that has to be seen."

"Then show me. I dare you to show me."

Jim glanced at the sky. "It's getting late. We have to leave for the mission."

The boy blocked his way. "Show me."

"Do you really want me to show you?"

"Yeah. Show me."

Jim hesitated. "Well, okay. But we have to hurry. First, lay down on your back."

The new kid looked surprised, but he stretched out on the ground as Jim had instructed. "Like this?"

"That's it. Now, hold your arms straight out above your head."

He held his arms up. "Like this?"

"Looks good. Here, hold her." Jim placed the pigeon in the boy's hands. "Not so tight. You'll hurt her. Loosen your grip. That's it. Okay now, move your arms in a big circle and say 'Spot the enemy' over and over."

The kid moved Squall Baby above his head in big circles. "Spot the enemy. Spot the enemy. Spot the enemy." He stopped.

"Keep it up." Jim grabbed his arms and forced them back into the circular movement. "You're doing a good job. She's getting closer all the time. She'll spot the enemy soon. Just make sure you don't cover her eyes so she can see the enemy."

He stared up into Jim's face. "Just how will I now when she spots the enemy?"

"You'll know." Jim smiled and winked at Mike. "You'll know."

He continued the circular movement. *Splat!* Squall Baby let loose a large edition of pigeon poop. It hit the bully between the eyes and ran toward his mouth. He let go of the bird and jumped up spitting. Squall Baby flew a few feet and landed next to Jim. The kid ran to the horse trough and splashed water on his face. Quackers quacked loudly, protesting the interruption of his afternoon swim, and waddle-stomped down the plank.

"The enemy has officially been spotted!" Jim laughed so hard he fell to one knee and held his stomach. The boy dried his face and hands in his shirttail while Mike and Jim continued laughing.

"That makes us even for your putting popcorn and bubble gum in my hair," Mike said.

"That was you? Well, you owe me big time. Aunt Shirley said whoever put gum on my seat was a hoodlum, and if she ever found out who it was, he'd be sorry." He clenched his fists and held them high. "It'll cost at least fifty cents to get those pants cleaned. Pay up, or I'll tell her it was you."

Jim put Squall Baby into the portable cage. "Don't pay any attention to him, Mike. He's just mad because Squall Baby knew he was the enemy, and she spotted him. Let's go. We have a secret mission to carry out." Mike and Jim started walking toward Waterworks Road.

"Wait!" The blond kid caught up with them. "I'll tell you what," he said. "Take me on this secret mission, and I'll forget everything."

Jim looked at Mike. "I don't know ... "

The boy pointed at Mike. "If you do, I won't tell Aunt Shirley you ruined my pants." He turned to Jim. "And I won't tell her you had your pigeon poop on me."

Jim thought for a moment. "I don't know. I mean, after all, you are the enemy. Squall Baby spotted you."

"The enemy and a bully," Mike said.

"Either I go with you, or I'll beat you both up right now, and I'll tell Aunt Shirley you ruined my pants."

Mike and Jim again looked at each other. "Okay," Mike said. "We'll take you on this one mission, but you have to promise never to say anything about the gum or the enemy-spotting. Promise?"

"Promise."

They shook hands, and two secret agents and one bully walked cautiously to the Potter Elementary School playground by way of the secret woods' hidden trails.

Chapter 10

THE THIEF

Two weeks later, Jim fed the last group of pigeons, shut the coop's door, and turned to Mike. "I'm ready. Just got to get my books." They walked to where he'd left them by the back stoop, and he grabbed them and held one up. "If this math gets any harder, we'll soon be doing college level work. Did you understand how to do it?"

"Yeah," Mike said. "It's not hard at all. They just added a step to what we've been doing for the last week."

Jim tucked the book under his arms with the others, and they started the long walk to school. "I keep forgetting you're a math genius. I should have called you for help last night."

"You should have. Next time you need help, let me know. If I'm not too busy writing spelling words I missed on a test or trying to understand geography or history, I'll be happy to help. Or maybe Steven can help."

Jim slowed. "You know, he makes a good secret agent. The missions have been a lot more fun since he's been coming with us."

"I agree," Mike said. "And he doesn't seem like a bully once you get to know him."

Jim shifted the books to his other arm. "And he is smart. Maybe even smart enough to sit in the bee row with the girls."

"Yeah, but it's still not right for him to sit in front of Heidi." Someone yelled a couple of blocks behind them, and Mike turned to see who it was. "It's Steven."

Steven caught up with them. "I've been thinking about the secret missions."

"Yeah? What about them, Agent Nevets?" Jim looked over his

shoulder to make sure enemy spies weren't listening.

"Well, they're fun, but we need to do something different. Something really exciting."

"Like what?"

"I'm not sure. It's just that we do the same thing every time. We always go through the secret woods to the schoolyard after school and let Squall Baby loose." He thought for a moment. "Tell you what. Tonight let's wait until after supper. We won't let her loose until dark. That'll make it more exciting. Can Squall Baby find her way home in the dark?"

"Sure she can." Jim paused. "At least I think she can."

Mike thought about Steven's idea. "You know, guys, tonight would be the perfect evening."

Jim kicked a rock from the sidewalk. It skipped across the street, bounced off the curb, and came to rest in the middle of the road. "What's so perfect about tonight?"

"Well, what's today's date, Jim?"

"I don't know. March thirtieth or thirty-first?"

"Nope. Try again."

"April first?"

"That's right. April Fool's Day. What better day to see if we can fool Squall Baby? I say we do it."

Steven put his arms around the others' shoulders. "Men, tonight we'll find out just how smart Squall Baby really is. The secret agent game is about to get more exciting."

***

When the three boys entered Miss Schneider's room, Mary was inspecting a ten-dollar bill Heidi held out. "She'll be surprised," she said. "I can't believe you're buying it for her."

Steven stared at the bill. "Buy what for whom and who will be surprised?"

"Show them."

Mike took the bill from her and examined it. "Wow! Where'd you get this?" He handed it back.

Heidi shoved it into her jacket pocket. "I've been saving for months and months. Tomorrow's my mom's birthday. I'm going to Brown's Drugstore after school and buy her a three-ounce bottle of

Moonlight on the Wabash perfume. It costs three dollars an ounce."

"She'll love it," Mary said. "And it sounds so exotic."

Someone tapped Mike's shoulder, and he turned. Skip, sporting an enormous grin, stared back at him. Mike rejoined the conversation, and Skip again tapped him. "Oh, Mike."

Mike turned a second time. "What, Skip?"

"Your shoe's untied."

Mike looked down at his shoe and instantly realized he had made a huge mistake.

"April fool! April fool!" Skip laughed his horrible, piercing laugh, and the entire grasshopper row joined in. "April fool. I got you on that one. April fool."

Mike rolled his eyes. He'd fallen for the oldest joke in the world. For the next several minutes he heard, "April fool. I got him on that one. Did you see it? I really got him. April fool."

School started, and time passed quickly, even though the grasshoppers constantly reminded him Skip had fooled him. The morning coolness had sneaked off, and a beautiful day welcomed the students when they went outside for noon recess.

Miss Schneider motioned for Mike to come to where she supervised the schoolyard. She talked without taking her eyes off the students. "On the shelf above where I hang my coat is a tissue box, Mike. Would you grab three or four tissues and bring them to me?"

He ran up the stairs and entered the second floor coatroom. Jerry Harders stood at the far end with his hand in a jacket pocket. Heidi's jacket! The boys stared at one another.

Mike considered options. He could tell Miss Schneider he couldn't find the tissues, and she'd probably ask someone else to get them. Or, he could pretend he never saw Jerry, grab the tissues, and leave without saying anything. Then he remembered what Mr. Jackson said that day he visited the classroom to watch the children do math: *Knowing someone is doing something terribly wrong and not informing proper authorities is also terribly wrong.*

A cold sweat formed on his forehead. He took a deep breath and heard himself say, "Jerry, we need to see Miss Schneider."

Jerry pulled his hand from the jacket pocket, and Heidi's ten-dollar bill came out and floated to the floor. Mike picked it up and walked from the room, down the steps, and out the door. He didn't turn to see if Jerry followed, in fear Jerry would grab him and beat him beyond recognition.

Miss Schneider yelled at two boys who were running in the distance. "You boys stop chasing girls with that toad and put it back where you found it." She watched until they placed it in the high grass by the back of the school. Mike waited for her to notice he'd returned. She placed her hands on her hips. "Where are the tissues?"

"I didn't get them. Jerry was in the coatroom. He had his hand in Heidi's jacket pocket, and when he pulled it out, this fell to the floor." He opened his hand to reveal the ten dollar bill. Miss Schneider took it from him. For the first time since he left the coatroom, Mike looked behind him to see if Jerry had followed him.

He had.

Miss Schnieder clutched the bill tightly. "Is that true, young man?"

"I thought it was my coat. I was just trying to get some candy from my coat. That's all."

She pointed to a spot two feet in front of her. "Sit! Jerry, it's rather hard to believe you mistook Heidi's coat for yours. Why, yours must be three times larger. Besides, you shouldn't have been in that coatroom in the first place. You know it's off limits to students during recess. You and I are going to see Mr. Jackson as soon as recess is over."

When the students returned to class, Miss Schneider escorted Jerry to Mr. Jackson's office. The sounds of seven whacks overflowed into the hallway, and Miss Schneider led Jerry to the red chair just outside her door. He didn't appear to be crying. He sat in the chair until the 3:15 bell ended the school day.

Chapter 11

THE ENCOUNTER IN THE SECRET WOODS

Trashman and Burly had been drinking most of the day. By the time Cinders pulled the green wagon up the driveway, they talked in slurs. Trashman grabbed two Sterling Beer six-packs from behind the seat, and the two stumbled inside and crashed on the sofa. Jerry walked in from the kitchen.

"Jerry," Trashman boomed, "take care of Cinders."

Jerry ran to the barn and got the horse ready for the evening. When he returned, his father sat on the sofa, drinking a beer and talking with Burly, and his mother prepared supper in the kitchen. He waited just inside the front door. Sweat from his scalp and face dripped onto his shirt. One drop slid over his upper lip and into his mouth. He spit.

Trashman looked up. "You get Cinders put away?"

"Yeah, I did."

Trashman continued talking with Burly. After a minute he looked back at Jerry. "Well, what? You want something?"

"I got a paddling at school. For something I didn't do."

Connie stepped from the kitchen and stood in the doorway. "You got a paddling? Who did it?"

"Mr. Jackson."

"If you didn't do anything, why'd he paddle you?"

"Mike Long told him I stole money, but I didn't. I just took some candy from my own jacket."

Trashman belched. "He paddled you for that?"

"Yeah. For getting a piece of candy. From my own jacket."

Trashman finished off the bottle and tossed it to the floor with a thud. "You sure you didn't do anything?"

"I didn't do nothing, Pa. Swear to God. Mike Long took that ten dollar bill out of Heidi Beck's jacket. He told Miss Schneider I took it."

Burly swigged from his beer and set the empty bottle on the floor. "Guys like that Jackson will push you as far as you'll let him." He wiped his mouth with his sleeve. "I know the type. Seen hundreds of 'em. He thinks he's hot stuff because he's a big war hero and has all that education. If no one stands up to him, he'll just keep pushing."

He opened another beer and tossed the opener to Trashman. "It's an insult to you, Seth. That's what it is. He takes that Long kid's word over your son's because he don't respect you. If you put a little fear in him, you won't have any more trouble with him." Burly glanced at Connie and then fixed his eyes back on Trashman. "Seth, you going to let him get away with it?"

Trashman stood. "No! By God, I'm not going to let him get away with it. It's time someone took care of Mister High and Mighty." He leaned against the wall to regain his balance and staggered to the door.

Connie ran after him. "Seth, don't go. I'll talk with him."

Burly stood, knocking his beer bottle over. The little bit of liquid that came out absorbed quickly into the wooden floor. "This ain't a job for a woman, Connie." He squinted at Seth, who still stood by the door. "Are you going to let your woman do your job for you?"

"No, I'm not. I take care of my own jobs."

"Want me to go with you?"

"I don't need no help."

"Suit yourself."

Both men left the house. Burly started the eight-block walk back to his home in Red Dog Pool Hall basement, and Trashman began an unsteady walk to Potter Elementary School.

Most of the teachers had already left. Lights in a few first-floor classrooms showed teachers were preparing for the next day. Trashman creaked up the stairs to the second floor where all the rooms were dark except for Mr. Jackson's office. He meandered toward the light and paused in the doorway. He cleared his throat.

Mr. Jackson looked up. "Oh, hello, Mr. Harders. Glad you stopped by. Did Jerry tell you about the problem we had with him today?"

Trashman squeezed the door frame to keep from falling. "As I understand it, Jerry had a problem with you today."

"What do you mean?"

71

"I'll tell you what I mean." He stumbled into the office. "That Long kid lied about Jerry stealing money. He didn't steal anything. I'll teach you to paddle my kid for something he didn't do, Mr. High and Mighty."

Trashman lunged at Mr. Jackson and swung his right fist with all the force he could gather. Mr. Jackson jumped back, and Trashman's haymaker found empty air and pulled him off balance. He fell forward, bounced off the desk, and knocked a chair over, before hitting the floor chin first. The fall knocked the breath out of him, and he lay groaning.

Mr. Jackson came around the desk and helped him up. Applying a half Nelson, he escorted him down the stairs and out the door where he released his hold and stepped back.

"Mr. Harders, you go home now. You hear? If you come back, I'll call Marshal Smart and have you arrested for trespassing. Now go home."

Trashman spit a wad inches from Mr. Jackson's left foot. "You haven't heard the last of me. Before I'm done with you, you'll respect me. You hear what I say? That Long kid's going to respect me, too. I'll see to that."

Trashman stumbled home. Once there, he sunk into a front porch chair and dozed off. Connie and Jerry stayed in the house and let him sleep.

***

Darkness was setting in when three agents entered the secret woods on a mission, one carrying a portable cage that held the famous Squall Baby. They said nothing as they followed the winding trails. Although some daylight lingered, they'd never before been in the woods so late in the day.

Mike looked around. "It's getting dark. Let's walk faster."

"Yeah. Let's walk a little faster." Jim picked up his pace.

"What's the matter? Are you scaredy-cats?" Steven also walked a little faster.

Mike hurried his steps even more. "No, we aren't scared. It's just that it's getting late."

"Yeah, it's getting late," Jim said. "And don't use the word 'cat' around Squall Baby. She hates cats."

The three wound their way down the secret paths until they exited the opening by the railroad tracks. Steven pointed to Carlton's Grocery, a block away. "Look—it's still open. Let's get some candy."

72

Agent Mij held up the portable cage. "Nevets, have you forgotten we're on a secret mission? We don't have time to buy candy."

"Agent Mij, I don't want to buy candy to eat," the blond agent said. "I have reason to believe communist spies hid secret messages inside some of the candy wrappers. It's our duty to find them. The world's safety depends upon it."

The fact they could save the world by buying candy made the purchase urgent. They entered the store and surveyed the candy assortment. Mr. Carlton came out of the back room and leaned on the counter, tapping his fingers as he waited for them to decide what they wanted. A bald man with a white fringe for hair, Mr. Carlton was about Grandpa's age and no stranger to their secret missions. They often stopped in for candy before or after setting Squall Baby loose, and he usually played along.

"I see we're on another secret mission, eh, boys?"

"Yeah." Jim looked around for spies. "We are."

"Kind of late for a mission, isn't it?"

"Not for this mission," Steven whispered. "It's a super-secret mission that can only be done after dark."

"That right? What makes this mission so different?"

Steven held a finger to his lips. "Shhhh. For one thing we understand enemy spies have put secret messages inside some of your candy. We have to find them before we can set Squall Baby loose." He looked over the assortment. "Problem is, we don't know which candy they're hidden in."

Mr. Carlton pursed his lips. "You know, when I came to work this morning, I saw a spy putting a secret message in one of these." He held up a Tootsie Pop.

Steven took the Tootsie Pop. "Thanks for the tip."

"What about you two? Do you want to see if there are any messages in these?" He held up two more Tootsie Pops, and Mike and Jim took them. Each boy gave Mr. Carlton two cents. He waved as they left. "Good luck on your mission. See you next time."

Outside, Jim unwrapped his Tootsie Pop, slipped it into his mouth, and peered around. "It's darker than I thought it would be," he said. "We'd better hurry." They quickly crossed Main Street and stopped by a large maple at the playground's edge. "Let's tie this Tootsie Pop wrapper on Squall Baby's leg instead of writing a message. After all, it does contain the enemy's secret message."

Mike took the pigeon from her portable cage and held her while

Jim secured the secret message. "Here, Agent Nevets," he said, holding the bird out. "It's your turn."

Steven threw her into the air, and the three shouted, "Fly home, Squall Baby! Fly home!"

***

Trashman lived just behind the grocery store. He'd woken himself up from his front porch slumber by swallowing the wrong way, and had just managed to control his coughing when he heard the shouting. He remained motionless for several seconds. "Squall Baby," he said. "That must be that Mackey kid with his bird, and I'll bet that Long kid's with him." He pushed himself out of the chair and headed toward Main.

***

Mike slowed his walk toward the secret woods. "You know what, guys? It's getting pretty dark. I say we go home the regular way."

"Okay with me," Jim said. "It'd be hard to see those paths."

"I don't care which way we go. I just want to see if Squall Baby can find her way home in the dark." Steven pointed to a figure running toward them. "Who's that?"

The fast-moving man yelled, "That's you, isn't it, Mike Long?"

Mike swallowed hard. "It's Trashman."

"I know that's you. My boy got paddled because of you." He ran faster, gasping loudly with each step. "I'll show you what a real beating's like, you worthless punk."

"Run," Jim yelled. Trashman was just a few steps behind them. The streetlights made it easy for him to follow them, even though he'd been drinking. If they were going to lose him, they'd have to get away from the lights.

Mike pointed toward the secret woods. "That way!" They cut through a yard, jumped the railroad track ditch, and scurried up the incline to the tracks, running as fast as they could toward the secret woods' opening. Trashman fell twice, once when he jumped the ditch and again when he got on the tracks, but the boys couldn't lose him. They went through the opening on the other side of the tracks and kept running. Darkness made it hard to see, and they ran on memory. Briars scraped at Trashman's clothes when he entered the woods, and he cursed.

"The peninsula," Mike shouted. "Run to the peninsula."

The three now ran as a unit, each within a couple of feet of the others. Trashman was twenty feet behind them when they jumped over the creek bank onto the peninsula. They pushed their backs against the bank and sat motionless in the dark woods. Brush swished close by as Trashman approached, then stopped. He stood within ten feet of their hiding place. For the next minute it was as quiet as it was dark.

Trashman's loud voice shattered the silence. "I know you're here, Mike Long. I'm going to give you the whooping of your life. You hear me? That goes for the rest of you brats, too. Then you won't tell lies, will you? Then you'll respect me."

What frightened Mike more than the Trashman's voice, more than his cursing and heavy breathing, even more than the threats of the beating, was what he did next. He laughed. It seemed so out of place and evil, it sent chills up his spine. The three remained motionless. Trashman slowly walked away, and the sounds of his footsteps grew fainter and fainter until they ceased to exist. Still the boys didn't move. A full five minutes passed.

Steven sat up slowly. Then Jim and Mike sat up, careful not to make a sound. Another minute passed. Steven whispered, "I think it's safe."

They stood. The muted moonlight made the woods eerie. Steven shook his leg. "My left foot's soaked," he said. They walked through the woods toward home. A loud snap resonated behind them.

"What was that?" Jim whispered.

"I don't know. Just keep walking."

"It's an animal. A big one."

"A bear," Steven said, softly.

"There aren't any bears around here."

Silence. They continued following the trail in the darkness. "Then it's a big wolf," Steven said.

Mike sighed. "There aren't any wolves either!"

Jim stopped in front of them, and they almost ran into him. "Boys, you know what that is? It's—it's a communist."

Another snap shot through the woods, this one closer. Whatever it was, it wasn't very far from them. They listened. Sounds of slow-moving steps, like an animal sneaking up on its prey, came from the trail behind them. Mike took off running, but had taken only two steps when something grabbed his shoulder. An arm wrapped around his waist and lifted him into the air. It laughed. "Let's see you get away now, Long."

Mike kicked. "Let me go. Let me go!"

"I'll let you go after I give you your whooping. I'll teach you to tell lies. I'll teach you to get my boy in trouble. When I'm done, you'll respect me and my family."

Trashman held Mike in a bear hug and used his free hand to unbuckle his belt for the whooping. Steven ran as fast as he could toward their voices and rammed into them with his shoulder. The unexpected jolt knocked both Trashman and Mike to the ground, jarring Mike loose.

"Run," Steven shouted. Mike scampered to his feet, and the three ran as fast as they could toward home in the darkness.

"You boys better not tell anyone about this. You hear?" Trashman yelled. "I'll just deny it. You hear me? Who're they going to believe—you kids or an adult?"

Tree branches slapped them as they dashed through the woods. Occasional logs and stumps reached out and tripped them. Although Trashman's voice became more distant as they ran, they could still hear his final advice. "If you tell, your folks won't let you out of the house until you're thirty years old. You'll be prisoners in your own homes."

The boys ran until they felt the sidewalk's firmness under their feet and saw the welcoming glow of a streetlight overhead. Their heavy breathing lessened as they approached headquarters at Jim's house and heard cooing from Squall Baby's cage. She'd beaten them home.

Jim closed the cage door and motioned for the boys to come closer. "Guys, Trashman's right. If we tell anyone, our folks won't let us out of their sight. We'll lose our freedom."

"You're right," Mike said. "This has to be our secret. We'll just have to be careful. No more going into the woods after dark. Things like that."

Mike looked at Steven. The boy he once considered a bully was a hero tonight. His bravery had saved him from a beating.

"I agree," Steven said. "It's our secret."

"It's getting late. I'd better go home before I get in trouble." Mike paused. "And Steven, thanks."

"You're welcome. That's what friends are for."

"Goodnight," the three said in unison. With that, Agents Mij, Ekim, and Nevets went their separate ways.

Chapter 12

THE SAVING OF THE HEATHENS

When Preacher Beemer accepted the call nineteen years earlier, he was a young man of twenty-four fresh out of preacher's college. He met his future wife Stella, an elementary education major, when they were freshmen at Oakland City College. They married soon after graduation and, after a brief honeymoon, began serving God at the Oak Street Baptist Church. The ensuing years molded them into distinguished and hardworking servants of God.

The Oak Street Baptist Church had been losing members for years, and the church council told Preacher Beemer they couldn't pay much. When he arrived in 1935 the church had only fifty-four members. Allowing for those who were too old, too busy, or just plain too lazy to attend, thirty-some made it to church on a somewhat regular basis. What with vacations, work schedule conflicts, and other complications, the average church attendance hovered around twenty-four.

To make matters worse, since the church attracted very few new members, the congregation had grown elderly. The death rate would very likely continue to outpace the new membership rate until the only person showing up on Sundays would be the preacher himself. They told him if he reversed the trend, they would increase his salary.

He and Stella began an outreach program within weeks of his first sermon. First, they concentrated on the youth. They held youth activities on a regular basis in the fellowship hall. They organized scavenger hunts, picnics, carnivals, and dozens of other activities. Youngsters came for the fun and later became church members. Then the Beemers convinced the council to purchase an old school bus they named God's Chariot. In addition to busing in those who'd otherwise be unable to attend church, it also provided access to entertainment for members and prospective members. The men used it to attend the Evansville Braves minor league baseball games, and once or twice a year they even ventured to Saint Louis to watch the Cardinals play. Women used it for shopping excursions to Princeton, Vincennes, Evansville, and other exotic cities. A few times they made it all the way to Indianapolis. The membership continued to increase.

The membership drive the Beemers instituted two years after they came proved to be the most successful part of the outreach program. They called the program *Planting the Seeds of Hope*. Each spring, Preacher Beemer asked the congregation to provide names and addresses of people they knew who had no church affiliation. The church women, under Stella's leadership, baked pies and cakes that Preacher Beemer took to the people on the list. He always presented at least two baked goods and even more to large families. He told them God loves them, he loves them, and his congregation loves them. He invited them to join the Oak Street Baptist Church and become a member of the congregation that loves them so much. If they allowed it, he gave a five-minute sermon and prayed for their souls. At the end of his visits he handed out tickets good for two more pies or cakes that had to be redeemed in person before or after any Sunday service during the three weeks following the visit.

Each year an average of seven families joined the church as a direct result of this program. Most families consisted of four or more people, and the church had been doing this for seventeen years. During that time, over three hundred people had joined the church because of this program alone. That's not even counting the children born to these new members after they were converted or the fact that, in a few years, those children would have children.

Members of some of the other churches joked about the program, and instead of calling it by its correct name, *Planting the Seeds of Hope*, they referred to it as *The Saving of the Heathens*. Preacher Beemer told them if it weren't for the heathens there wouldn't even be an Oak Street Baptist Church. He also pointed out that once they accepted God, heathens became children of God.

***

Preacher Beemer's 1947 Plymouth smelled like a bakery when he backed out of his driveway on the first day of the annual three-day

Planting the Seeds of Hope outreach program. He and the car were familiar sights in town, and people could identify both blocks away. No matter how cold or hot the weather, he always wore a blue suit with a white decorative handkerchief, a white long-sleeved shirt, a tie with a picture of Christ, blue socks, and shiny black shoes. On hot days he carried his suit coat over his shoulder, and on cold days he added a gray overcoat and perhaps a hat.

He parked his Plymouth in front of Trashman's house and took a cherry pie and an angel food cake from the trunk. The place hadn't changed since his last visit. Several sheets of tin roofing that covered Cinder's dilapidated dark gray barn had long ago rusted through. Some were missing completely. The house wasn't any better. The gutters had fallen off years ago. Firewood for cooking and heating rested against the shack. The pump that supplied the water and the leaning outhouse that served as the bathroom hid behind the house. Inside, kerosene lamps supplied light after sunset.

He knocked gently on the screen door so it wouldn't fall off. Connie answered with a slight smile. "Why, if it isn't Preacher Beemer out saving us heathens."

Preacher Beemer chuckled. "Now Mrs. Harders, you know you aren't a heathen—you're a friend and a child of God. And just look what the church ladies made for you and your family." He held out the pie and the cake. "Is there someplace I can set these? They're getting heavy, and they smell so good I'm afraid I might be tempted to eat them."

"Sure. Come on in and put them on the table." She shooed the big gray cat from his tabletop lounge to make room. The cat slipped through a tear in the screen door and onto the porch, sniffing the air and stretching. Preacher Beemer placed the offering on the table.

"I know your family will enjoy eating these as much as the church ladies enjoyed making them." He sat in a kitchen chair next to the table and motioned for Connie to sit in the chair next to his. "Mrs. Harders, may I ask a question?"

"Sure."

"Have you thought of where you will spend eternity?"

"Not really. I mean there are still just two choices, aren't there? Either one will be better than this."

Preacher Beemer frowned. "Are you okay, Mrs. Harders?"

"Yeah. I'm okay, Preacher."

"Are you safe? Is Jerry safe?"

"Yeah, we're safe. You don't have to worry about us."

Preacher Beemer studied her. "Promise if you need help, any kind of help, you'll come to my house. I don't care if it's in the middle of the night. Will you promise me that?"

"I promise," she said. "If I need help, I'll let you know."

"I sure would like to see your family in church. We have a lot of activities I'm sure Jerry would enjoy. Here." He pulled a ticket from his inside coat pocket. "When you come to church don't forget to redeem this for more baked goods. You have to admit, the church ladies know how to bake." He handed her the ticket. "Before I go, may I pray?"

Connie hesitated. "Well, you can if you want to, but I don't expect it'll do much good." She bowed her head.

Preacher Beemer prayed for her salvation, for Jerry's salvation, and for her husband's salvation. He prayed Mr. Harders would stop drinking demon liquor and attend church. He prayed they would all get baptized at Lake Dundee and stroll down the golden streets of heaven after they leave this earthly world. When he finished, he said, "Remember, the Lord loves you. Don't forget, if you ever need help, see me—day or night."

"I won't forget."

He waved from his car. He had presented the seeds of hope to her sixteen times before. Someday one of the seeds just might take root.

Chapter 13

A DREAM OF CIRCUS MAGIC

Mike had just entered the classroom when Heidi approached him with a smile even bigger than usual. "Did you hear about the circus this weekend?"

He nodded. "Grandpa told me about it. Brown's Drugstore sells Saturday matinee kids' day tickets for fifty cents if you buy them in advance. That's when I'm going."

"Me, too. Just think—this'll be the last time we'll qualify as kids. Mom keeps saying how fast I'm growing up."

Mary placed an armload of books on her desk. "Are you talking about the circus?"

Heidi's eyes danced. "Yes, I'm going on Saturday. Isn't it exciting? Are you going?"

"I wouldn't miss it for the world. I bought my ticket yesterday."

Miss Schneider entered the room, and the kids took their seats. She opened a book to a page marked with a piece of paper and leaned against the front of her desk.

"Children, today we will study math we use while shopping. You'll be adults before you know it and will have to buy everything you need yourself. If you don't understand how to do the math involved, the store might overcharge you by mistake, and you wouldn't even know it."

Mike tried to listen to the math lesson, but it got mixed up with his circus thoughts. He folded his arms, leaned back, and stared at the ceiling. *A circus. What would happen if I bought Heidi a ticket, and she sat with me? We'd have a good time, and then every time she sees me she'll think of all the fun we had. Grandpa said it worked for Mom. I'll buy her peanuts and cotton candy, and we'll laugh at the clowns and enjoy the acts. It will be a day we'll*

81

remember forever. Magic, Grandpa called it.

With a great deal of effort, he pushed his circus thoughts toward a temporary holding region where they could be easily recalled later. He stared at a pencil and concentrated on thinking *Miss Schneider, Miss Schneider, Miss Schneider.* He finally called up the very small region of an eleven-year-old boy's brain that deals with teacher lectures, but Miss Schneider appeared somewhat blurred.

"You will have to make out budgets and pay bills," she was saying. "You must become wise consumers and understand how to calculate the cost of various purchases. I'll pass out a worksheet for you to work on at home tonight."

She handed a stack of worksheets to the students sitting in the front desks. After they took their copies and passed the rest to the students behind them, she looked about the class. "Is there anyone who did not receive a worksheet? Good. Now before I discuss the worksheet, let's look at the problems on page 213 in your math book."

Keeping the thoughts of circus magic with Heidi separate from Miss Schneider's math lecture proved exhausting. The effort sapped so much energy that Mike became sleepy, and Miss Schneider's voice drifted into the distance. Circus thoughts seeped through a small crack in the teacher lecture region wall until it crumbled completely, and they flooded in. Mike knew he'd soon be unable to follow the lecture. He turned to page 213, held the book tightly in both hands, and angled his body to make it appear as if he were following the lecture.

Her voice droned on. "Look at the sample problem on that page. It says, 'The department store sells boys' shirts for a dollar and fifty cents each ... '"

His eyelids got heavier and heavier until they closed. He tried to open them, but didn't have enough eyelid power. Miss Schneider continued. "If you buy three shirts, and your friend *bue* two *tenfer ouden flunding*, how many *ettens* do you *flabbet* together?" Sleep won out. His subconscious rerouted Miss Schneider's voice to a little known abyss in a distant, unnamed brain region. That allowed Mike to dream about circus magic with Heidi without fear of being interrupted by the math instruction taking place in the fifth grade classroom.

***

Mike's bed creaked as he shook his amber glass piggy bank. Every so often a coin fell through the slot and clinked against those that had already fallen on the bedspread. Soon the remaining coins escaped pig prison and formed themselves into neat one-dollar stacks. He counted the money. *One, two, three, four, five. Ten, twenty, thirty, thirty-five. Five dollars and thirty-five cents.* That would be enough to buy two circus tickets plus cotton candy, pop, peanuts, and everything else two people needed to have a magical time at the circus.

He put the coins into his pocket and flew backwards through space and walls to Brown's Drugstore. A clerk stood with his back to him making click, click, click sounds as he stirred a soda with a long spoon. When he turned, he held a three-foot tall strawberry soda. "I believe this is what you want, young man."

Mike's mouth flew open. "I don't believe it!"

The clerk laughed. "I don't blame you. It's not every day you see a soda this big."

"No. No. That's not what I don't believe. Grandpa, what are you doing here?"

Grandpa smiled, squeezing his eyelids into all-knowing slits. "I'm here to help you achieve circus magic. I know what you want, and this isn't it." He threw the soda high into the air and out of the dream. "You want to buy two circus tickets so you can take her." Grandpa pointed to a girl standing motionless in the perfume section holding a bottle of Moonlight on the Wabash perfume. It was Heidi. Her lips were pursed like George Washington's in that picture in Mr. Jackson's office, and the sparkle was missing from her black eyes.

"Do you think she will sit with me at the circus if I ask her, Grandpa?"

"I don't know, son. You'll just have to buy the tickets and find out for yourself. But if she does, it will be magical. Every time she thinks about clowns, cotton candy, and good times, she'll think of you. When she smells freshly popped popcorn or hears calliope music, she'll think of you. She'll be yours forever, all for the price of two circus tickets. It's the magic of the circus." He held something out in his hand. "Here are two tickets to the kids' day performance. Now, that will be a thousand dollars."

"A thousand dollars? I don't have a thousand dollars."

"Sure you do. Reach into your pockets."

Mike reached in and pulled out a wad of hundred dollar bills.

"Here, Grandpa." He handed him a fistful of bills. "Keep the change."

Grandpa stuffed some of the money into his overall pockets and the rest under his straw hat and vanished through the drugstore wall on the back of a trumpeting elephant.

Mike held the tickets out to Heidi.

"Oh, you've bought your circus ticket." Her expression hadn't changed from the first time he saw her in the store. "I still have to get mine. That is, if I have enough money left after buying Mom's perfume. I may not be able to go."

"You don't need to buy a ticket. I bought one for you."

"You did?"

"Sure. Here."

Heidi took the ticket. The sadness left her face, and the smile that made her Heidi returned. Her black eyes sparkled. "Thank you. That's so sweet of you."

"Will you sit with me at the circus?"

"I wouldn't want to sit with anyone else."

"Then let's go."

He took her hand, and they flew backwards through time and space from math class reality to the Saturday afternoon circus performance. Clowns rode unicycles and stuffed themselves into tiny, brightly painted cars. Mike and Heidi ate cotton candy and popcorn. Just one more treat would complete the magic—circus peanuts.

He pointed to the vendor who hawked peanuts several rows away. "Would you like some peanuts?"

"I'd love some, but you've spent too much money already."

"For you, my dear, money is no object." Mike raised his hand to get the vendor's attention. Then he stood and waved, but the vendor ignored him and tossed peanut bags to other kids. The only way to get his attention would be to yell as loud as he could.

***

Miss Schneider continued teaching math. "Look at problem four. The store has boy's pants on sale. Each pair costs four dollars. If you buy five pairs of pants, how much will it cost? Let's see. Mike why don't you take this one? What would the five pairs of pants cost?"

"PEANUTS!"

Miss Schneider stepped back and held her hand to her throat. Her voice, which had been rerouted to the little-known abyss up to this point, found a direct route back to the teacher lecture region. Mike's circus magic thoughts vanished. The changeover happened so suddenly it exploded, awaking Mike with such a start his left arm spasmed outward and upward. His hand stopped when his arm reached its full extension, but his fingers continued their outward movement until they resembled fingers of a five-year-old telling his age.

The math book they had clutched an instant before rocketed from his open hand, missing the head of the person sitting to his left by twelve inches. It sailed a good three feet above Jerry Harders and Skip Gander in the grasshopper row, and was still gaining altitude when it hit the window frame. The book fell onto the bookshelf below and knocked the globe to the floor, where it careened off the radiator and came to rest less than a yard from Miss Schneider's feet.

She shifted her gaze from the globe to Mike. Her hand moved slowly from her throat and found her hip.

"Mike, I will not put up with your throwing books in my classroom. Go sit in the hall until you can behave as a fifth grade student should. And when I ask a question, I want an answer, not a joke."

Snickering peppered the room. "Class, be quiet this instant!" She aimed her scowl at the students. "Don't encourage him. He is not funny." Hands went over mouths as students tried to stifle further laughter.

Mike didn't get up. What's going on? A minute ago he sat next to Heidi at the circus. Now Miss Schneider is telling him to sit in the hall, and everyone is laughing at him. There must be some mistake. He's never had to sit out in the hall in his entire school career.

"Up, up. Let's go."

"But I, uh—"

"Young man ... " She pointed toward the door.

No use trying to explain now. She'd already "young manned" him. Besides, what could he explain? That he dreamed he sat next to Heidi at the circus instead of following the lesson? He failed to pay attention, and now he had to pay the price.

He trudged to the door. The hardest steps were the ones in front of Heidi. He looked back at Miss Schneider just in case she had changed her mind, but she still pointed toward the door. Heidi looked sad, just like she did before he took her to the circus in his dream. He walked out of the room and sat in the red student chair put there for those who acted up. Everyone who walked by would know he had caused trouble in Miss Schneider's class.

Jerry Harders sat here. I'm no better than Jerry Harders. Heidi will never want to sit with me at the circus now. The day that had started off so promising with hints of circus magic had turned into one he just hoped to get through somehow.

Chapter 14

THE FUNERAL

Betsy ran into the house and down the basement stairs. "Mom, what time is it?"

Ever since Donna Mackey's husband died in the power line accident three years ago, she supported her family by cleaning houses and taking in laundry. Today she faced fifteen loads of dirty clothes. She added soap to the washing machine's churning water and tossed in another load. "Betsy, it's five minutes later than the last time you asked."

"But I'm bored."

"If you can't find something to do, I have a job for you. You can dust the living room furniture."

Betsy made a face. "I hate to dust."

Donna emptied another bag of dirty clothes on the floor and began separating the lights from the darks. "Then I suggest you go outside and play. If you ask what time it is once more, you'll be dusting."

Betsy moseyed outside and sat in the sparse backyard grass. She broke a twig into small pieces and flicked them away as hard as she could, mentally marking each new distance record she set. After launching the last one, she lay on her back with her head resting on her hands and watched the clouds float by, describing what each one reminded her of. "A bird ... A car ... A dragon."

Quackers waddled up to her wagging his tail and nibbled her nose, quacking quietly. She laughed and scratched her nose and petted him. "That tickles. Are you bored, too?" Doodles, the green-tailed rooster, pecked at the invisible morsel trail until he stood next to Quackers and Betsy, and she petted him, too. Quackers waddled up the plank to the horse trough and eased in for a swim.

The temperature was more like mid-July than early April. She turned on her side and watched Doodles peck the ground. "You look hot. If you could swim, you could cool off. All you have to do is float like Quackers does and kick your feet now and then. Do you want to learn how to swim?"

Doodles clucked.

She jumped up. "Come on—I'll teach you how."

Doodles clucked again and followed her to the trough. She picked him up, placed him on the trough's platform, and pointed at the duck.

"You can't swim because you've never watched Quackers swim, right? You can't see him from the ground. See how he floats? That doesn't look so hard, does it?" She didn't say anything for a while, giving the rooster ample time to concentrate on the duck's swimming techniques.

"Think you can do that?"

Doodles clucked.

"Do you want to try it?"

He clucked one last time.

Betsy lifted the duck from the water and placed him on the platform. "Doodles wants to swim." Quackers wagged his tail and flapped his wings.

She picked up the rooster. "Now, remember to float like Quackers did. If you want to move around, just kick. That's how Quackers does it." She placed Doodles in the water and stepped back.

Doodles didn't float gracefully. In fact, he didn't float at all. Once in the water, he panicked. Instead of floating the way Betsy had instructed him, he beat his wings on the water and made loud noises.

"Float," Betsy shouted. "Float. Don't beat your wings. Float!"

Doodles didn't listen to a word she said. The rooster went under several times, but each time managed to come up for air.

She continued providing swimming instructions. She didn't know what else to do. She tried to pull him out of the water, but his flailing wings slapped her and made saving him impossible. "Float, Doodles. Float. Oh, don't go under the water. Float on top of it."

Doodles ignored her. He continued struggling a while longer. Then all movement stopped, and, like a rubber ball, he floated in the trough.

Betsy poked several times at the portion of Doodles that protruded above the water. He didn't move. She hoisted the heavy, water-soaked bird from the trough and placed him gently on the ground. She poked him again. The bird showed no signs of life. She poked harder. He still didn't move.

"Don't hold your breath. Quit sleeping, will you?"

Betsy held her hands over her eyes and cried. She sat beside him on the ground and waited for Jim to come home from school, occasionally looking at Doodles to see if he showed any sign of coming to. She heard a familiar voice. Jim! Mike and Steven walked on either side of him. She ran to her brother.

"Doodles won't wake up."

Jim stiffened. "What?"

"Doodles won't wake up." She took Jim's hand and led him to the motionless bird.

He knelt and pressed the bird's chest several times. He lifted Doodles's head and pulled his hand away. The head fell limp to the ground. He looked up at Betsy. "What happened to him?"

"I was teaching him to swim." Betsy continued crying.

Jim pointed at the trough. "In there? How long was he in there?"

"I don't know. A long time."

"How did he get there?"

"I put him in the trough so he could swim."

Jim let out a deep sigh. "Betsy—Betsy, roosters can't swim."

Her chin quivered. "I know. That's why I wanted to teach him. I wanted him to cool off."

"Betsy, it's not just that roosters don't know how to swim, they *can't* swim. Besides, you don't know how to swim, either. How could you teach him if you don't know how?"

"But I told him to float. He wouldn't listen." She looked at Mike. "Please, Mike, find a magic rock to wake Doodles up."

Steven wiped tears from his eyes, and Mike shook his head. "Betsy, this isn't like the spider story. This is real. Doodles is dead. Nothing, not even a magic rock, will bring him back to life."

Jim also wiped his eyes. "You've really done it this time, Betsy. You killed Doodles."

Her face looked stricken, as if she'd just seen a real monster. "He's dead? But—but I didn't mean to hurt him. I loved him." She threw her arms around her brother, and they sobbed, holding one another. Mike hugged them both. Except for the crying, the backyard was quiet. Even Quackers was quiet.

"Well, he needs a decent burial," Mike said. "But first we have to tell your mother."

***

Six people, a duck, and a pigeon gathered in the Mackey's backyard that evening for the burial. Quackers stood by Betsy and wagged his tail and quacked when appropriate. Squall Baby sat on Jim's shoulder and cooed while the other pigeons watched from their cages. Also attending were Donna Mackey and Grandpa.

Betsy wore her Easter dress, bonnet, and white shoes. The three boys wore ties that were too long for them, which they had borrowed from Mike's dad. Betsy had convinced her mom to wear her Sunday-go-to-meeting dress. Mike even talked Grandpa into wearing a black tie with his overalls.

Mike's dad couldn't come because he had to attend a union meeting to talk about a strike that might happen at the packing plant. Mike tried to convince his mom to attend, but she said, "What would people think if they saw me all dressed up to watch a bird being buried? They'd think I was as crazy as Bertha Kramer. That's what they'd think."

Grandpa had made a coffin from wood scraps. He picked up Doodles, placed him in the coffin, and closed the lid. Once he finished digging a grave with a spade from the Mackey's shed, he placed the coffin in it. After everyone sang *Amazing Grace*, Grandpa said, "Let us pray." He bowed his head. "God, please watch after Doodles. He's as fine a rooster as you'll ever meet. He's leaving behind people who love him more than words can express. Amen."

"Amen," the congregation echoed.

Grandpa grabbed the shovel and scooped up some dirt. Before he could toss it onto the coffin, Mike stepped forward, waving a piece of paper. "Wait. I want to say something about Doodles."

"Do you want to say a eulogy?" Grandpa asked.

"Yes. A eulogy."

He stood next to Grandpa and read the words he had written. "When the angels created you, they gave you a heart that contained three times the amount of love as usual. God knew you were special and that you had to be where you could best share all that love. That's why He put you here with us. Nowhere else in the world could you have shared more love.

90

We will cherish your memory forever. Thank you for being you, and thank you for loving us." He picked up a handful of dirt, tossed it on the coffin, and stepped back.

Grandpa filled in the hole and turned to the others. "Mrs. Mackey has prepared some delicious refreshments. Let's go inside and enjoy them."

Everyone followed him to the house. Just before they stepped onto the front porch, Steven pulled Mike aside. "That was beautiful. When I die I want you to give my eulogy."

"Sure. I'd be happy to." Mike stepped toward the porch. Steven grabbed his arm and pulled him back.

"I'm serious. Promise?"

Mike studied him. "You *are* serious, aren't you?"

"I'm dead serious."

The boys laughed at his unintentional pun, and Mike held out his hand. "I'd be honored." They sealed the agreement with a firm handshake.

"Thanks." Steven looked toward the backyard. "You know, something seemed missing."

"Missing? What do you mean?"

"Oh, I don't know. Like something else should have happened. Something good should have come from his death."

"Like what? What good can come from death?"

Steven looked toward the backyard again and didn't say anything for a long time. "I don't know," he said, finally. "Something. Maybe Mrs. Mackey could have given Betsy a little yellow chick. You know, and said something like 'Doodles, this is Doodles the Second. We can only hope he becomes half the bird you were.' Betsy might feel better, and another chicken would be loved like Doodles was."

Mike frowned. "That actually makes sense."

"You know what else?"

Mike let out a long, exaggerated sigh. "I'm afraid to ask, but what?"

"Wouldn't it be neat if you knew when you were going to die so you could plan your own funeral?"

Mike made a face. "That doesn't sound like fun at all. I'd just as soon someone else planned my funeral. Why would you want to plan your own funeral?"

"Think about it," Steven said. "You could do anything you wanted at your funeral if you knew when it would happen. You could even write your own eulogy. You know, say how great you were, things like that."

Mike stepped onto the porch and reached for the doorknob. "You're creeping me out. You can stay out here and plan your funeral if you want. I'm going to check out the refreshments."

They joined the others in the house. Mrs. Mackey had made a chocolate cake, which she served with vanilla ice cream and iced tea, and they talked about the good times they'd had with Doodles.

For a few minutes Mike's thoughts drifted. The paper on which he had written the eulogy sat on the table in front of him. He picked it up and read it again to himself and then folded it and tucked it into his billfold.

***

"I miss him," Jim said on their way to school the next morning. They walked more slowly than usual. "Squall Baby misses him, too. You should've seen her this morning. You know how Doodles always stood on our fence and crowed early every morning?"

Mike nodded.

"Well, something woke me at sunrise. I looked out the window and realized I forgot to close Squall Baby's cage. She stood on the fence where Doodles always stood going, 'Coo coo coodle coo. Coo coo coodle coo.' It was like she was giving Doodles a tribute."

"Can I stay at your place tonight?" Mike asked. "I'd like to see her do that."

"Your mom won't let you stay over on a school night. Besides, Squall Baby may never do it again."

The boys walked the next block without talking. Mike pulled two circus tickets from his pocket and showed them to Jim. "I bought these at the drugstore yesterday. I'm going to ask Heidi to sit with me."

"Do you think she will?"

"Why wouldn't she, if I paid for the ticket?"

"No reason. She probably will."

The day ended without his asking Heidi to sit with him at the circus, as did Wednesday, Thursday and Friday. Maybe Jim's doubts had made him afraid to ask. Maybe she would say no. Maybe she'd laugh at him.

On Saturday afternoon he went to the circus with both tickets and a plan. When he saw Heidi he'd say he just happened to have an extra ticket, and she may as well use it or it would go to waste. It would be natural for her to sit with him under those circumstances.

He waited for her to show up, but she never did. After the circus started and he still hadn't seen her, he entered the tent by himself. Once inside, he saw her in the third row of the middle section with a bunch of other kids from his class. He sat back and tried to enjoy the circus. He had very little fun, and the magic Grandpa had talked about never happened.

Chapter 15

THE SECRET AND DANGEROUS MISSION

Steven walked into the classroom grinning and motioned for Jim and Mike to come to his desk.

"What do you want, Smiley?"

Steven's grin got even bigger. "You may call me Smiley now, but you'll call me Mr. Genius in a minute. I've thought up the perfect secret and dangerous mission."

"What's that?" Mike checked behind him. Miss Schneider was still out of the room.

"Well, we take Squall Baby to Good Shepherd Cemetery at midnight tonight and see if she can beat us home. It's the perfect secret and dangerous mission."

Jim laughed. "There are a few problems with your mission."

Mike laughed with him. "I'll say there are."

"Such as?"

"Such as, there's no way our folks would let us out of the house at midnight. And they sure wouldn't let us walk all the way to the cemetery at night by ourselves. I'm no Mr. Genius like you, but it's two miles to the cemetery, and if I figure correctly, that's a four-mile round trip."

"Yeah." Mike used his outside voice to emphasize the correctness of Jim's statements.

"That's what makes it a secret mission. You can't tell your parents. I can't tell my aunt. The mission will really be secret."

Mike shivered. "I'm not going to a dark cemetery way out in the country, with all those spooks and goblins floating all over the place. We might never make it back alive."

Steven leaned forward and lowered his voice. "That's what makes it dangerous. We'll set Squall Baby loose in the exact center of the cemetery. It'd be like we really are agents going on a secret and dangerous mission."

Mike waited for Jim to come up with another reason not to go, realizing butterflies sometimes have a hard time winning arguments with bees. At these times they need to work together. But Jim didn't speak next. Steven did.

"Jim, I know you aren't scared. You get your pigeons from farmers' barns late at night, right?"

"Right."

"You don't believe in spooks, do you?"

"Well ... no ... "

"I didn't think so. You know what that means? You don't want to go because you don't think Squall Baby is smart enough to find her way home in the middle of the night from two miles away."

"She is too smart enough."

"Then prove it. Talk is cheap."

"Okay, I will. Midnight. Tonight. My house. But if you aren't there at the stroke of midnight, I'm going back to bed, and I will never consider going on this mission again."

"Fair enough." Steven patted Mike on the back. "Jim's not chicken. What about you, Mike? Are you chicken?"

It was déjà vu all over again. Mike was at least as chicken now as he was when Tony talked him into riding to school on the forbidden street. He shouldn't sneak off to the cemetery at midnight, just as he shouldn't have ridden to school down Main Street. If his mother ever found out about it, she'd get all upset. He could hear her now. *What kind of a mother will people think I am if they find out about the cemetery episode?* Even Grandpa couldn't defend him on this one.

But these were his friends. If he didn't go with them, they might not want to be seen with him ever again. Who wants to be friends with a chicken? They'd have a special bond by doing something secret and dangerous that he wouldn't have. If friends you love and trust want you to do something that you don't think you should, is it wrong to do it?

"Well? Chicken or man?"

Mike gritted his teeth. "I'm not chicken."

"That means you'll go on the secret and dangerous mission with us tonight?"

"Yeah. I'll go."

Stephen stood back and smiled. "Okay. We meet in Jim's backyard at midnight. Anyone who doesn't show up is chicken for life. And remember, don't tell anybody. This mission is super-secret. Right?"

"Right," the other two said in monotone.

Steven flipped through his previous evening's homework, and Mike and Jim sat at their desks. Class would start in less than a minute.

***

Jerry Harders grinned as he passed the boys and went to his own desk. He sat and ripped a piece of yellow paper from his Big Chief tablet and wrote, "2 butterflies and 1 bee cemitary midnite." He folded the paper in half and then folded it again and stuffed it into his shirt pocket.

***

Going on the secret mission bothered Mike even more than riding his bike down Main Street. He hadn't thought long about peddling down the forbidden street. It was just a spur-of-the-moment reflex when Tony called him chicken. This secret and dangerous mission, on the other hand, had been planned since eight o'clock that morning.

At bedtime he put his pajamas on over his jeans and shirt and placed his shoes and socks within easy reach. He sneaked his dad's flashlight from the kitchen cabinet junk drawer, hid it under his pillow, and stepped into the living room.

"Good night, Mom. Good night, Dad. Good night, Grandpa."

"Good night, Mike."

"Good night."

"Don't let the bedbugs bite." Grandpa chuckled just as he did every evening, as if it were the first time he'd given the bedbugs warning.

Martha closed her Good Housekeeping magazine and placed it on the end table next to her. "You know, I do believe Mike's putting a little meat on his skinny body."

Grandpa looked at Mike. "He does seem to fill out those pajamas a little more than usual."

Mike went back to his room and shut the door. He slipped into bed and stared into the darkness outside his window, concentrating on staying awake. He didn't dare let an alarm go off in the middle of the night. That would wake everyone, especially his mom, who was a light sleeper anyway. Yet he didn't want to be late and risk being called chicken for life.

He woke with a start. Had he overslept? He pulled the clock to his face. Eight minutes to ten. His folks hadn't even gone to bed yet. It was going to be a long night. He tried to stay awake, but he dozed in and out.

Mike got up at half past eleven to avoid falling asleep again and missing the meeting time. He took off his pajamas, slipped on his shoes and socks, and grabbed the flashlight. Before leaving his bedroom he put on a light jacket to fight off the night's chill.

A floorboard in the hallway by his parents' bedroom squeaked when he stepped on it. He froze and waited a full minute before taking another step. That step made another board squeak, and again he stood motionless in the darkness. Another minute passed, and hearing nothing from his parents' room, he took another step. Silence. Once outside, he pulled the door shut slowly until it made a muted click. His shadow became longer and fainter as he walked away from the streetlight on his way to Jim's.

He leaned against the tree in Jim's back yard and stared up at the moon that drifted in and out of clouds. It must be a quarter to twelve. Nothing stirred except for a lonely duck asking to be petted.

Jim finally came out carrying a flashlight and Squall Baby's portable cage. They exchanged whispered greetings.

"Jim, you have a watch?"

Jim patted a chain that hung from his belt and disappeared into his front, right pocket. "Yeah, I brought my dad's old pocket watch."

"What time is it?"

He pulled the watch out and angled it toward the streetlight. "Five minutes to twelve."

The two boys stood silently in the yard for several seconds. "Well, aren't you going to get Squall Baby?"

"Not yet."

"Why not?"

Jim's voice became louder. "Because if the mastermind of this secret and dangerous mission isn't here by twelve o'clock sharp, I'm going back to bed. No use waking Squall Baby unless I have to."

Four minutes to twelve and still no Steven. Maybe he was all talk. Three minutes to twelve. Still quiet ... no Steven. The only sounds were occasional quacks and yawns.

Two minutes to twelve. Still no Steven. Wait. What's that shadow under the streetlight? The form came closer. Steven showed after all. The mission would proceed.

He stopped before them. "Okay, men. You ready?"

Jim's response was almost a sigh. "Yeah, I'm ready."

Mike pointed to the western sky. "Isn't that lightning way in the distance?" A faint light appeared briefly in a remote cloud. "See, there it is again. Maybe we ought to forget about it tonight."

Steven placed an arm on Jim's shoulders. "That's just heat lightning, Mike. Heat lightning never brings rain." He squeezed Jim's shoulder. "Is Squall Baby ready, buddy?"

"I'll get her." Jim went to the pigeon cages and pulled out a protesting Squall Baby. She didn't seem to want to go on the mission any more than Mike did. Jim put her into the portable cage and latched the door. "She's ready. Let's go."

The three secret agents walked in and out of shadows through the town's dark streets without using flashlights. They'd need them when they left the town limits where there were no streetlights. They kept to the less traveled streets and watched for cars. After all, people—and especially Marshal Smart—would wonder why three kids were out so late by themselves.

They crossed Highway 41 and made it to the cemetery, just over a mile east of town, without being spotted. Mike shined his flashlight on its eight-foot-tall iron fence and then on the entrance gate. He turned to the others. "Now what? They lock the gate at night, and climbing that fence won't be easy."

Steven walked toward the main entrance. "Let's try the gate just to make sure it's locked."

Steven left no doubt he was in charge of this mission. They followed him and studied the gate in the flashlight's brightness. It wasn't locked. Mike shined his light on the ground, and the beam struck a loose chain and lock. "Look. They forgot to lock it."

Steven pulled the gate open, and Mike shivered at its ghostly squeal. Steven stepped inside and turned to the others, reaching his hands out to Jim. "Here, let me carry Squall Baby. I want to be the one to let her loose."

"Sure." Jim handed him the cage, and they entered the cemetery.

Three flashlights shone in all directions as they walked close together toward the cemetery's center, their eyes darting from tombstone to tombstone looking for ghosts. Each step changed their fast-moving, flashlight-beam angles, creating illusions of spooks rising from one hiding place after another.

Jim paused, holding a hand up to stop the others. "Look. Head-lights. Someone's coming."

Steven turned off his flashlight and stuffed it under his belt. "Quick! Hide behind a tombstone."

The boys crouched as darkness again overtook the cemetery and watched a pickup truck approach. It stopped by the cemetery entrance, its brakes making a loud, grating sound like chalk on a blackboard. The truck door slammed, and someone with a flashlight walked toward the open gate.

Mike peeked over the grave marker that shielded him. The intruder shut and opened the gate several times, making it squeal its ghostly response. "They cut the chain," the man said. He shined his light over the rows of tombstones. Mike ducked.

"Who is it?" Jim whispered.

"I don't know. I couldn't tell."

"What's he doing? Why's he shining his light in here?"

Steven grabbed Jim's arm. "Shhh. He'll hear you."

The moving light flashed on tombstones, and the boys hunched down further as it passed by them. "I know you're in there. Come on out. Right now."

Mike hugged the ground. "It's Emil Hoff." Emil was the cemetery's caretaker. He mowed the grass, dug the graves, and plowed the snow in the winter.

"Come on out!" His voice echoed through the cemetery. No one moved. Light from his bright flashlight, apparently the kind with a big battery and large reflector, bounced against tombstones on the left and right. "I know you're in there. You come out."

Still no one moved.

"If you don't come out, I'm coming in after you."

Thunder rumbled as Emil Hoff entered the cemetery. The boys stayed low and moved to other tombstones. By the time Emil reached the cemetery's center, they'd maneuvered around in a semicircle to the front gate. As Steven pulled it open, it squealed. Emil shined his light at him. "Stop right there!"

The boys ran as fast as they could, following a road lit by their flashlights' galloping beams. The clouds from the quickly approaching storm now blocked any light the moon may have provided. Thunder rumbled louder and more frequently, and the wind blew dust in the boys' eyes. Emil ran from the cemetery, jumped into his truck, and aimed it toward town. His headlights flashed from dim to bright, highlighting the three boys. The truck roared louder.

"To the field!" Jim jumped a small roadside ditch, climbed over a fence, and continued running at top speed. The other two followed him. The storm, once resembling harmless heat lightning in the distance, had arrived. With it came heavy rain. Mike's right foot found a hole, and he fell hard to the suddenly wet ground, his flashlight flying ahead of him as he slid face-first.

The others stopped. "You okay?" Jim helped him up.

"Yeah, I'm okay." Mike picked up his flashlight and continued running. His right leg throbbed where it had slammed against the ground, and he ran with a limp.

Emil stopped at the fence by the road's edge. "You boys come back here right now," he called. "You hear me? Right now!"

His voice became fainter and fainter as they ran. Out of breath, they stopped just short of the highway. Jim gasped and reached out to Steven. "Okay, I'll take Squall Baby now."

Silence, except for the wind throwing rain at the ground.

"Come on. Give her to me."

Steven shifted to the other foot. "I don't have her."

Jim's shoulders slumped. "What do you mean you don't have her?"

"Why should I? She's your pigeon."

"Because you told me to give her to you when we got to the cemetery, and I did."

Steven hesitated. "I ... I left her behind the tombstone."

"What?"

"I forgot all about her. I left her by the tombstone we hid behind."

Rain now slapped the boys' faces relentlessly, and thunder boomed. Jim turned toward the cemetery. "Well, we have to get her."

"You guys get her. It's starting to storm. I'm going home." Steven began walking toward town.

Mike planted his hands on his hips and spread his feet far apart. "Stop!" Steven turned and faced him.

"Steven Culpepper, when I met you, you were a bully. You put popcorn and bubble gum in my hair. You even cheated Heidi out of her rightful place in the first desk of the bee row. But we took you on our secret missions anyhow."

"So?"

"So, you thought up this mission. You said heat lightning never brought rain. You left Squall Baby in the cemetery, and if we don't get her, she'll drown. If you're a friend, you'll come with us. If you're still a bully, then just go home and stay out of our lives."

Mike and Steven stared at one another in the downpour. Steven held out his hand. "Friend."

The three friends ran back toward the cemetery. They didn't know if Emil Hoff was still there or not, so they kept their flashlights tucked in their pants. At least he wouldn't expect them to go back to the cemetery in the storm. The lightning brightened their path, and they ran as fast as they could. Each fell several times and slid on the grassy mud. The wind blew harder, and the rain stung their faces. The once-rumbling thunder now cracked and boomed, and lightning strikes snapped close by.

Emil Hoff had left. They turned their flashlights on and ran to find Squall Baby. She was alive in her portable cage. Jim picked it up, and they again ran toward home.

The rain had let up when Mike reached his house. He crossed the squeaky floor cautiously to his room and walked toward his bed in the darkness.

A sudden click. His bedroom light flashed on, and he turned. Grandpa stood with a hand on the switch. His mom sat in a chair next to him by the door. She stood.

"Where have you been? I'm deathly ill from worry."

"Well, uh—we took Squall Baby to the cemetery on a secret mission."

She frowned dark thoughts at him. "At this time of night? I started to call Marshal Smart, but Grandpa said to wait. In another five minutes I would have called him. Do you enjoy making me worry?"

"No." He could think of nothing else to say. What he had done was so wrong he couldn't even defend himself. "I'm sorry."

Martha's hands shook. "Steven Culpepper isn't any better than that Jim Mackey. I don't care if his aunt is a teacher. I heard his parents got a divorce, and his father married some young floozy and moved to Brazil, and they carted his mother off to the nut house."

She leaned against Grandpa. "You're making me old before my time, Mike. Now, dry yourself off and go to bed. We'll decide your punishment tomorrow. I'm simply too upset to think about it tonight, but rest assured, you will be punished."

She left his room, and Grandpa lingered in the hallway. He shook his head and walked away. Mike stood in his room alone. Water dripped from his clothes and formed small puddles on the linoleum.

Chapter 16

HONEST ABE

Miss Schneider entered the classroom the next day, placed a stack of papers on her desk, and turned to the students. "I have a surprise for you. We are going to put on a play for the school next Thursday and perform again that night for all the parents. We'll have to work very hard to be ready in time, but I know we can do it."

Mike sat up. A play? This could be just the break he needed. He'd heard that some of the big Hollywood actors got their start the very same way. Something minor like a part in a school play started a chain reaction that became bigger and bigger until Hollywood called, and they became rich and famous. Why, he could be the next Jimmy Stewart or Bing Crosby. Well, maybe not Bing Crosby because Bing could sing. But he could be the next Jimmy Stewart. Jimmy couldn't carry a note either.

Mike leaned back and thrust his legs out under his desk. Once he became rich and famous, Heidi would notice him. He wouldn't have any problems talking with her then, and she'd be proud to be seen with him. Mom and Dad and Grandpa would respect him when he became a famous actor. They might forget about his midnight visit to the cemetery in the storm, and his mom might even regret she'd forced his dad to spank him.

"The play's name is *Abe, the Boy*," she said. "It demonstrates Abraham Lincoln's honesty, even as a young man. In this play young Abe walks a mile from his simple log cabin to the general store to buy provisions. After he walks the mile back carrying those heavy provisions, he discovers the store owner gave him a penny too much in change. Because he is so honest, he walks the mile back to the store and gives the man the penny back. Then, of course, he has to walk the mile back to his cabin. Abe did all this because he received a penny too much in change. Can you imagine being so honest? That is why he grew into a great man and made an outstanding president."

Mike had never before paid more attention to what Miss Schneider said. Maybe she'd choose him to play the part of Abe.

"Now class, there are only eight parts in this play, so everyone won't be able to act in it. If you aren't selected, just remember you might have another chance next year or the year after that."

Mike knew Miss Schneider had already decided who would be in the play, and nothing he could do would change her selection. Still, it wouldn't hurt to play it safe. He crossed his fingers. After a few seconds he also crossed his toes, his arms, and his legs, just for good measure. He wouldn't budge an inch until she either called his name or handed out all the parts. As long as he'd gone this far, he might as well go all the way and cross his eyes, too. *Oh, my. Seeing two Miss Schneiders talking at the same time is spooky.*

The two Schneiders picked up the scripts and approached the class until they stood between the teacher's desk and the students' desks less than a foot from Tony's middle row front seat. "Okay now, when I call your name, please come up and get your script," they said in unison. "I want you to take it home tonight and practice your lines. I have chosen Tony to play the part of Abe Lincoln. Tony, here's your script."

The Tony twins stood, and each took a script from the Schneiders' outstretched hands. As much as he'd wanted the lead, choosing Tony made sense. He was tall and slender like Abe, although he'd need at least a ton of makeup to look as homely.

"Mike, what in the world are you doing?"

Mike shifted his eyes from the Tony duo to the Schneiders. What was she concerned about? He was just sitting there hoping his name would be called.

"Ma'am?"

"I said what are you doing?"

"Sitting here."

"Mike, I asked you a serious question, and I expect a serious answer. Just what do you think you are doing?"

She had changed her wording. The first time she asked what he *was* doing, and this time she asked what he *thought* he was doing. Was there a difference between the two questions? "Sitting here" wasn't the correct answer, at least to the first question. It could be the correct answer to the second one, though. After all, he did *think* that was what he was doing. Maybe she wanted more detail.

"Well?"

"Sitting here ... quietly?"

"You know what I mean. Why are your eyes crossed? Don't you know they could stick that way and you'd be goofy looking the rest of your life? Is that what you want?"

"No, ma'am."

Mike eased his eyes, and the two Miss Schneiders slammed back into one, causing him to flinch. The remaining Miss Schneider stared at him for several seconds. She then resumed calling names. She selected Mary to play Abe's mother and Jim to play the store owner. Soon, only one part remained.

"And Mike will be farmer number two."

Unbelievable. He was one of The Chosen. Although feelings of greatness engulfed him, he'd act as if honors like this came his way all the time by walking up to accept the script without a smile. He uncrossed his fingers without incident, but when he uncrossed his toes and legs, his right foot plopped to the floor, sending a shockwave throughout his body. His leg was asleep—severely asleep. It didn't bother him when it was crossed, but now he had no control over it, and it hurt. A lot.

The pain forced his eyes shut and drew his lips back, exposing his teeth. He barely managed to fight off the urge to let out a loud and prolonged scream. Efforts to hold his legs still with both hands proved minimally successful. A couple of times his leg moved just a little, releasing more body-filling pain and causing his face to become even more distorted.

Tingles signifying his legs were waking up hadn't begun yet. It would be impossible to stand, let alone walk, without having more pain than he had ever experienced thus far in his life. No way would his leg support him. If he tried, he'd fall like a wounded deer. No, it would be foolish to even think about getting up until at least after the tingles came. Maybe he could wait it out.

Miss Schneider tapped her foot. "Mike, come up and take your script." She didn't appear to be in much of a waiting mood.

"Yes, ma'am."

He couldn't tell her his leg had fallen asleep. She'd think he had done it on purpose, just as he had crossed his eyes on purpose. She'd tell him if he'd sat properly as she'd instructed him to do a thousand times, this would never have happened. Then, to teach him a lesson, she'd give his part to someone else. He'd never get the first in a series of bigger and bigger breaks that would end in his being a famous movie star like Jimmy Stewart.

If he didn't grab this opportunity, he may never become someone Heidi would look up to. Yet, Miss Schneider must never suspect his leg fell asleep. He calculated the distance between his seat and where she stood in front of Tony. He might be able to make it in three giant strides. Three steps up, grab the script, three steps back, and collapse in his seat, all the while fighting the pain. If he started with his left foot, he'd have to put weight on his right leg two times for the round trip.

Wait, he could do this. How many times had he seen movies where doctors removed bullets from cowboys without giving them something for pain? Ten? At least. Twenty? Maybe. And what did the cowboys do to withstand the pain? They bit down on bullets.

Mike peered at the items on his desk. Just his luck. No bullets. There were two pencils, a pair of scissors, and one of those hollow erasers you put on a pencil when its original eraser wore out. It looked something like a bullet. It just might work. He should have paid more attention during those cowboy movies. Did they chomp down on the bullets with their front teeth or their back teeth?

"Mike, do you want this script or not?"

Miss Schneider held the script in one hand and rested her other hand on her hip. She pursed her mouth and held one eyebrow abnormally high.

"Young man, if you don't come get this script this instant, I am going to select another boy to play the part of farmer number two."

He had to act now. The eyes of every grasshopper, every butterfly, and every bee in the class, including the sparkling black bee eyes of Heidi Beck, were fixed on him. He picked up the eraser, stuck it into his mouth with part of it protruding from his lips, and bit hard with his front teeth. Wanting to get as far as possible before he had to step on his right foot, he pushed off with his right hand on his desk and his left hand on the desk to his left and propelled himself up and forward. He landed on his left foot and leaped with all his strength. It was just as he had pictured it, graceful like a gazelle.

Then, he landed on his right foot.

Never before in the history of the world had there been such pain. He didn't take the third step to reach Miss Schneider. Instead, he let out a scream heard around the world of the Potter Elementary School's second floor. The eraser shot from his mouth, grazed Miss Schneider's right ear, bounced off the blackboard, and fell to the floor. Mike fell hard to the floor, too, and grabbed his leg.

For half a minute he rolled and screamed. Soon, Mr. Jackson appeared in the doorway and stared at him, his mouth open. Mike lay curled up, moaning. Miss Schneider stood almost trancelike in front of the class, still holding the script, and the students stared at Mike with wide eyes.

Mr. Jackson ran to were he lay and knelt next to him. "What is it, son? Where are you hurt?"

Mike opened his eyes, and the magnitude of what had happened struck him. Everyone, including the principal, his teacher, and Heidi Beck, stared at him as he moaned on the floor. His leg no longer hurt. It still tingled, but he could walk if he were careful and took his time. He had no choice but to tell Mr. Jackson what had happened, even though Miss Schneider would yell at him for being dumb enough to let his leg fall asleep in the first place.

"My ... my leg fell asleep."

"May I help you up?" Mr. Jackson offered his hand. Mike took it and soon walked in a small circle, his leg feeling better with each step.

"You okay?"

Mike put as much weight as possible on his leg as a final test. "Yes, sir. I'm okay now."

Mr. Jackson let out his breath. "You had me worried, son."

Mike pried the script from Miss Schneider's still outstretched hand and returned to his desk. Her expression hadn't changed since the moment he went to the floor. He sat and put the script on his desk.

Mr. Jackson left the room. One by one the children took their eyes off of Mike and looked at Miss Schneider. Her hand fell to her side.

She looked up. "It's time for spelling class. Don't forget to practice your scripts tonight. And be sure to bring them to school each day because you'll need them for play practice. Does everyone understand? Bring your scripts to school every day." She looked around to see if there were any questions on script responsibility.

Mike picked up his script and sniffed it. Very few things smelled as good as newly mimeographed paper, especially a newly mimeographed script of a play he had a part in. He sniffed again. Was this what heaven smelled like?

He glanced at Heidi. She was flipping through her spelling book to find the lesson. He had lost ground. He'd have to be the best actor in the play to help Heidi forget what happened today.

***

Mike ran toward the backyard swing waving the script. "Look at what I have."

Grandpa took a couple fast puffs on his pipe. "What is it? Did you finally get an 'A' on a spelling test?"

"No, it's better than that. I'm in a school play. We're going to perform in front of the entire school and for all the parents." Mike smiled so much the corners of his mouth hurt.

"A part in a play? You have a part in a play?" Grandpa held the pipe in front of him, and the smoke curled toward his face. "This could be the start of something big. Why, one of these days, I just might be watching your latest smash hit movie. What's the play about?"

"It's about Abe Lincoln's honesty as a boy. I've read the entire script, and it's really interesting. It tells how he walked all the way back to the general store just to return a penny. The store owner gave him a penny too much in change."

"That does sound interesting. What part do you play? Abe?"

"Well, no ... "

Grandpa put the pipe in his mouth and studied Mike. He snapped his fingers. "The store owner. I'll bet you play the store owner. I've always thought you had a businessman look about you. I'll bet Miss Schneider noticed it, too."

"No, I don't play the store owner. Jim got that part. I'm a farmer."

Grandpa reached out and shook his hand. "Congratulations. That's a very important part. Without farmers we'd all starve. Seems to me farming was the number one industry back in Abe's day. What's the farmer's name?"

Mike shifted from one foot to the other. "Actually, Grandpa, he doesn't have a name. He's called farmer number two so people don't confuse him with farmer number one. But he has some great lines." He thrust the script in Grandpa's face. "See here? I underlined all my speaking parts. Read them, Grandpa."

Grandpa took the script. "Let's see now. 'Hi, Abe. Kinda hot isn't it? ... See you later, Abe ... I'm surprised to see you again so soon, Abe ... '" He handed the script to Mike. "You've got some good lines there, all right."

Mike pushed the script back. "Wait, Grandpa. You missed one."

"Oh, yeah. I see it now. 'Fine boy.' I don't know how I could have missed that one. I'm sure you'll be the best one in the play."

Mike took the script from Grandpa. "I don't know about that, but I do want to do the very best I can. Will you help me? Please?"

Grandpa rumpled Mike's hair. "I'd be honored. When you become a famous actor I'll tell all my friends I knew you when you were farmer number two talking to Abraham Lincoln. That'll impress them."

The two sat in the swing and practiced Mike's lines for over two hours without taking a break. The practice paid off. Mike could say his lines without looking at the script. The bright sun that shined when they began rehearsal had sunk deep in the sky.

Martha's voice echoed in the outdoor rehearsal hall for the third time in the last fifteen minutes. "Grandpa. Mike. Your supper's getting cold. This is the last time I'm going to call you." She slammed the door.

Grandpa winked at Mike. "Good. I'm glad she's quitting. I don't know about you, but I was getting pretty tired of her calling us every five minutes. But we may as well go in. A little supper break sounds just like what the director ordered."

"Can we practice some more after supper?"

"Sure. But you already know your part pretty well. In fact, you know everybody's part pretty well, even Abe's. I don't think you need much more practice."

"I know, but I want to do a good job."

Grandpa eyed him. "Trying to impress someone, Mike?"

"No."

"A little girl maybe?"

"I just want to do a good job, Grandpa."

Grandpa puffed his pipe. "Her name wouldn't happen to be Heidi, would it?"

"Oh, Grandpa."

The door pushed open again. "Will you two get in here? Come eat your supper before it gets ice cold."

Grandpa looked at Mike. "I thought she wasn't going to call us anymore." He stood from the swing. "We're coming, Martha dear."

"Don't you 'Martha dear' me, Grandpa. Come on in and eat."

When Grandpa and Mike got to the table, Martha and Charles were almost finished eating. Charles topped off his meal by scooping several large spoonfuls of peaches into a bowl. Grandpa speared a minute steak, cut off a small portion, and placed it in his mouth. "Kinda cold." He winked at Mike.

Martha slammed her fork on the table. "It wouldn't be cold if you came in when I first called you."

"Just kidding, Martha. It's exactly the temperature I like."

"And just what were you two doing out there all evening, practicing that play Mike has a bit part in?" Mike continued eating without looking up. He always stayed out of it when his mom got into it with Grandpa.

"First of all, Martha, it's not a bit part. He has lines to say. Important lines. And he plays a very prominent farmer who knew Abe Lincoln. Talks to him, too. You know, we could use your help rehearsing after supper. What do you say?"

"This house doesn't clean itself. I do it, and I get very little help out of anyone. You would be more useful around here if you helped me do the dishes instead of spending time with Mike on that little play."

Grandpa handed the script to Mike's father. "What about you, Charles? Want to help us?"

Charles flipped through the pages and laid the script on the table. "Sure, I'll help."

Martha's voice softened. "I'll tell you what, Charles—help me with the dishes, and we'll both help the boy."

Mike felt special when he got ready for bed. The front porch had become a stage, and Grandpa, his dad, and even his mom helped him rehearse all evening. He knew his lines well, and he knew how to say them. Grandpa told him to emphasize certain words and put motions—he called them gestures—into his acting. When he said the line "fine boy," he'd say "*fine* boy" and shake his head for emphasis.

He had accomplished so much. He had memorized not only farmer number two's lines, but the lines of every character. If Miss Schneider were to ask him tomorrow, he'd be able to stand in for any of the actors and do an outstanding job acting out that person's part without ever looking at a script. He'd even be able to take over Tony's Abe role and use the right gestures if Tony became sick. Why, if she wanted to, she could tell the rest of The Chosen to sit down because Mike had decided to act out all the parts. He could do it, too. He could put on a one-boy show and do every part in the play from memory. Wouldn't that make Hollywood sit up and take notice?

Never before had he accomplished so much in such a short period of time. If it wasn't a miracle, it was a double cousin to one. Even his mom seemed to look at him with pride when he went to bed. He pulled the covers back. Maybe he'd dream about the play all night.

Chapter 17

THE PLAY PRACTICE

When Mike awoke the next day, he'd never felt better. Even his oatmeal and prunes breakfast tasted good.

He sauntered into Miss Schneider's room feeling confident and in control. This was his day. He'd accomplished a miracle last night, and soon everyone—Heidi included—would see the results of that miracle. He'd dazzle them with his amazing acting. They'd find out he knew his lines by heart and see him say them on cue with emphasis and gestures, while everyone else struggled with their lines by reading them from the script. Yes, he'd remember this day forever.

Heidi sat at her desk working math problems. Ordinarily, Mike would say "hi" or something like that and move on to his seat before he made a fool of himself by becoming tongue-tied and unable to think of anything to say. Today he'd make up for yesterday's fiasco.

"Working on your math, I see." He sported a toothy movie-star smile and added a little drawl to his voice for a Jimmy Stewart effect.

She marked her place with a piece of paper and closed the book. "Yes, I'm working ahead to see what's coming up. How's your leg? Can you walk okay?"

"Sure. It's not a problem at all anymore." He did a mock two-second tap dance that ended with his holding his arms out as if he'd just done something great. "See? All better. It just fell asleep." He hadn't stopped by to talk about yesterday's embarrassment. "I practiced my part last night."

"Good. You'll make a fine actor."

"I know my lines by heart. I know the other kids' lines, too. Will you watch us practice? Afterwards you could tell me what you think. You

112

know, about my acting. You could tell me what I'm doing right or wrong." He knew he wouldn't do anything wrong. If she watched, she'd think she was seeing a young Jimmy Stewart.

"Sure I'll watch. I'm not very good at offering advice, but I'll tell you what I think."

"Great. Well, it's time for the bell. See you later."

"Okay, see you."

The morning dragged by. After all the students returned from noon recess, Miss Schneider stood by her desk and waited for them to settle down. "Class," she said when the last person took his seat, "it's time for play practice. Those of you who are not in the play should read your history assignment at this time. Those of you who are in the play, come up to the front of the room."

Mike waited until the rest of The Chosen were well on their way before he got up. He deserved to walk up by himself. While all the others struggled with their lines, he'd sail through his with feeling—and from memory, no less. When he took his first step to join the other actors, he peeked through his eyebrows to see if Heidi was watching. She was.

Mike's pace slowed, and then stopped. Miss Schneider stood in front of him with both hands on her hips, an indication a problem existed in the fifth grade world.

"Mike, where is your script?"

"What?"

"I said, 'Where is your script?'" Her stance didn't change.

At least she'd asked an easy question, and his answer would impress her. He'd left his script on his nightstand. Only an actor who doesn't know his part needs a script. Once he's memorized every word, every comma, and every period on it, it's of no further use. She'll be amazed when he tells her he knows not only his lines, but everyone else's, too.

"It's at home, but—"

"I don't want to hear any 'buts.' I specifically told everyone to bring his script to practice every day. Are you telling me you left yours at home and don't even have it here for the first practice?"

She made it sound like a bad thing. Sure, for the average child actor it would be a bad thing, but he wasn't just any child actor. He'd accomplished more last night than he'd ever accomplished in his life. More than he'll be able to accomplish ever again. He'd memorized the entire script. Sure he left it on his nightstand, but he also brought it with him. He'd transferred it to his brain, and that made the paper script obsolete.

"Yes. It's at home, but—"

"I said not to 'but' me, young man."

How was it possible for her to have "young manned" him so soon in the conversation? He didn't even have a chance to tell her why he didn't have it with him. She'd understand if she'd allow him to explain.

Miss Schneider changed her stance. Now, only her left hand rested on her hip. Normally that would be a sign things were getting better, but her right index finger pointed directly at Mike's desk. "If that's all you care about this play, then you can just sit down and read your history assignment."

How could this be happening? It was supposed to be his day. The miracle—

"Go ahead, now. Sit. I am going to give your part to someone who actually cares."

Mike walked to his seat like a condemned prisoner walks to the gallows. Heidi stared at the book in front of her. She didn't smile. She didn't move. What happened to his day? She was supposed to be proud of him today.

Miss Schneider scanned the Non-Chosen. "Is there anyone in this room who actually cares about this play enough to bring the script to practice with him? Someone who would like to take the part of farmer number two?"

Maybe all the Non-Chosen would refuse to raise their hands out of respect. Mike's dad talked about sit-down strikes he'd read about in the *Courier*. Maybe everyone without a part would go on a hands-down strike. If they refused to raise their hands, she just might give the part back to him out of desperation to save the play, and he'd be able to show her and the entire class how much he did care.

Hands shot up, and Miss Schneider studied the students. "Skip, would you like to play the part of farmer number two?"

"Me?" Skip pointed to himself.

"Yes, you. You are the only Skip in the class, are you not? Do you want this part or don't you?"

"Yes, Miss Schneider. I want the part."

"Well, come on up. The part's yours. Mike obviously doesn't care about it. You'll have to share a script with someone else until I can run off another copy. I don't have any more copies because I thought I had chosen people who would be responsible enough to bring their scripts to school each day." She paused and looked at Mike. "But I was wrong."

Skip had the same expression he had when he correctly answered the math question the day Mr. Jackson watched them work. He ran up to the front of the room and stood where Mike should have been standing. Mike's day had become Skip's day. Couldn't she at least have chosen someone other than Skip to take his part? Things just couldn't get any worse.

For the next hour Mike found it impossible not to watch The Chosen rehearse. When Miss Schneider looked in his direction he averted his gaze to a blank piece of paper on his desk and moved a pencil up and down on it to make it look as if he were writing. Miss Schneider stopped practice several times because Skip couldn't say a line correctly even though he read from the script. She said she might have to change farmer number two to a non-speaking part and later said she just might drop farmer number two from the play altogether.

Mr. Jackson appeared in the doorway. Miss Schneider motioned for The Chosen to be quiet while she and he exchanged whispered words. "I'll get him," she said after the brief discussion. She walked to Mike's desk and stood over him. "Mr. Jackson would like to see you."

When Mike reached the classroom door, the principal placed his arm on his shoulder. "There's someone in my office who wants to talk with you."

Chapter 18

HONEST MIKE

A middle-aged man rose from a chair next to Mr. Jackson's desk. Mike's jaw fell. It wasn't the man's size that stood out, although at well over six feet tall and a good two-hundred thirty pounds of today and yesterday's muscle, he made quite a presence. And it wasn't the brown uniform or the badge, either. Mike stared at a gigantic pistol that protruded from his huge leather holster as if it were a 3-D movie prop.

Mr. Jackson patted the man's back. "Mike, this is Sheriff Frank Conners. He's the Gibson County sheriff. He has some questions for you."

Mike's gaze moved from the gun to the man's face. A short, red crew cut accented his round, ruddy face. Sheriff Conners held out his hand, and Mike shook it. It felt huge and rough.

"Glad to meet you, Mike. Have a seat."

He moved a chair from the wall for Mike to sit in and sat in a chair facing him. Mr. Jackson's desk separated him from Mike and Sheriff Conners, giving the illusion that they were alone in the room.

The sheriff stared directly into Mike's eyes. "Mike, I'm investigating something that happened at the Good Shepherd Cemetery a few nights ago. It seems someone, or several someones, pushed over grave markers and scattered flowers. The caretaker said they caused over a thousand dollars of damage."

"Yes, sir?"

The sheriff shifted his bulk. "Mike, I am going to ask you some questions, and I want you to answer them truthfully. Do you understand?"

"Yes, sir, except ... " He looked around the room. "Where's Mr. Smart? I thought he was the law in Potter."

"You're right. Marshal Smart is the law in Potter. But since the cemetery is outside of town, it's under county jurisdiction." He leaned in and spoke slowly. "Son, were you at the cemetery late Tuesday night?"

Mike spoke without hesitation. "Yes, sir."

"What time were you there?"

Mike thought for a moment. "Just after midnight, I guess."

"Were you there by yourself?"

"No, sir. A couple friends went with me."

Sheriff Conners pulled a slip of paper from his shirt pocket, looked at it, and returned it to his pocket. "Are their names Steven Culpepper and Jim Mackey?"

Mike stiffened. "Yes. How did you know?"

The serious look on Sheriff Conner's face remained unchanged, as did his tone of voice. "That's not important. Do your parents know you left the house that night?"

"Yes, sir. They do."

"So you told them you were going to the cemetery in the middle of the night, and they let you?"

Mike trembled. He tried to control it, but couldn't. "No. I sneaked out. When I got back, Mom and Grandpa were awake. The storm woke them up."

Sheriff Conners rubbed his chin. "You say you sneaked out around midnight without telling anyone so you could walk two miles to a cemetery. Do I understand that correctly?"

"Yes."

The sheriff leaned in even more. "You have to help me understand something. Why would three eleven-year-old boys sneak off to a cemetery in the middle of the night? If you didn't plan to vandalize it, why did you go there?"

Mike's eyes widened. "We didn't vandalize it. Honest. We have this game we play. We pretend we're secret agents, and we take Jim's pigeon someplace, tie a message to her leg, and let her go. She flies back home. That's all we were doing that night."

The sheriff sat back. "Let's see if I understand this. You sneaked out of your house in the middle of the night to take a pigeon to the cemetery—in a driving rainstorm—so that it could fly back home again. Is that it?"

Mike sighed. "Well, almost. The rain hadn't started when we left.

When you say it now, it sounds stupid. I didn't want to go from the beginning."

"Then why did you?"

Mike rubbed his eyes. "I don't know. I guess I just didn't want to be called a chicken for life."

"How'd you get into the cemetery? Mr. Hoff said he locks the gate every night."

"But the chain was on the ground," Mike said. "He must have forgotten."

"Actually, someone cut the chain. Mike, I have two more questions." He held up one finger. "First question. Did you boys cut that chain?"

"No, sir. We didn't."

He held up a second finger. "Did any of you push over grave markers or do any other damage?"

"No, sir. Honest. We didn't."

The sheriff crossed his legs and tented his hands. "Let me tell you something. Emil Hoff said he got an anonymous telephone call that three boys were at the cemetery destroying markers. The caller gave him your names. You yourself say you were there, and you tell a ridiculous story about setting a bird loose there after midnight. Anyone could come up with a better story."

Mike sniffed. "But it's true. We really did."

"Mike, the county prosecutor would call this an open-and-shut case. A jury would find you three boys guilty in a heartbeat. No doubt about it." He didn't say anything for a long time. Finally, he said, "In spite of all that, I do believe you. I don't think you vandalized the cemetery."

After hearing the sheriff sum up the situation, Mike had a hard time himself believing he didn't do it. For the first time since he entered the room, he smiled. "You do? You believe me?"

"Yes, I do. And do you know why?"

Mike shook his head. He couldn't imagine why he'd believe him over someone as important as a cemetery caretaker who'd received that phone call. If he were Sheriff Conners, he sure wouldn't believe him.

"I believe you because of this man." He nodded toward Mr. Jackson, who was staring down at his desk blotter, motionless. "We served in the war together, and I found him to be a very honorable and honest person. What's more, he risked his life to save mine. I trust him completely. He told me you are a very honest young man and that you'd be truthful. So if he believes you, I do, too. I hope you'll someday have a special friendship like Mr. Jackson and I have. Such friendships are rare."

Mike no longer noticed the badge or the 3-D gun or the brown uniform. He saw instead a compassionate man who believed him when many others, including his own mother, wouldn't. He sprung from his chair and gave Sheriff Conners a hug, the kind you give a friend you hadn't seen for a long time or who you might never see again. "Thank you, Sheriff Conners. Thank you for believing me."

"You're welcome, young man." He patted Mike's back.

Mike looked at Mr. Jackson, who still sat behind his desk. "May I go now?"

The principal rose from his chair. "Not yet." He walked around his desk and sat on its corner with his hands on his knees. "I told Sheriff Conners you were truthful, but you still have a lot to work on. Just because we believe you doesn't alter the fact you shouldn't have been in that cemetery. You knew it was wrong when you did it, didn't you?"

Mike dropped his head. "Yes, I did."

"But you did it anyway. That's what concerns me. Do you remember when you rode your bicycle down Main Street?"

Mike fidgeted in his chair. "I'll never forget it."

"You confessed. You told the truth. That's great, but you shouldn't have ridden your bike down Main Street in the first place. You knew it was wrong before you did it, didn't you?"

"Yes," Mike said. "I knew it was wrong."

"Do you understand what I'm saying? I don't know how you developed such a strong commitment to telling the truth, but you have. Now you must develop your character to the next level by not doing the wrong things in the first place."

"Yes, sir." Mike paused. "But I don't always know which choices are right."

The principal nodded. "You're right. You can't always tell. But you can start with the obvious ones."

"Like not going to the cemetery in the middle of the night?"

"Right. And not riding your bike down Main Street. On the tough choices, where right and wrong aren't as obvious, you have to trust your conscience. If something doesn't seem quite right, don't do it. Go with your heart." Mr. Jackson walked Mike to the door. "It's something to work for, son."

Chapter 19

THE COMMUNIST THREAT

Charles sat in his porch chair and patted his stomach. "Martha, that was a delicious dinner. I'll bet you fry up the best minute steak in the tri-state area. And the mashed potatoes and gravy never tasted better. I'm so full, I didn't think I'd make it to the porch."

Martha looked as if someone had just jumped from a hiding place and yelled, "Surprise!" "Why, thank you, Charles. Why are you in such a good mood? You're not usually so talkative."

"Oh, no reason. It's just that the food tasted so good." He bent down to pick up the newspaper from the floor, but his full stomach blocked the move. "Mike, would you get the paper for me?"

Martha pointed toward a person walking in their direction. "Hang on to your seats, everyone," she whispered. "Judy Brown is out for one of her lumbers."

Judy neared the Long's front porch, and Martha tossed her a smile. "Why, Judy. Getting some exercise, I see. You're looking good."

Judy veered into the yard and stood just outside the screened-in porch. Sweat streaks lined her face. Her right arm trapped a large brown grocery bag against her chest.

"Thanks for the compliment, Martha." She breathed heavily for half a minute. "Right now I don't feel so good, but I'll feel better when I get home and sit a spell."

"Won't you join us? I could get some iced tea."

"No thanks, Martha. I've got some things I need to put in the refrigerator. But look at me! I made it all the way to town and back."

Grandpa stood. "You didn't!"

"I did. This is the first time since—well, I guess since my teenage years. And we all know that's been a while." She laughed a teenage giggle.

Grandpa stepped off the screen porch and slammed the door behind him. "Judy, it seems like only yesterday you were a teenager. I remember you used to walk to school every morning."

"Lumber." Martha flinched and appeared surprised she had said the word aloud.

Grandpa flashed a just-sit-there-and-don't-say-anything look. "Yes, *number*," he said. "I remember seeing you walk to school a *number* of times when you were a teenager. It's so good to see you walking again. And all the way to town and back. That's such a big accomplishment, you need a hug." He hugged her and stepped back. "You've lost more than a few pounds, I'd say. How many? Twenty-five? Thirty?"

She blushed. "Why Grandpa, thank you for noticing. I've lost thirty-three pounds so far. But I've got a long way to go."

"But thirty-three pounds, Judy. That's fantastic. It looks like you're doing a good job sticking to your diet and exercise."

"So far, but its hard. It's just so hard. I hope I can stay with it."

"I'm sure you will. I can't see you stopping now."

She grinned. "Well, good talking with you all. I've got to go put this milk away." She adjusted the bag and began the last leg of her journey.

Grandpa watched her for a few moments and returned to the porch. He sat in the swing and patted his stomach. "You know, I ought to join her. I've put on quite a bit of weight myself. She's looking better, don't you think?"

Martha sighed. "I suppose. But is it worth killing herself over?"

"What on earth do you mean?" Grandpa puffed his dry pipe slowly and shoved it back into his pocket. "How is she killing herself? She's on a healthy diet and getting plenty of exercise."

"That's what I mean." She picked up the sweater she'd been working on for the past week and eyed it critically. "I have nothing against a healthy diet. I've been on hundreds of those myself. It's the exercise that does you in, Grandpa. It's a proven fact that God allots everyone just so many steps, and when they're used up, that's it. The person dies. Not even doctors know how many steps God has allotted until someone takes his last one."

Grandpa narrowed his eyes. "You can't be serious."

"Oh, but I am. That's why I prefer car rides to walking. Just remember—the next time you drive me somewhere, you're prolonging my life. I figure all Judy Brown is doing is getting her size down to where she'll fit into a casket when she takes her last step."

Grandpa watched Martha knit for a while. "You're making this up as you go along, right? You're making a joke."

"A joke, Grandpa?" She sorted through a Ben Franklin dime-store bag and pulled out a skein of red yarn. "It's common knowledge."

"Well, it's not *my* common knowledge." He patted his stomach again. "Still think it might do me some good."

"Haven't you heard of someone being on his last leg?" she asked without looking up.

"Sure I have," Grandpa said. "It's an old saying that people use all the time."

"Well, what does it mean?"

Grandpa considered that. "It means the person is in bad shape and is going to die soon."

"Right. You walk with your legs, and when your legs take the last step, it's known as being on your last leg. You've reached the number of steps allotted, and you die. Last leg. You die." She went back to her knitting. "Common knowledge."

"I think you're kidding with me, Martha. At least I hope you are. I think I detect a little smile. In any event, I'm going to take my gift of gab elsewhere."

He shifted his weight in the swing and angled toward Charles, who hadn't said a word since he began reading the paper. "Say, Charles. You're awfully quiet over there. Anything interesting in today's paper?"

"The newspaper's always interesting." He pointed to the front page headline. "Like those McCarthy hearings."

"What's old Charlie up to now?"

Charles looked up from his paper, his face frozen in disbelief. "Are you serious?"

"No, I'm not serious. I know you're talking about Senator Joseph McCarthy and his search for communists. But Charlie McCarthy's funnier, and at least he knows he's a dummy." He made a face and exhaled sharply. "If Senator McCarthy is right, the communists are about to take over everything. It scares me. It really does."

Grandpa leaned back in his swing. "The whole world scares me nowadays. The Rosenbergs sell the atomic bomb formula to the Soviets. We develop the hydrogen bomb. And the communists are about to take over the world. That's why we need Charlie McCarthy more than we need Senator McCarthy. We should enjoy life, not be afraid of it. I laugh every time I hear Charlie on the Philco. There's never been a better ventriloquist than Edgar Bergen." He eyed Charles, who held the paper close to his face. "So tell me. What's happening in Senator McCarthy's communistic world?"

Charles ran a finger down the columns until he found the section he wanted. "Well, it says here he's presiding over hearings investigating the army. Says they're too soft on communism, and that some high-ranking army officers may even be commies themselves. He's trying to save our army from the red threat."

Grandpa thrust his arms into the air. "Now they're in our army. I like to read the paper, too, but I couldn't read it practically word-for-word every day like you do. It would scare me to death."

Charles looked up briefly and then went back at the paper. "But don't forget the paper also has sports, comics, and Dorothy Dix's advice column. It all averages out."

"Maybe." Grandpa took out his pipe again. "I hear everything I need to know on the Philco."

Martha pointed toward Grandpa's pipe. "I hope you're not going to smoke that thing. It would bring us all closer to our deaths."

"And just how will it do that?"

She continued knitting. "Well, it would stink up the porch so much we'd all have to leave."

"So?"

She yanked on the red yarn, flipping the skein over on her lap. "Well, just think about it. By walking away we'll all be that much closer to hitting the number of steps allotted to us and closer to being on our last leg."

Grandpa stuck the pipe in his mouth. "Very funny, Martha. No, I'm not going to smoke it here. I like to save it for the backyard when it's just me, the swing, and Chirper the robin." He took a couple of deep draws from the pipe. "Though I admit it's much more satisfying when it's lit."

He put it back in his pocket. "You're quiet over there, Mike. You going to Tony's tonight?"

"Yeah. Steven, Jim, and I are going to watch *I Led Three Lives* at Tony's and then play chalk the rabbit."

Martha stopped knitting. "Did you do your homework?"

"I only had a little math to do. Just took a few minutes."

"Did you write the spelling words you missed on Friday's test ten times each?"

"I did that in school."

She held up the sweater and examined the sleeves. "I don't like your watching that TV program. It puts goofy ideas into your head about communists and spies." She placed the sweater back on her lap, and the needles once again moved rapidly. "You and your little friends already seem to think you really are secret agents and believe we have communists right here in Potter."

Grandpa scratched his beard and leaned back. "I beg to differ, Martha. I haven't seen the program, but they say it's based on a true story. Besides, Senator McCarthy says communists are everywhere. Right, Charles?"

"Pretty near."

"See there, Martha? They're pretty near everywhere. And that comes from a man who reads the paper every day." Grandpa pointed up the street to Bertha Kramer, who stood on a stepladder clipping her hedge. "For all we know, she's a communist. If she is, the boys and Squall Baby will use their finely-honed spying skills to bring her to justice."

Martha watched the old lady a moment and then went back to her knitting. "I don't think she is. You'd have to actually know something to be a communist."

"I'm just saying she could be. I think *I Led Three Lives* is education-al, and we should be grateful Tony's folks let the boys watch it." He winked at Mike. "Maybe Trashman's a communist."

Martha laughed. "I doubt that they let drunks join. They'd be afraid they'd let important secrets slip out."

Grandpa swung a little slower. "That's the beauty of it." He used the all-knowing voice he used when he wanted someone to believe the impossible. "What if I told you Trashman's not really a drunk and that he doesn't even drink?"

Martha's needles stopped. "Trashman doesn't drink? Really?"

"I said, 'What if I *told* you?' I don't know. He probably is a drunk. But it makes you stop and think, doesn't it? His shack may be a cover. Maybe he's not poor. Maybe Connie's not his wife. Why, she could be an-other communist. Little Jerry could be a huge communist midget. Maybe they're getting ready to take over Potter."

Martha's knitting needles remained stationary. "Why in the world would they want to do that?"

Grandpa shrugged. "I don't know. Lot of reasons. Maybe they want Squall Baby on their side, and the only way they can get her is to take over Potter."

Martha's knitting needles began moving again. "Grandpa, I don't believe a word you say."

Steven ran up the brick sidewalk. "Hi, Mike. Ready to go to Tony's?"

"Yeah. Okay, Mom?"

"I guess so. I still think it gives you boys goofy ideas."

"I think it's educational," Grandpa said loud enough for Martha to hear.

She rolled her eyes in Grandpa's general direction. "Whatever."

"Thanks, Mom." The screen door squeaked, and Mike left.

"You got the chalk?" Steven asked.

"Right here in my pocket." Mike tapped it for emphasis. "You got the flashlight?"

Steven pulled a flashlight from his blue jeans pocket and switched it on and off.

"Great. Let's get Jim. We don't want to miss the program."

"Don't stay out too late," Martha yelled. "Remember, tomorrow's a school day."

***

When the boys arrived at Jim's house, he was throwing his knife at the ash tree in his front yard. They watched him throw it five or six times, and each time, it stuck with authority.

"You're pretty good at that," Steven said. "I've never thrown a knife. May I try?"

Jim handed him the knife. Steven brought his hand back, aimed at the tree with one eye open, and threw. The knife missed the tree by two feet and landed six feet behind it. He retrieved the knife and threw again. This time the knife hit handle first and fell to the ground.

Jim laughed. "Well, what do you know? I finally found something I'm better at than Steve." He picked up the knife, closed it, and slid it into his pocket. "It's getting late. We'd better go or we'll miss the program."

Chapter 20

DROPPING THE BOMB

Four figures slinked from Tony's house into the dark April night. Tony pushed the door closed. "I've never seen a more exciting *I Led Three Lives.*"

Jim turned his back to the streetlight and faced the other three. "Makes you think, doesn't it? Who'd have guessed a school teacher could be a communist?"

Steven shined his flashlight around the house and yard, forming mysterious, silent shadows. "But it makes sense. Did you notice how she said things to make the kids think like communists?"

Mike froze. "You don't suppose—"

"Suppose what?" Steven held the flashlight under his chin and pointed it skyward. Its beam lit parts of his face, but the rest formed eerie shadows. "That I'm a communist? BWAHAHAHAHA."

"No, not you. But what about your aunt? She could be one."

Steven clicked off the flashlight. "Aunt Shirley? Nah. She's no communist."

"You sure?"

"Sure I'm sure. She loves being an American. You know what she told me the other day? She said President Eisenhower just signed a bill to build an Air Force Academy in Colorado. She wants me to go there. You know, so I can learn to defend our country against communism. She said if I expect to have a chance of being accepted I'll have to keep making good grades and stop doing dumb stuff like sneaking off to cemeteries in the middle of the night."

"Come on, guys," Tony said. "Let's stop talking about a forced air academy and play chalk the rabbit. Jim and I'll be the rabbits."

Steven raised his voice. "It's Air Force Academy, not forced air academy."

"Air force, forced air, it's all the same to me. Who's got the chalk?"

Mike pulled the chalk from his pocket and tossed it to Tony. "Here. Now, take off. We'll give you five minutes, and then we'll track you rabbits down and show you no mercy."

"You don't have a watch," Jim said. "How will you know when five minutes are up?"

"We'll know." Mike raised his left wrist and pretended to look at a wristwatch. "You have four-and-a-half minutes left. You'd better go before you lose more time."

Tony made a chalk arrow on the sidewalk next to Mike's foot. "Catch us if you can. Remember, five minutes."

They took off running. Tony knelt under the streetlight at the end of the block and made another arrow on the sidewalk. He and Jim vanished in the darkness.

Mike sat on Tony's front lawn. The dew had not yet made its evening visit, and the grass felt soft and inviting. He peered at Steven in the dim streetlight. "What would you do at the Air Force Academy?"

Steven sat next to him. "Well, I'd learn to be an air force officer and to fly airplanes. Just think—I'd fly like Squall Baby, only higher and faster. I might even get into dogfights and drop bombs."

Mike quickly surveyed the area to make sure a communist wasn't listening to their classified conversation. He leaned in and whispered. "What kind of bombs would you drop? Atomic?"

"Maybe."

"What about hydrogen? Would you drop the new hydrogen bomb?"

"If I had to. By then there'll probably be bombs we haven't even thought of yet, like an oxygen bomb or a sulfur bomb."

"What's sulfur?"

"It's a gas." Just as Mike had done earlier, Steven made sure a communist wasn't near enough to overhear future bomb ingredients. He put his finger to his lips. "Shhhhh." He picked up the flashlight, switched it on, and aimed it at the bushes near Tony's front porch. Just as the light had done when he shined it on his own face earlier, it made weird and creepy shadows. Something moved in the shadows, and Steven adjusted the flashlight to shine on the interloper.

"Meow."

It was Tony's black cat, Whitey. Steven exhaled and moved the beam from one end of the porch to the other. Satisfied Whitey was alone and posed no threat, he leaned closer to Mike. "It smells just like rotten eggs."

"Rotten eggs?" Mike snickered.

"What are you laughing at?"

"Nothing. I'm not laughing at anything."

The snicker evolved into a snort and then a laugh so uncontrollable it came out almost silent. Mike gasped for air. He rolled in the grass and pounded his fists into the ground.

Steven laughed, too. He didn't know why, but he'd caught the laughter from Mike like he'd caught a cold from his mother during Christmas vacation, by just being there. Steven managed to stop laughing. "What? Tell me."

Mike held his stomach with both hands. "Oh. Wow. My stomach hurts." He laughed again. Every time he laughed, Steven laughed. He held his stomach tighter. "Oh. Give me a minute. Don't say anything." Mike sat for a while taking deep breaths.

He gradually regained control and removed his hands from his stomach. "When you said sulfur smelled like rotten eggs, it made me think of a fart bomb."

"A fart bomb?" Steven laughed harder.

"That's right, a fart bomb. I can see it now. Your first assignment as an air force officer is to pass gas into an empty bombshell. In spite of your natural talent, it takes you weeks to complete the assignment, but finally, it's full. You couldn't force another ounce of gas into it if your life depended upon it."

"That sounds like something Tony would say," Steven said between spells of laughter. "He was the one who thought I wanted to attend a forced air academy."

Mike waved his hand. "Shhhh. Let me finish. On the day of the big mission, you fly over a bunch of communist soldiers and drop this huge, pressurized, personally made fart bomb. The communists aren't worried because they have the latest uniforms to protect them from the atomic bomb, the hydrogen bomb, the oxygen bomb, and even the sulfur bomb. They know they're going to feel quite a sting when the bomb hits, and it's going to be pretty warm for a while, but their uniforms will protect them from being hurt too badly."

Steven rolled on the ground, laughing. Mike talked louder so Steven could hear him over his laughter. "A few point at the bomb when it's released from your plane. They make fun of it as it whistles toward the earth." He moved his opened hand down to represent the falling bomb and made a whistling sound that started out high and got lower and lower. His hand slapped the grass. "Boom! It releases the most awful stench in the history of the world. That's right, Steven—it smells just like you.

"Soldiers fall by the hundreds. 'It's a fart bomb!' someone yells. 'Save yourselves.' The few not killed by the smell on the spot try to run, but die in mid-step. Animals as big as cows die. Leaves turn brown, curl up, and fall off trees. Nothing is left alive within a fifty-mile radius. Not a plant, not an animal, not a person. People just outside the fifty-mile smell zone manage to live, but they develop terrible headaches. Their cows seem okay, but when they drink the milk, they notice a strong taste that interferes with the enjoyment of homemade cookies."

Steven lay holding his stomach. "Where do you come up with stuff like this, Mike?"

"Wait. Wait. I just thought of more. You leave the air force, get married, and have a little kid. But you can't forget the terrible destruction you caused or the people who died. Twenty years later, you and Steven Junior visit the spot where the bomb hit. He's our age and, unfortunately, looks just like you. You get out of the car and walk to the exact spot where the bomb hit and look around. The trees are all dead and rotten, and there's no grass or animals or anything. You cry, and tears drip down your face and onto the ground.

"Then you hear something. 'Sniff. Sniff.' You look around. Maybe something's alive, after all. Maybe there's hope. You hear it again. 'Sniff. Sniff.' It's your son, Junior. He looks up at you and says, 'Eew, is that you, Dad?'"

Steven was the first to stop laughing and the first to speak. "I wonder what Heidi Beck would say if she heard you telling that story."

Mike sat up. "If Heidi were here right now, I know exactly what she'd say."

Steven grinned. "Yeah? What would she say?"

"She'd say—Eew, is that you, Steven?"

"Ha ha. Very funny."

"No, I'm serious, Steven. Are you making fart bombs?"

"Well—maybe."

"Yuck."

Steven looked in the direction the other boys went. "Do you think the time is up yet?"

"It's up as far as I'm concerned. Let's go get those rabbits. And when we get back we should make sure Tony's folks are still alive."

Chapter 21

CHALK THE RABBIT

Steven and Mike jogged down the sidewalk to the spot where Tony had chalked the arrow under the streetlight. They turned left and went to the end of the next block where an arrow pointed east on Stoner Street and followed more arrows until they crossed the railroad tracks that divided the town. The tracks sat atop a rocky six-foot bank that blocked streets from entering from the west all the way to the south end of town. A big, white arrow there pointed right, down narrow Railroad Street, which had no sidewalks. The boys followed arrows drawn in the middle of the street, watching closely for potholes.

Steven shined the light on the arrow at each intersection entering Railroad Street from the east, and Mike expected to eventually find one pointing that direction toward civilization. Scrub trees and thick brush covered the three-block stretch where Trashman's shack and barn were the lone buildings. Because the town never bothered to put up streetlights along this stretch, the only light finding its way to this part of the planet at night came from the moon and stars on a clear night, from the streetlights a block over, and from the dim flame of Trashman's kerosene lamp that flickered through the window.

Tony and Jim had drawn the final chalk-the-rabbit mark, a circle with four arrows pointing north, south, east, and west, directly in front of Trashman's shack. That meant they hid nearby waiting for Mike and Steven to find them. Steven turned off the flashlight and put it into his pocket. The sliver moon provided little light, and patchy clouds blocked most of the stars. The distant streetlights cast long, dim shadows.

Mike looked west at the railroad tracks, and imagined the secret woods that lay beyond them. Surely the rabbits didn't hide there. No, they had to be hiding in the other direction.

He pointed at Trashman's shack and barn. "They've got to be there," he whispered. They crept along the rutted driveway that led to the barn, and then veered right toward the house. Feeble light from Trashman's kerosene lamp reflected from Steven's features. He pointed toward a burn barrel, an old wagon, and a horse trough, all places rabbits could hide.

Mike's right foot hit something hard. It rolled and clanked loudly when it struck something else. He froze. A whiskey bottle. Bottles were probably scattered about the yard like land mines in a war zone. They'd have to be sure not to kick another one and get Trashman's attention. Picking his yard to hide in was dumb, just plain dumb.

"Psssst."

The noise came from near the shack's front window.

"Psssst. Come here."

Mike glanced back at the street, ready to run. "Who are you?"

"Jim. Come here."

"No. You come here. Let's get out of here."

Jim walked to them and grabbed Mike's arm. He spoke in a whisper. "You have to see this. You have to. It's important." They followed him to the front window, put their hands on the sill, straightened, and peered inside.

Burly sat to the right, his chair angled enough for them to see the left side of his face. Trashman stood to his left with his back to the boys, shouting at his wife, who was in front of him facing the window. Jerry stood behind his mother.

Connie put her hands to her eyes and cried. "I didn't do anything. I didn't."

"Don't give me that crap. You told that preacher man things about me. You told him lies." Trashman stood with both hands on his hips. During the loudest point of his yelling he swung his right hand in the air and returned it to its resting place.

"I didn't do anything. I went to get a ham hock and some navy beans for your supper."

Jerry's eyes darted from one to the other.

"Liar."

She looked down. "I'm not a liar."

"You can buy ham hocks a block away, over at Carlton's Grocery. Burly seen you downtown. Didn't you, Burly?"

Burly fisted his right hand and slammed it into his opened left hand. "I saw her downtown, Seth."

She looked up, her eyes pleading. "Mr. Carlton didn't have any good ham hocks left, so I went to Big John's Market. I went to get a good ham hock for your supper."

He stepped closer to her. "You went to meet that fancy preacher man. The one who gives you pies and cakes so he can talk to you and turn you against me. Burly seen you with him. Didn't you Burly?"

"She talked to the preacher man, Seth." Burly pounded his fist hard on a small table to the right of the chair, jarring an apparently empty beer bottle to the floor. "Right downtown."

Connie rolled her eyes. "Sure, I talked with him. I ran into him on my way to Big John's Market. What was I supposed to do, ignore him when he said 'Hi?'"

"I saw them meet," Burly said. "I was sitting on the bench in front of Brown's Drugstore. They stood right there and talked about you, Seth. Right there in front of Brown's Drugstore."

Trashman's entire body trembled. "And just what did you tell the preacher man about me?"

Tears streamed down her face, and she wiped them with her hands. "Nothing. I didn't tell him nothing. I didn't."

"Burly?"

He pointed to Connie. "She told him plenty. He asked her if she was safe. Safe from you, her husband. He asked if you still came home drunk and if you hit her and Jerry."

Trashman reared back. "Why is he even asking you those questions? That's all private stuff between a man and wife."

Connie's voice softened. "He just wanted to make sure I was okay."

"And what did you tell him?" Trashman's hands were still on his hips, just as they were when the boys first started watching.

"I told him I was okay, Seth."

Trashman looked back at Burly.

Burly leaned forward. "Yeah, she said that. She also said you came home drunk last night and yelled at her and Jerry. She promised she'd pack her things and go to him if she couldn't stand it any more."

Trashman removed his hands from his hips and stepped toward Connie. He slapped her, and her head snapped back. "You don't talk to other people about me. You understand, woman?" He slapped her again.

"I said do you understand?"

"Yes." Her voice was quiet, almost calm. She stared at the floor. He slapped her again. And again. Again.

Jerry's hands curled into fists, and he stepped in front of his mother. "Stop hitting her. Stop hitting her."

"Stay outta my way." Trashman shoved him, and Jerry hit the floor hard. "This is between me and her. Stay out of it, elephant."

Jerry jumped up and ran toward his dad. "You stop hitting her!" His fists found Trashman's midsection, and the man held his arms in front of him to ward off the attack. Then he struck Jerry's head hard with his closed fist. The blow knocked him to the floor where he remained, whimpering. Burly crossed his legs. Like the boys, he was merely a spectator.

Connie fell to her knees and wrapped her arms around Jerry. "Don't. Please don't."

"You get up. We're not done yet." He grabbed her arm and yanked her up.

Mike ran from the house. Bottles clanked as he ran. When he reached the street, he put his hands on his knees and threw up. The sour liquid burned his mouth. He threw up again, spit, and wiped his lips with the back of his hand.

The shack's front door opened. Trashman stood on the front porch, swinging his fist. "What are you doing in my yard? If I catch you, you're in trouble. You hear me?"

Mike ran down Railroad Street as fast as he could in the darkness. The others followed close behind.

"Where are we going?" Jim yelled.

Before Mike could answer, his foot found a pothole, and he slammed hard against the rugged gravel and asphalt, breaking the fall the best he could with his hands. He knew from the pain and the dampness that they were bleeding. Jim and Steven helped him up. "Where are we going?" Jim said again.

"We're going to Marshal Smart's. What's happening in that house is terribly wrong."

Marshal Smart lived on the north end of town, some fourteen or fifteen blocks away. When the boys arrived, they were out of breath. Mike pounded on the door. Mrs. Smart opened it about ten inches and peered out. "Yes? Can I help you boys?"

"We need to see Marshal Smart." Mike talked as fast as he could so he could take another deep breath. "It's important."

They followed her to the living room where the marshal sat in an overstuffed chair watching *Truth or Consequences* and drinking Royal Crown Cola from a bottle. A five-cent Planter's Peanuts bag lay empty on the coffee table, its missing peanuts floating in the nearly full RC bottle. He swigged the drink, chewed the peanuts, and swigged again to wash them down. He looked up at them.

"Boys, can you wait until the commercial? This is my favorite program, and I want to see what consequence Jack Bailey has cooked up for these people."

"No, we can't wait." Mike had caught his breath. "Trashman's beating up Mrs. Harders and Jerry. Unless you stop him, he's going to kill them."

"Let's go." Marshal Smart pecked his wife on the cheek and ran to his car with the boys close behind. "Get in."

Mike jumped into the front seat, and the others piled into the back. The tires squealed when the marshal backed the car out of the driveway and again when he slammed it into first. The car slowed when he turned onto Railroad Street, but still found nearly every pothole. He pulled into the Harders' driveway and killed the engine.

"Boys, stay in the car. Is that clear? Stay in the car." He walked toward the house with his pistol pointed skyward next to his right ear and looked into the window. A few moments later Marshal Smart shoved the pistol back into its holster and walked to the door. He knocked with his left hand and kept his right hand on the gun's handle. "Open up. It's Marshal Smart." Soon, he disappeared inside the shack.

Mike opened the car door. "Hurry up. Let's go."

"Go where?" Steven asked. "Marshal Smart said to stay in the car."

Mike was out of the car. "We've got to see what's going on in there. It could be a trap. Maybe Burly and Trashman are going to jump him and beat him up."

Steven and Jim slipped out of the back seat, and the three maneuvered through the bottles to the window. Inside, Burly still sat in the easy chair, his hands folded over his substantial stomach. Trashman, Connie, and Jerry held playing cards and sat in folding chairs around a dilapidated card table. The rest of the cards were spread face down in front of them. The marshal stood next to Trashman.

"Hey, Marshal." Burly offered a fake-looking smile. "Don't you love seeing a family play games together? What brings you to this part of town?"

"I came to see Seth and his family here." He studied the man. "I understand there was a little problem here tonight, Seth."

"Problem, Marshal? I don't know what you're talking about." He looked back at Jerry. "Any sevens?"

"Go fish."

Trashman pulled a card from the facedown stack and slid it in with his other cards. "Nope. That ain't it."

Marshal Smart removed the kerosene lamp from its shelf and took it to the card table. He knelt by Connie and moved the lamp around her face. Mike caught his breath. The light's closeness made her wounds stand out. Both eyes were swollen and dark. Her lower lip was puffy and cut, and blotches marred her face.

Marshal Smart knelt next to Jerry. His eyes were also dark and swollen nearly shut He put the lantern back on the shelf and returned to the table.

"Have you ever watched *Truth or Consequences*, Mr. Harders?"

Trashman's face furrowed. "Now Marshal, we don't have electricity. Unless they make a kerosene television I don't know about, we can't watch TV."

"Well, let me tell you about it. I was watching it just before coming here. It's a program where people have to either tell the truth or pay the consequences. That's what you're going to do right now. Seth, what happened here tonight? Remember, I want the truth."

"Nothing, Marshal. We've just been playing cards. It's family night."

The marshal turned to Connie. "Did he beat you?"

Her eyes remained fixed on the cards she clutched. "Like he said, we've been playing cards."

"Mrs. Harders, how did you get those bruises?"

She talked in a monotone. "I walked into a tree limb in the dark."

"I see," Marshal Smart said. "What about your eyes? How did they get swollen?"

She didn't answer.

The marshal stepped toward her and spoke in a firm voice. "Mrs. Harders, it's important you answer my questions."

She looked away. "I have a bad cold. They always get this way when I get a bad cold."

He lowered to his knees. "Your lips, Mrs. Harders. Why are they bleeding?"

"Chapped."

"Your son has similar injuries. How do you explain that?"

She fixed her gaze on her cards, and her voice sounded as if it came from way in the distance. "Tree limb ... bad cold ... chapped lips."

The marshal stood. "That's it. Time for the consequences. Stand up, Seth." He took the handcuffs from his belt.

Trashman stood. "What are you doing, Marshal?"

"Put your hands behind you. You're under arrest for battery." He snapped the handcuffs on the man's wrists and turned to Connie. "I'm taking you two to Gibson County Hospital to be checked out."

"I don't need—"

"This isn't a suggestion. It's the way things are going to be. It's time you started thinking about yourself—and your son."

He looked at Jerry, who sat in a chair with his head in his hands, and then back at Connie. "You need someplace to go. You have any relatives you can stay with for a few days?"

Connie shook her head.

"How about friends?"

"Well, there's Preacher Beemer. He might take us in or find a place."

"I'm sure he would." The marshal reached out to Jerry and pulled him from the chair. "Tell you what, we'll stop by the preacher's on the way to the hospital and make arrangements." He patted Jerry's shoulder. "That sound okay to you, young man?"

Jerry didn't say anything.

"Let's go." He nudged the man toward the door and stopped next to Burly, who still sat in the chair by the window. "Family night's over, Burly. Time to go home. And put the light out when you leave."

"Back to the car," Mike whispered. The three raced back and waited for the others. The marshal held onto Trashman's arm and led the handcuffed man to the car. "Boys," he said when he opened the door, "got to take Mr. Harders to the county jail and Mrs. Harders and Jerry to the hospital. Can you make it home on your own?"

"Sure." Mike motioned across the railroad tracks with a quick hand movement. "We just live eight or nine blocks from here."

Marshal Smart helped Trashman into the front seat and Mrs. Harders and Jerry into the back. He walked to the boys and leaned down with his hands on his knees. "Thanks for getting me. You may have saved a life. Maybe two. It's getting late. You boys need to go home now."

Soon everyone had left, and darkness reclaimed Railroad Street. Mike looked back over his shoulder as the three walked toward Stoner Street. Trashman's house was dark. A distant streetlight's dim glow faintly highlighted a large figure standing by the willow tree in the front yard.

Chapter 22

A LIGHT IN THE DARKNESS

In many ways, church service that Sunday was like every other church service. Members filled the pews, forcing latecomers to stand along the back and side walls. The choir belted out beautiful and inspirational songs. Preacher Beemer sat in his chair to the pulpit's right, and Stella sang.

Yet it was completely different. For the first time, Connie and Jerry Harders sat in one of the pews. Jerry was all cleaned up and dressed in a white shirt and a red tie. Connie wore a beige dress and white shoes. Had she ever worn a dress before? Their faces, although still discolored from the beatings, no longer appeared swollen.

Following a rousing choral rendition of *Amazing Grace*, Preacher Beemer stood and took his place behind the pulpit. "Welcome to the Lord's house. I especially welcome two visitors—Mrs. Connie Harders and her fine son, Jerry—whom I hope will turn their lives over to the Lord. Welcome, and God bless you both."

"Amen!"

The "amen" came from one of the old men sitting in the front left pew next to the upright piano. For some reason, years ago that particular pew attracted the congregation's most vocal old men who took turns yelling "amen" whenever the preacher said something they agreed with, and they agreed with almost everything he said. Everyone called the pew Amen Corner, and the "amens" became a part of each Sunday's church service. The supply of old men never seemed to dwindle. When one died, another took his place, as if there were a waiting list to join.

Preacher Beemer continued. "Mrs. Harders and Jerry will stay with Stella and me for a few days before visiting with her sister in Grayville,

Illinois. I trust the Lord will touch their souls and protect them while they are there."

"Amen!"

He opened his Bible. "I begin today's sermon by reading from the fifteenth chapter of Proverbs, verses one through three and twenty-five and twenty-six." He held the book at eye level and read the sacred words. "'A soft answer turneth away wrath: but grievous words stir up anger. The tongue of the wise useth knowledge aright: but the mouth of fools poureth out foolishness. The eyes of the Lord are in every place, beholding the evil and the good.'" He paused for only a second, which proved long enough for the latest Amen Corner member, an eighty-year-old youngster, to respond.

"Amen!"

"'The Lord will destroy the house of the proud: but he will establish the border of the widow. The thoughts of the wicked are an abomination to the Lord: but the words of the pure are pleasant words.' The word of our Lord."

"Amen!"

As usual, Preacher Beemer's sermon was riveting. He told how God saw everything everyone did, both the good and the evil. He loved everyone, including the evildoers, but did not like the actions of the wicked. He explained how God appreciates people who use words to help others and how He is hurt when words and actions bring harm. His voice became quiet when he concluded his sermon by saying, "It may appear the proud and the evildoers are never punished. They may think they are getting away with their actions, but they are not. God sees all. In the end, He will destroy their houses."

"Amen!"

Mike counted nineteen "amens" from Amen Corner, down from the average of twenty-five, and a far cry from the record of thirty-seven set on Easter Sunday two years ago. As the congregation left the church, Preacher Beemer shook Mike's hand. "Good to see you, Mike. Bless you, son."

As he shook hands with the preacher's wife, Mike noticed Connie and Jerry Harders standing next to her. Mike's mom shook their hands without speaking, using her unenthusiastic "fish" handshake. She let them shake her hand, but shook back so passively, it resembled a catch-and-release fishing program. When Connie and Jerry caught her hand, it became a lifeless bluegill until they tired of moving it up and down and let it go. She wiped the bluegill on her thigh, first one side and then the other. Like a miracle, the fish disappeared, leaving behind a normal hand.

Mike's dad also shook the newcomers' hands. "Welcome," he said, first to Connie and then to Jerry. Grandpa sandwiched Connie's hand between his. "Welcome to the Oak Street Baptist Church. I hope this is the first Sunday of many that find you in a church of the Lord." He shook Jerry's hand. "Good to see you, son."

Mike had mixed feelings. He was glad they were there, but it somehow didn't seem right that Jerry got to shake everyone's hand. When he stepped out of the church, Grandpa was talking with Widow Benson.

Martha leaned against the car with her arms crossed. "Are you coming or what?" Grandpa tipped his straw hat to the widow and walked to the car.

"Don't you embarrass me enough by wearing those overalls to church? Do you also have to make me stand around while you talk with that brazen woman?"

Grandpa winked at Mike. "First of all, Martha, these are my brand new church-meeting overalls from Sears and Roebuck, a fine and reputable company. I also put on clean white socks this morning. And second, be careful how you talk about the Widow Benson. Someday she just might be your stepmother."

Martha's eyes popped open wide. The suggestion Maud Benson could somehow end up being her stepmother never failed to ignite a reaction in her. She sniffed. "The day that woman becomes my stepmother is the day I leave."

Grandpa again winked at Mike. "How about that? Two birds with one stone."

"I see you winking, Grandpa. I'm not blind."

"Just have something in my eye, Martha. I think it's getting better."

***

Grandpa rushed into the house following a late Tuesday night smoke in the front yard. Mike looked up from the floor where he was doing his homework. Grandpa had something important to say. He could always tell by the way he held his mouth, and never before had it been this stiff. Mike laid his pencil down and waited.

"You're not going to believe this."

Martha motioned for Charles to turn the Philco down. "What won't we believe?"

"Judy Brown just told me Trashman is dead."

"Dead? Trashman's dead? I don't believe it."

"See? I knew you wouldn't. She said she heard it from reliable sources. Shot himself in his shack. Burly found him. He was just a couple of blocks away from Trashman's shack when he heard a gunshot and ran in and found him. He had placed his twelve gauge shotgun up to his—"

"Shush, Grandpa!" Martha nodded toward Mike. "Little pitchers. Big ears."

Grandpa placed a hand over his mouth. "We'll talk about it later."

"Trashman ... dead." Martha sat without moving or saying a word for a full minute. Then she rose slowly. "Time for bed, Mike. Tomorrow's a school day."

"I just have a few more spelling words to write ten times each."

"Let me see that paper," she said. "My goodness, Mike. How many words did you miss?"

"Eight. But it was a hard test."

"Eight out of twenty? How could you miss that many?"

Grandpa held up a hand. "Shhhh."

"Grandpa, don't you shush me. I'm talking to my son here. If I don't keep after him, he'll grow up to be the village idiot."

"Shhhh. Listen."

Martha cocked her head. "What is that?"

Charles jumped from the sofa. "It's sirens." He stepped onto the front porch. The sirens continued. "Come here. Look at this. Hurry."

The three joined Charles on the porch and saw the eastern sky's orange brightness. For several seconds they stood speechless.

"Fire," Grandpa said. "Let's go."

"Go where?"

"To the fire. We might have neighbors in trouble."

***

Grandpa backed his black '49 Ford from the old, leaning garage and motioned for the others to get in. Mike jumped into the front. "Hurry!" he shouted to his parents when they opened the rear doors. Grandpa began backing before Martha shut her door.

"Just a minute, Grandpa. I'm not in yet."

He kept backing. "Can't wait. People may need our help."

The traffic going east on Stoner Street resembled a parade. The line of cars moved at a speed even Cinders could match, their drivers honking, hoping to somehow speed things up. Grandpa inched his car onto Stoner until a driver motioned him in.

The fire had attracted people like light attracts moths, and the sleepy town had become a city of excitement. People ran on the sidewalks and in the street, passing up the cars, yelling to one another.

"It's over there. See it?" People, some running, some walking, pointed toward the orange sky.

"Bobby. Come back here. Stay with Daddy." The child waited until his father caught up, and then darted off again.

Like football running backs, several teenagers veered left and right, picking holes in the crowd to run through. "Run faster," the lead boy yelled to the others. He misjudged the size of an opening and ran into several people, almost knocking them over.

Charles pointed toward the crowd. "It's down Railroad Street, Grandpa. Park the car. Let's see what's happening."

Grandpa raised his voice to be heard over the crowd noise. "There's no place to park."

Martha shook his shoulder. "Well, do something."

Grandpa took a sharp left and parked in a driveway. Martha peered at the house and then at Grandpa.

"Goodness, Grandpa. Why'd you stop at the widow's house?"

He shut off the car. "Either we park here, or I drive around for another fifteen minutes trying to find a place to park on the street. Besides, Maud said I could stop by any time."

They joined the march, and when they reached the Stoner and Railroad Street intersection, they saw the burning building. Fire trucks, police cars, and a couple hundred people had overtaken the area. The section known for its solitude and darkness had become the busiest and brightest place in town.

Grandpa pointed at the railroad track. "The road's too crowded. Let's walk down the track." He ducked his head to make sure he didn't trip on a tie and led the way to the fire. It glowed brighter as they neared a spot where other trackwalkers had stopped, their faces an eerie yellow glow.

Martha pointed. "Why, it's Trashman's place. The shack's on fire."

Mike watched with the rest of the gapers as flames shot skyward, consuming the building. Shouts rose to the elevated tracks, mixing with the fire's own crackling. "Over here. More water over here ... Don't let it spread to the barn ... Keep that barn wet ... " Some firemen sprayed the house while others aimed hoses at the barn. And constantly, the shouts rolled over Mike.

"Where's the horse?"

"Burly took him to the schoolyard."

"That house is a goner."

Marshal Smart walked toward the crowd, waving his arms. "Get back and let the firemen do their job. Go on. Get back."

The crowd moved back. Some jumped the ditch and climbed the railroad bank to stand on the tracks. Before long, darkness settled in again.

Little remained of the shack. In the embers' glow, Mike recognized some of the bystanders. Connie Harders stood by Marshal Smart's car, next to Preacher Beemer. The marshal walked up to the firemen, who now slumped together holding limp hoses, watching the ashes. "Good job, men. Harry, go tell Burly he can bring the horse back to the barn."

Like an audience leaving a movie theater, the crowd walked slowly back down the tracks, discussing the action and speculating on motives. Martha turned to Grandpa. "I wonder how it started. Why, that was awful."

"I think someone started it on purpose."

"How do you know that, Grandpa? Maybe it started by accident."

"I don't think so, Martha. There was no lightning. The shack didn't have electricity, so it couldn't have been electrical. Connie and Jerry are staying with the preacher and his wife, and Trashman's dead, so no one was using the kerosene lamps or cooking dinner on the stove. No, I think someone started it on purpose."

No one spoke when they got into the car. Grandpa backed out of the widow's driveway and drove toward home.

Chapter 23

THE KIDNAPPING

The three agents ran to the burned-out shack as soon as school let out. Neither Jim nor Steven had seen it burn. They both saw the bright light, but Jim had to stay home and help his mom catch up on the laundry, and Miss Schneider had told Steven working on the math problems she had given him was more important than gallivanting all over town to find the light's source. The three stood in the middle of Railroad Street and stared at the spot where the old shack once stood. The only thing left was green grass surrounding an area of black ashes and debris. An old farm truck with an attached horse trailer was parked near the barn. Cinders neighed from inside.

Steven stared at the black ashes. "It's hard to believe Trashman's gone and his shack's burned down. I wonder what caused it."

"Grandpa says it was arson."

"He may be right," Jim said. "But why would someone want to set it on fire?"

"Well, not for the insurance money. Grandpa said the whole place wasn't worth more than a buck-fifty."

Jim gazed at the burnt spot. "I'll bet I know who did it—Jerry."

Steven shook his head. "I don't think so. Why would he set his own house on fire?"

"Because he's Jerry. Why does Jerry do anything?"

"Grandpa thinks Connie Harders did it. He says she wanted to destroy the house of the evildoer like what the preacher talked about in his sermon."

As they watched, Jeb Johnson led Cinders from the barn, and Burly helped load him into the trailer. The two talked a minute, and then Jeb

146

drove down the bumpy street. Cinders let out a loud whinny, as if saying goodbye to the only home he knew.

Steven motioned to the others. "C'mon. If we're going on a secret mission tonight, we've got to get Squall Baby." They climbed the rocky bank, crossed the tracks, and entered the secret woods through the briar-protected opening.

***

Burly watched the boys disappear through the briars, and went back into the barn. Moments later he came out shouldering a coiled rope that hung almost to his knees and carrying a large seine in a bear hug. He crossed the road, jumped the ditch, and climbed up to the tracks. Briars pulled at the bulky fishnet as he entered the secret woods.

***

The three agents left Jim's house and followed the secret path through the woods, carrying Squall Baby in the portable cage. They were on a routine mission to the schoolyard and should easily make it back to headquarters at Jim's house by suppertime.

Jim slowed. "What's that?"

Steven and Mike stopped behind him. "I didn't hear anything."

"Shhh. Listen."

Steven took a hesitant step. "You're hearing things."

"Ohhhhh." The sound came from ahead of them.

"There it is again. Did you hear it?"

Mike pointed toward the creek. "It came from the peninsula. Sounds like someone's hurt."

"Ohhhh."

They ran to the creek bank and peered down. A man lay face down on the peninsula. His feet and part of his legs were submerged in the water, and his left arm angled awkwardly under his body. His right arm stretched out in the tall weeds that surrounded his shoulders and head. A large seine lay under his stomach and legs.

"Ohhhh."

"He must have come for some minnows and fallen," Steven said. "His arm looks broken or something."

Mike pursed his lips. "That net's too big for this little ditch. I'll bet he cut through here on his way to Jones' Creek."

The man groaned again. "Help me. Please help me."

"Mister, we'll go get help. Grandpa will know what to do."

"Don't leave me. My arm's broken. It's killing me."

The three slid down the bank to the peninsula. "We don't want to hurt you more, Mister," Jim said.

"Just roll me on my back. That'll get me off my arm and get my face out of this mud. I can hardly breathe."

Mike and Jim put their hands on the man's shoulder and Steven gripped his hip, and they rolled him toward them. When he was half-way over, he flipped the rest of the way by himself. His quickness startled them.

"It's Burly," Steven yelled.

The man jumped up. Before the boys could move, Burly grabbed the net and threw it over them. He pulled it tight and encircled his arms around the boys.

"Let us go," Jim shouted. Burly tightened his grip.

"That hurts," Mike yelled. "Let us go."

"Shut up, kid. Every time you say something, I'll squeeze tighter. When you shut up, I'll let you go. Your choice." Except for moans, the boy's protests stopped.

"That's better." Burly loosened his grip. "Now listen good. You try anything funny, you're going to get hurt. Understand?"

Burly freed them from the net one at a time. Using his pocketknife, he cut lengths from the rope he'd hidden in the brush and tied their hands behind them. Then he shackled them together in a line like pearls on a string by tying the remaining rope around their waists. Five feet of extra rope dangled from the first and the last boy.

He finished the last knot. "There. That'll hold you. Sit, boys. We're not going anywhere until dark."

Jim struggled against his knots. "What do you want with us?"

"Yeah," Mike said. "We haven't done anything to you."

Burly leaned against a sycamore tree, scratched his back on its sparse bark, and crossed his legs. "Might as well make yourselves comfortable. We're not moving until dark."

A squirrel chirped overhead. Way in the distance a dog barked, and Mike turned to the sound. Was this how it would end? Would he see his mom and dad again? Or Grandpa?

Or Heidi?

He never did tell her he liked her. Would she miss him? Would she even care? If he got out of this alive, he'd tell her. He'd say, "Heidi, I like you a lot. Always have." Even if she laughed at him, it would be worth it. It'd be awful if he died and she never knew how he felt. He'd end up being just some kid she used to know. He leaned back against a tree and waited for darkness.

Finally, Burly spoke. "Okay boys, get up. We're going for a walk." He gathered the rope's loose ends and tugged. The boys tried to obey his command, but being tethered together at the waist with their hands tied behind them, moving was difficult.

Steven pointed his right foot at Squall Baby. "You can't leave the pigeon here."

Burly kicked at the cage. "I can leave it if I want to, kid. And maybe I want to."

Steven stepped tentatively up the narrow path. "It's up to you. I'm just surprised you'd leave a clue behind."

Burly frowned. "A clue? How would the pigeon be a clue?"

"Well … well, when Marshal Smart comes looking for us, he'll see the bird. 'There's the pigeon,' he'll say. 'It's an open and shut case now. Burly's got the boys.'"

The man stood for a moment, biting his lower lip. "You're right. He's a pretty sharp guy." He walked back to the creek bank, picked up the portable cage, and thrust it into Stephen's hands, bound behind him. "Here. You carry it. I'm not carrying a stupid pigeon."

Burly again grabbed the rope ends and snapped them, as if the boys were Cinder harnessed to the wagon and he was Trashman sitting on the wagon seat. They turned up the trail, and he followed. He jerked the ropes. "Follow the path just like you were heading for the schoolyard."

They trudged up the trail toward the railroad tracks with vines grabbing their feet and branches slapping their faces. A tree branch hit Jim's head, knocking his cap off. He kept on walking.

They reached the tracks and followed them south to Lake Dundee Road, where they turned west. Occasionally, Burly pulled them into the weeds to hide as cars went by. Each new road they turned onto was narrower and more remote than the one before it.

They made one last turn, and Burly followed the boys down a dirt and gravel trail overgrown with weeds. They trudged for half a mile through the weeds and underbrush until they reached an opening. Burly jerked the ropes, and they stopped. "Watch out for that chain," he said. "We got to go around it."

They walked around the roadblock and stopped. Moonlight-silhouetted buildings loomed in front of them. "Welcome to your new home, boys. This is the old Kaden Coal Mine. I know it like the back of my hand. Worked here for years, until one day the owners just packed up and left. They still owe me money."

Mike moved his hands in an attempt to ease the pain caused by the rope. "Why'd you bring us here?"

"You'll see soon enough. In fact, I want you to know so you'll suffer just like you made Seth suffer." Burly turned toward a building in the distance. "That old dynamite shed's going to be your new home. Now, get over there."

He shoved Mike, and the rest followed in the dim moonlight to the building's metal door in the murky shadows. He tugged on it, and its hinges creaked as it slowly opened.

"There," he grunted. "Go in."

The boys didn't move.

"I said go in." Burly pushed Jim to the door. He stumbled and fell, jerking his two friends, shackled together like a chain gang, toward the ground. They caught themselves awkwardly, unable to use their hands, and entered Burly's dungeon. Steven stopped just short of the door to take one last look at their captor.

"Get in there, kid." He shoved him with his foot, and Steven hit the doorframe and bounced off, dropping Squall Baby's portable cage. Burly kicked it to the side, forced the door shut, and flipped the hasp.

"Open the door," Steven shouted. "I dropped Squall Baby."

"Too bad. You should have taken better care of it." He slid something that sounded like metal through the hasp to lock the door, probably an old rod from the heap of junk scattered in front of the building.

"I know I don't have to worry about you boys blowing the door off to escape. The county hauled all the explosives away years ago. See you at sunrise."

The boys huddled in the darkness. "Guys," Steven said after a long silence, "this is what our missions have been about. We've survived them before, right? Remember the cemetery? We survived a storm, Emil Hoff, and Frank Conners."

"That's right," Mike said. "But Sheriff Conners was nice."

"He was," Steven said, "but he didn't have to be. He could have locked us up and thrown away the key. Remember, he said it was an open-and-shut case. Besides, the storm wasn't nice, and neither was Emil Hoff."

"Yeah, that's right ... " Mike looked around. The room was pitch black, except for an occasional pale glimmer from the moon after clouds crossed it.

"We also survived Trashman," Steven said. "Remember that night in the woods when he was drunk and wanted to beat us with his belt? We've got to approach this like it's the mission we've been training for."

Steven leaned toward the other two and spoke quietly. "Here's the situation, guys. Burly's a communist. He just found out we're secret agents and that we've learned all of his evil secrets, so he wants to destroy us. We can't let that happen, right? Our mission is to escape and bring him to justice. We have until sunrise to come up with a plan."

"If one of us can get free, he can untie the other two," Jim said. "Burly didn't search us. My pocketknife is in my right front pocket. Mike, see if you can get it out."

Mike stepped closer to him and felt about Jim's waist with his hands tied behind him. Finding Jim's right front pocket was harder than he'd expected. He worked his fingers into it, and after several tries grasped the knife and pulled it out. It dropped to the concrete floor. Had Burly heard it? He listened for Burly's footsteps. Silence.

He felt about with his foot until it touched the knife, and then he lay on the floor and wiggled his fingers, scooting an inch or two at a time until he touched its cold metal. He opened the knife, touched the blade to the rope, and started cutting. Burly had bound his hands tightly, making cutting difficult. Occasionally the knife jabbed his arm, and he felt blood trickle down his wrists. He gritted his teeth to keep from crying out and continued the slow, methodical task.

Finally, he cut through. He wiped his bloody arms on his pants and freed Jim's and Steven's hands. They huddled together, each rubbing his wrists, breathing heavily, and listening for Burly outside the door. There was no sound.

Mike took a deep breath. "Now, I'll cut the rope around our waists."

Jim touched his hand. "No. Don't cut it. We need to untie it and then put it back around us to make Burly think we're still tied together. Here, give me the knife."

151

Mike closed it and handed it to him. They untied all the knots, and for a minute they stood unbound. The only sound besides their breathing was an owl, way off in the distance.

Jim broke the silence. "Now, we need to put the rope back on. Don't tie knots. Just tuck the rope inside your pants. It'll look as if we're still tied together, but we'll be able to remove it in a second."

Mike tucked the rope into his pants and sat on the floor with the others. "Now what, Jim? Burly's planning something terrible. What do we do next?"

Jim motioned for them to huddle closer. "He's going to take us somewhere else at sunrise. This is just a holding area."

"What makes you think that?" Steven asked.

"Well, otherwise he wouldn't have a reason to come back. He could have just left us here to die. He's going to do something, for sure. Look—when he opens the door, we have to catch him by surprise."

"That's easy to say, Jim," Mike said. "But how?"

"Well, we'll jump him. I'll shout 'now!' and we'll drop the rope and jump him at the same time. You two hit him as hard as you can, and I'll stab him. Then we'll tie him up and go for help."

Mike swallowed hard. At sunrise, Burly might kill them, or they might kill him. This wasn't a game. It was a real mission, as secret and dangerous as any he could imagine.

"Sounds like a good plan." Mike shut his eyes and waited.

Chapter 24

SUNRISE

Mike jumped. A falling-off-the-cliff dream had awakened him, and for a second he wondered why he wasn't in his bed. The concrete floor's hardness jerked him back to reality, and memories of the night before flooded in. Burly had locked him and his buddies in a Kaden Coal Mine shed.

Birds, probably sparrows, chirped in the trees and bushes outside. Why are they up so early? If he had a choice he'd be asleep, that's for sure. And why are they so happy? Don't they know it's the end of the world? If he had wings like they did, he'd fly as far away as possible.

A hint of a light appeared. The rope tightened as Steven pushed up and leaned against the wall. He stretched and moaned softly. The morning's first rays seeped through a lone window and made his face appear strange. Jim sat up, too.

Steven stretched. "I've been thinking about all the things I'm going to do when we get out. When I grow up, I'm going to the Air Force Academy. I'll become an air force pilot and protect the world from communism by shooting down enemy planes and bombing enemy entrenchments. That's why I can't die here."

He stopped talking. Only the birds made sounds, happy sounds that seemed out of place. "What about you guys? What'll you do if—when we make it out?"

"I've always known what I'll do," Jim said. "As soon as I can, I'll hire on at Morrison's. Mom won't have to take in laundry or clean houses anymore. And I'll pay for Betsy to go to college. She'll make a good nurse or a teacher."

Faint, ghastly tree shadows, which weren't there just minutes

153

earlier, had sneaked in through the window. Steven moved a little, and the rope tugged again.

"What about you, Mike?"

What a ridiculous conversation. They'd been kidnapped and locked in a building in the middle of nowhere. They should be yelling, kicking the door, crying. After all, they were eleven-year-old kids, not the trained secret agents they pretended to be. Yet here they were, calmly talking about what they would do with their lives *if* they made it out alive and waiting patiently for the chance to hurt or kill Burly. What chance did they have against him, anyway?

Mike didn't have any grand plans like going to the Air Force Academy and saving the world from communism like Steven did. He didn't even have ordinary ones like Jim, who wanted to support his mother and sister. He thought about it as he watched the ghostly limb shadows waver on the concrete floor.

"Well, when I get out I'll hug my family," he said. "Mom, Dad, and Grandpa. I'll tell them how much I missed them. And I'll tell them I'll do my best to make them proud of me."

"That's it?" Steven asked. "You wouldn't do anything else?"

"I'd do one more thing. I'd tell Heidi how I feel about her. I'd tell her I like her. I don't want to die without her knowing how I feel. I'd tell her I *always* liked her."

"You'll never do it. Every time you try, you chicken out."

Mike couldn't argue with Jim's logic. How many times had he planned to tell her?

"But it's different now. If Burly kills us, we'll all be dead forever. Isn't that worse than telling her how I feel? I used to think if she laughed it'd be the end of the world. Now I know it wouldn't be."

"So now you wouldn't mind if she laughed at you?" Steven asked.

"Sure I'd mind. It'd hurt a lot, but I'd rather be laughed at than dead forever."

"Good point."

"At least I would've given it a shot, and she'd know how I feel."

"Another good point."

Mike studied their prison in the dim light. The building was square, about twelve feet by twelve feet. The concrete slab floor and block walls were solid. Orange rust blotched the metal door, but it appeared solid. He tugged the rope to see if it had enough slack to get within kicking distance without removing it from his pants. He scooted to the door and brought his legs up until his knees almost touched his face, and slammed his feet hard against the door. Rust specks fluttered to the floor, but the door didn't budge. He did it again with the same results. Escaping through the door seemed impossible.

Mike glanced up at the lone window. About a yard wide and a couple of feet high, it was located just above their heads, its glass pane yellowed with time. He chuckled.

"What?" Steven asked.

"That's our escape route. All we have to do is climb through the window." He took a deep breath and lunged upwards, catching his forearms and elbows on the ledge. The window was hinged on top. He unhooked it, pushed it up, and rested it on top of his head. His heart skipped a beat. Burly knew what he was doing when he locked them in the shed. Steel bars about four inches apart, evidently designed to prevent anyone from sneaking in through the window to steal dynamite, would now prevent them from escaping through it. He grabbed one in each hand and tried to shake them. They were solid. He tried the rest of the bars with the same disappointing results.

"Steel bars," he said. "We won't be able to escape through the window."

He'd seen pictures of ancient civilization ruins in history books. The portion of the Kaden Coal Mine he could see from the window resembled those pictures. Weeds and trees had reclaimed the land. The buildings showed years of neglect. The smokestack loomed overhead like a majestic temple.

A rocky hole thirty feet long and twenty feet wide stretched halfway between the shed and the smokestack. Maybe one of the tunnels caved in, creating its own version of Crater Lake without the water.

"What do you see?"

Mike looked down at Jim. "Buildings. The smokestack. And roads, or at least what used to be roads. They're all covered with underbrush now. And a big hole."

"Let me see."

The boys maneuvered so Jim could pull himself up. After Steven took his turn, they sat again on the concrete floor to wait for Burly. Jim pulled the pocketknife from his pocket, opened it, and placed it on the floor next to him.

"It's got to be after eight o'clock," Steven said. "What's keeping him? He said he'd be here at sunrise."

Mike sighed. "I don't know, but I'm ready to get this over with."

Jim rubbed his knife back and forth on the concrete floor as they waited. Another hour passed.

"Boys?"

Burly! Jim gripped the knife tightly. Burly's voice came from under the window.

Mike stood. "What?"

"Want to know what's going to happen?"

"You're going to take us somewhere," Mike said.

"Lucky guess, kid. Know where?"

"Where?" Jim asked.

"I'm taking you to Little Jane."

The boys looked at each other, then at a spot below the window where Burly stood on the other side of the wall. "Who's that?"

"It's a tunnel we started just before the place shut down. We never finished it, and it's a big accident waiting to happen. I worked on it this morning. It took longer than I thought it would, but guess what. That accident's ready to go. If they ever find you, they'll think you sneaked in, and it just caved in on you."

Steven stood. "Why are you doing this, Burly? We've never done anything to you."

"Seth's dead because of you. If you hadn't contacted Marshal Smart that night, he'd still be alive. Like the Bible says, 'an eye for an eye.' In this case, three eyes. Or is that six? You made him suffer—now you'll suffer. He died—now you'll die. And everyone will think it was an accident."

"Right." Mike sounded as sarcastic as he could, hoping Burly would rethink his plan. "They'll find us all tied up together, and they'll think it was an accident."

Burly snorted. "You won't be tied together. 'It's a real shame,' I'll tell everyone. 'They were such nice boys. We all knew Little Jane was just an accident waiting to happen.'"

The swish-swish of weeds sounded as Burly walked away from the window. "Okay, boys. I'm going to open the door. Walk out slowly and in single file." The lock hasp sounded, and the door creaked open. The boys, appearing to still be tethered with the rope, stood with their hands behind them.

"Come on out. Let's go."

They walked single file through the door—Steven, Mike, and then Jim, all staring at the ground.

Mike's heart pounded. Could Burly hear it? If so, would he know they were up to something? He looked away from Burly, fearing if his attacker saw into his eyes he'd see all the way to his soul and know they were going to try to kill him.

Burly grabbed the rope that hung in front of Steven and tugged on it. "Let's go, boys. Move it."

"Now!" Jim pulled the knife from behind him and lashed at Burly. Burly brought his hand up, and the knife sliced deep into his forearm. Mike and Steven jumped Burly and slammed him with their fists. He lost his balance and fell backwards with his hands in front of his face.

Jim's second and third stabs also found Burly's arm, slicing deep into flesh. All four had Burly's blood on them. He tried to get up, but Mike's fist hit his left eye, and he fell back. Steven and Mike continued hitting Burly hard. Jim brought the knife above his right ear, closed his eyes, and forced it toward Burly with all his might. The blade hit his cheekbone and sliced a six-inch gash. Blood gushed out.

For a second Burly lay quietly, surprise on his face. Then he yelled and got up with such force, he knocked all of the boys to the ground. The knife flew from Jim's hand and landed between Mike and Steven. Mike grasped it, and the three again rushed Burly.

Burly grabbed Jim and flipped him around. He pressed his left hand against his own wounded face and threw his right arm around Jim's neck. Blood covered everything.

"Take one step closer, and I'll break his stinking neck." He tightened his grip, and Jim made a throaty sound.

"I swear to God I will. I'll snap his neck in two." His arm was like a giant boa constrictor ready for the kill. He shouted at Mike. "Drop the knife!"

The weapon fell from Mike's hand.

"Now kick it toward me."

Mike kicked it, and Burly picked it up.

"What else you got in your pockets? Empty them."

Mike patted his pockets. "We don't have anything else."

Burly squeezed his arm tighter around Jim's neck. Jim didn't move or make a sound.

157

"I'm not playing games, boys. This kid's as good as dead if you don't empty them now."

Both boys pulled out the few items they had in their pockets and dropped them to the ground. Loose change, a pocket comb, several pieces of hard candy, some string, and four pieces of Dubble Bubble gum soon lay in front of Mike. He glanced at Steven's items, and his heart skipped a beat. Included in the discard pile were the paper and pencil they had planned to use to write the secret message for Squall Baby to take to headquarters from the Potter schoolyard. They now had no way of leaving a note telling the police who killed them. Burly would get away with murder. Burly's gaze washed over the boys and stopped at their shoes. "Take off your shoestrings. And your belts, too. Let's go."

The boys sat on the ground and pulled the laces from their shoes. "Why do you want our laces?" Mike asked.

"I'm not taking any chances this time. I've been locked up a few times and they always took my shoelaces. I've seen how you boys work. You're just sneaky enough to figure out a way to use them. I ought to strip you naked."

Burly continued his tight grip on Jim. Soon four shoelaces and two belts lay on the ground in front of Burly along with the items from their pockets. He motioned to the shed. "Okay, now get back in there."

On their way in, Mike saw Steven glance at an object on the ground a couple of feet from the door. Squall Baby's cage! Then, even though the ground was smooth there, Steven tripped and fell hard on top of the cage.

"Get up, you clumsy oaf." Burly, still holding Jim in a chokehold kicked Steven's leg.

"Sorry," Steven mumbled. He got up, staggered into the door jam, and stumbled inside. As Mike followed him into the shed, he looked back at where the cage had been. It was gone.

Burly stood at the entrance, blocking most of the sunlight. He pointed at the floor. "Now sit."

Mike sat and squinted in the low light level. What had happened to the cage? He looked around. Steven was lying on his side, his head propped up on the palm of his hand. The cage was on the floor behind him, hidden from Burly's evil eyes.

"Change of plans." Burly carried Jim by the neck. They were both red with Burly's blood. Jim's eyes darted as if he were looking for something. Burly pushed the door shut, and the hasp closed.

The sounds of Burly walking through the weeds became fainter and fainter. Up to this point Jim had been quiet. That suddenly changed. He yelled for Burly to let him go. His yells became fainter and fainter. Mike pulled himself up to the window and looked out.

"Can you see anything?"

Mike looked down at Steven. "Yeah. Burly's still carrying Jim. Jim's kicking and hitting and yelling."

Steven stood and leaned against the wall next to Mike. "Where's Burly going? What's he going to do?"

"I don't know. He's walking toward that crater. He's still walking. He's almost there. He's stopped. Now he's holding Jim above his head—like ... like King Kong. Oh, no!"

"What, Mike? What?"

"Noooo!" Mike's shout filled the shed. "He threw Jim into the crater. I can't see Jim. He threw him into that hole, Steven."

Steven stepped closer and reached up and touched the window. "Now what's happening? Is Jim okay?"

"Shhh. Listen."

Steven tilted his head. "What? I don't hear anything."

"That's what I mean," Mike said. "Jim's not yelling anymore." He looked out the window again. "Burly's coming back. He—he's staggering."

"Maybe he's lost too much blood. Do you think Jim's okay?"

"I don't know. Burly's almost here."

Mike saw blood ooze from the gash on Burly's face. His arms and shirt were covered with it. He stopped under the window and looked up. "I'm going to toss you down that pit, too."

He walked toward the door but after a few steps stopped, bent over, and put his hands on his knees. He breathed in gasps, gradually looking up at the window.

"But not now. I'm going to let you think about it a while. I'll be back. I'll toss one of you into that pit and a couple days later I'll toss the other one in. Then you'll know what it's like to suffer." He added what seemed to be an afterthought, "And what it's like to be dead."

Silence followed. Burly straightened, took off his shirt, and tied it around his face, covering everything below his eyes. The part covering the gash became red, and he pressed his hand against it and staggered away. Just before reaching the road, he shouted back at the shed. His words were faint, but they carried the same sting they would have had he

159

been a foot from them.

"I'll be back. You're going to die."

Mike slid down from the window. The boys stared at each other for a long time.

"What are we going to do?" Steven asked.

Mike sat on the concrete floor and studied the block walls that surrounded them. "Well, we're going to think of a way out. There's got to be a way."

"Yeah, there's got to be."

"Steven, we have to get Jim out of that pit. If he's still alive, he's probably badly hurt. And even more scared than we are."

The two boys sat facing one another, both deep in thought, trying to come up with a plan to save Jim and themselves. Nearby, Squall Baby cooed a lament.

Chapter 25

THE SEARCH

When Skip ran into the classroom just before the bell was to ring, he saw a red-haired lady writing math problems on the board. He stopped abruptly and stared at her. "Who are you?"

Her hand paused in mid-word, and she smiled. "I'm Mrs. Stunkel. I'm subbing for Miss Schneider." She continued writing problems.

"She sick?"

She again looked at him. "Who?"

"Miss Schneider. She sick?"

Mrs. Stunkel glanced at the clock by the coatroom door and wrote faster. "I don't know. Mr. Jackson called this morning and asked me to come in."

"She must be sick. Awfully sick."

"Why do you say that?" She continued writing.

"Because she hasn't missed a day of school in over fifteen years. She must be real sick to miss today."

The substitute teacher paused. "You may be right." She started on another problem.

"You've got pretty handwriting."

Again she stopped writing and smiled at him. "Why, thank you, hon. By the way, I like your hair."

"You do?"

"Sure do. It's bright red—the same color as mine."

Skip laughed. The bell rang, and he ran to his seat. The other students stopped talking and sat quietly waiting for the teacher to start class.

Mrs. Stunkel placed the chalk in the tray and stepped in front of the desk. "Good morning. Miss Schneider couldn't be here today, so I will

161

teach instead. My name is Mrs. Stunkel." She pointed to her printed name on the board. "Today we will begin with math."

Mr. Jackson appeared at the door with a big man in a policeman's uniform and motioned for Mrs. Stunkel to join them. They spoke quietly, and she and the uniformed man shook hands. The two men followed her to the front of the room. Mr. Jackson cleared his throat. "Class, this is Sheriff Conners. He's working with Marshal Smart on a situation he'd like to discuss with you."

Mr. Jackson stepped back. A piece of paper made crinkly sounds when Sheriff Conners removed it from his shirt pocket. He dropped his hands and held the paper just above his right knee. "I'm afraid I have some bad news." He paused, waiting for the murmuring to stop.

"I'm sure you've noticed Miss Schneider is not here today. She isn't here because her nephew—" He brought the paper up to his face. "—Steven Culpepper—didn't come home last night."

The students gasped and talked among themselves. Sheriff Conners stood almost at attention until the talking stopped.

"Two other boys—" He again looked at the paper. "—Mike Long and Jim Mackey—were with him. They, too, are missing."

"Oh, my goodness!" Tears appeared in Heidi's eyes. Mary put her arm around her, wiping tears from her own eyes.

Sheriff Conners held up a hand for silence. "I know this is a difficult time, but we all have to be strong. Will you help me find these boys?"

Some students nodded; some said 'yes;' and most blotted tears with handkerchiefs or shirtsleeves.

"Good. We know they met at the Mackey house after supper and left with a pigeon in a small cage. Can anyone add to that?" Hands went up.
"You."

"That was Squall Baby," Heidi said. "They turn her loose at different places, and she flies home."
"You."

Mary took her hand down. "They usually turn her loose right here in the schoolyard. Maybe they came here last night."

"Did any of you see them last night?"

All of the hands went down. Tony raised his hand.

"You saw them, son?"

"No, but—well, when they come here to fly Squall Baby, they usually walk through the secret woods."

162

"The secret woods?"

Tony pointed out the window. "It's the woods on the other side of the railroad tracks."

The sheriff stepped toward the window and studied the woods. He again faced the students. "Who's familiar with the secret woods?"

Every student's hand went up.

He moved again to the front of Miss Schneider's desk. "This secret woods seems to be pretty well known. Is there anything there that might harm the boys?"

"No. Nothing I can think of," Tony said. "A creek runs through it, but it's barely a foot deep."

Another hand went up. "You. The redheaded boy. What information do you have?"

"Maybe a bear got them. Or a monster. Or a spy. They're always looking for spies. Or maybe—"

Sheriff Conners cut Skip off in mid-maybe. "Thank you for your help. We'll check out the secret woods. If any of you think of anything else, tell your teacher or Mr. Jackson."

Mr. Jackson stepped forward. "Thank you, class. You've been a big help. You can help us the most now by doing your very best in school today. Do everything Mrs. Stunkel tells you."

The men left, and Mrs. Stunkel held an open math book, watching the crying students. She placed the book on the desk and stared out the window at the woods beyond the tracks.

***

Martha sniffed and wiped her nose with a tissue. Charles sat next to her on the couch and stared at nothing in particular. Grandpa paced.

"Grandpa, you're going to wear a path in the linoleum."

"You're right, Martha. I'm not doing any good in here, anyway. I'm going out for a smoke." He walked to the door and paused. "Why, Sheriff Conners just pulled up."

Martha and Charles followed Grandpa to the porch and watched the sheriff exit his car and walk briskly up the sidewalk. He stopped at the porch, and Grandpa opened the door. Martha motioned toward a wicker chair next to the swing. "Come in, Sheriff Conners. Any news?"

He sat and removed his hat and turned it slowly in his hands.

"No, ma'am, no news yet." He looked up. "We just finished searching the woods."

"What woods?"

"That little ten-acre plot over by the tracks. The kids said the boys go that way to let the pigeon loose in the schoolyard."

Martha's eyebrows shot up. "Mike walks through a woods on the way to school?"

"Yes, ma'am. At least that's what his classmates say. They call it 'the secret woods.'"

She blotted her eyes. "That Mackey boy puts him up to things like this. I just know he does."

Grandpa slipped his tobacco into his pocket and leaned closer to Sheriff Conners. "You didn't find any ... remains, did you?"

"Grandpa!"

"No, we didn't. But we did find something that belonged to one of them. A cap."

"A cap?" Martha said, "You found it in ... that woods?"

"Yes, ma'am. Mrs. Mackey said her son wore it when the boys left with Squall Baby last night."

Grandpa pointed at the sheriff with his pipe stem. "You think someone kidnapped them?"

"Grandpa! Don't say things like that." Martha blew her nose.

"Martha, I'm just trying to understand what could have happened."

The sheriff looked down at his hat, then back at Grandpa. "All we know is they went to the woods. There's no ransom note, so we can't say it's a kidnapping, at least not yet. We don't know what happened."

***

Lightning from a sudden evening thunderstorm flashed through the dynamite shed's window, lighting Mike and Steven as they processed the water they'd gathered in their makeshift water accumulator. Two hours ago, they'd taken off their trousers, stuffed their outer shirts inside them, and hung them from a steel window bar with tightly wound undershirts they'd threaded through the belt loops. The clothing soaked up the wind-blown rain, and they were now ready to harvest it.

Mike, naked except for his jockey shorts, pulled himself up to the window and untied Steven's undershirt. He dragged the soaked clothing in through the open window. They worked quickly, twisting as much water as possible from the pants and shirt into a waiting shoe. Mike returned to the window, pulled in his own clothing, and they repeated the process. When they finished, he looked around. "Where's the toilet?"

Steven pointed. "Over there in the far corner."

Mike picked up the shoe, peed in it, and flung the shoe's liquid through the window's bars. He returned the shoe to the corner. "I'll tie our pants to the bars again so they'll soak up more drinking water."

"Mike, don't get that shoe mixed up with the others when you get thirsty." Steven laughed at his joke.

***

Grandpa pushed the wooden backyard swing slowly back and forth, listening to its rhythmic "creak ... creak ... creak" as he occasionally drew on his pipe. The smoke swirled around his face and danced away slowly.

The grass and leaves looked greener from last evening's thunderstorm. An occasional cloud briefly blocked the sun, and a robin by Morrison's fence performed its three-step dance. Three hops—stop. Three hops—stop. She pecked at the ground, pulled out a big worm, and flew to the nest in the cherry tree where her four children greeted her with opened mouths. A farmhand drove an old beat-up, doorless, mufflerless, truck past one of the large barns beyond the fence, and in the distance a John Deere tractor's chug chug announced the fields were being plowed. A flock of sparrows flew into a nearby tree, chirped loudly, and flew away.

Grandpa sat up abruptly. "Squall Baby!"

He struck his pipe several times on his shoe heel to dislodge the burning vegetation and ran into the house, slamming the door.

Martha ran to the kitchen. "What is it, Grandpa?"

His hands shook. "Squall Baby!"

"What about Squall Baby?"

"The boys took Squall Baby with them. If they're in trouble they might send her home with a message."

He left the house with Martha giving chase. "Grandpa, slow down! You'll have a heart attack!" He half ran and half walked to Donna Mackey's house and pounded on the door. "Donna. Donna. You home?"

Donna stepped out onto the porch. Betsy followed. "What is it?"

"Is Squall Baby here?"

Donna dried her hands on her apron. "No, the boys took her. Why do you ask?"

"If they're in trouble, they might send her home with a note." He walked quickly toward the pigeon coops, pausing once to catch his breath. Squall Baby's cage was open. He looked inside. She wasn't there. He turned to Donna. "Watch for her, will you? That bird may tell us where the boys are."

"I will."

Betsy pulled on his trouser leg. "I'll watch, too."

Grandpa knelt next to her. "I know you will, Betsy. This could be Squall Baby's most important mission. Your job on this mission is to let your mom know as soon as you see her. Okay, Agent Ysteb?"

She hugged his neck. "Okay."

A car stopped in front of the Mackey house, and Sheriff Conners exited and walked toward them. Grandpa and Donna met him on the sidewalk.

"Any news about the boys?" she asked.

"Afraid not. I just stopped by to ask a few more questions." He shook hands with Donna and extended his hand to Grandpa. "Glad you're here, Mr. Barton. I was going to stop by your place next."

Grandpa shook his hand. "What kind of questions?"

"Just routine ones. Did either of you notice a '47 or '48 Packard in the neighborhood around the time the boys disappeared?"

They glanced at one another and then back at the sheriff and shook their heads.

"Have you seen a stranger with a heavy German accent?"

They shook their heads again.

"Well, thanks for your time. I'll let you know if—"

Grandpa waved his hand. "Just a minute, Sheriff. Those aren't routine questions. You got a lead?"

"Well, there may not be a connection, but we're checking all possibilities. Burly Thompson was attacked by four men in what he thought was a '47 or '48 Packard. He said the driver had a heavy German accent."

Grandpa stepped back. "Burly? Who would attack Burly Thompson? Who could attack Burly?"

"We don't know yet. He's hurt bad, though."

"What happened?" Donna's voice cracked.

166

"Well, Nate Simpson at the pool hall says Burly just up and takes off a day or two at a time, so he didn't worry when Burly came up missing. A farmer found him lying out in the middle of nowhere, a mile or so from the old coal mine. Burly said four men jumped him when he was walking home late Tuesday night. He—"

Grandpa interrupted. "Tuesday? The night the boys disappeared?"

"The same night. They forced him into the car and took off. He said he'd fought off the two in the back seat when the front passenger stabbed him several times. They pushed him out and took off, probably thinking they'd killed him or he'd bleed to death. It took over sixty stitches to patch him up. He said the driver with the German accent seemed to be the ringleader."

Grandpa whistled softly. "Burly Thompson. It *would* take four men to beat him up. Will he make it?"

"The doctors said if he'd been found half an hour later, he would have more than likely died. He's pretty stable now and should be going home soon.

Donna rubbed Betsy's hair. "Why would anyone kidnap Burly?"

The sheriff shrugged. "Why would anyone take the boys, if they did? Burly's kidnappers may have done it, though. But it was dark, and Burly's not even sure the car was a Packard. The only thing he's sure of is the driver's German accent."

Donna leaned against Grandpa. "This just keeps getting scarier and scarier."

"It sure does. That's why we're setting up a curfew for everyone under eighteen. If they can take Burly, they can take anyone." Sheriff Conners smiled at Betsy. "We've got to protect our children."

She looked up at him. "I'm watching for Squall Baby. I'll tell mom if I see her."

***

Mike and Steven sat on the concrete floor with their backs against the wall. Squall Baby sat in front of them in the portable cage. Except for their shoes, they were once again dressed.

Two drinking shoes were empty, while the third was still nearly full. Their pants and shirts had been dry for almost two days. Mike kept track of the days by scratching faint marks in the door's rust with a button that had fallen from his shirt. Three lines appeared there.

"I'm thirsty." Steven's voice sounded raspy.

"Me too, but we don't have much water left. We have to ration it."

"I know. I'm hungry, too."

"I'm beyond hungry."

"Funny, isn't it?"

"What?"

Steven shifted his weight against the wall. "We had a pencil and paper to write a note and string to tie it to Squall Baby's leg, but we didn't have her. Now we have her, but we don't have the pencil, paper, or string."

"Yeah, funny."

"She's our only hope." Steven stuck a finger into the cage, and Squall Baby pecked at it. "I don't think a pigeon can live as long as we can on just water. Maybe she'll get too weak to fly home."

"I know." Mike stood and looked toward the window. "And Jim's out there in that pit all by himself. He probably has some broken bones. I'll bet he's getting weak, too."

"We've got to think of something soon."

Mike looked down at him. "You're the big air force man. You should be able to come up with an idea."

Steven stood and put his arm around Mike. "Hey, we're both secret agents, right? We should be able to get out of a shed, even a concrete one with steel bars and a steel door. All we have to do is figure out how before Burly comes back."

Chapter 26

FLY HOME, SQUALL BABY

Four marks now decorated the rusty calendar. The boys huddled on the floor with the portable cage in pieces between them. Steven pulled off another leather strip from the cage and held it up. "I think your idea will work," he said. "I guess we'll find out soon."

Squall Baby stood between them, watching Steven unwind another thin leather strip from her cage and lay it alongside those he'd already untied. She eyed them a moment and grabbed one in her beak. Steven yanked it from her.

"Squall Baby, those aren't food." He knotted two strips together, tugged the ends to tighten it, and picked up another one to add to the developing rope. Maybe they'd have enough to tie Burly up, if it came to that. But first they had another use.

"How's your punch coming?" Steven asked without looking up.

"Almost ready." Mike rubbed the end of one of the cage's wooden bars back and forth on the concrete floor and held it up. "Yep. It'll soon be as sharp as a needle. Before we break the window, we've got to put something up there to keep Squall Baby inside. How about your shirt?"

Steven removed his shirt, hoisted himself up to the ledge, and pushed the window upward, allowing it to rest on his head. With his forearms on the ledge, he secured his shirt to the bars with leather strips from the cage. He eased back to the floor, shutting the window gently, and leaned against the far wall.

Mike smacked the window pane with an empty water shoe. It broke into several pieces that resembled isosceles triangles. He pried one out and handed it to Steven, who tested it on his finger.

"Sharp as a knife. Now we need to cut your shirt."

Mike removed his shirt and stretched it tight against the floor. He moved his finger over a section about one by twelve inches. "About this size?"

"Looks about right," Steven said. "Any bigger, it'd be too heavy."

Mike punched a hole next to its hem with the glass knife, and moved it back and forth until it cut through. Soon he had a jagged section of cloth about the size they wanted. "Okay, what do we want the note to say?"

Steven studied the cloth strip. "How about—'We're in the dynamite shed at the Kaden Coal Mine. Burly is going to kill us.'"

Mike waved the cloth in front of Steven's face. "Look how small this is, Steven. Squall Baby'd have to carry my entire shirt if we wrote that much."

"You're right. How about 'Kaden Mine. Burly's going to kill us.'" Steven studied the cloth. "Still too long, isn't it?"

"Afraid so."

"That's seven words. Let's see. How about this? 'Kaden Mine. Burly kill us.' That's five words. Can we do that many?"

"I think so. We can try."

Steven stretched the cloth, and Mike punched holes into it to make the capital letters for the five-word message, making each letter as perfect as possible. He finished and smoothed it out on the floor. Steven grabbed the message and held it toward the window's light. "It's just a bunch of holes. I know what it says, and even I can't make it out."

Mike took the strip from Steven and inspected it. He threw it on the floor. "How's anyone going to read it if we can't?"

They again sat on the floor, and Mike stared at the random-appearing holes. "It's just a bunch of dots. I thought at least the 'E' would be easy to read, but it's not. The 'N' doesn't look like anything, either. Just a bunch of dots."

Steven slapped his hands together. "Just a bunch of dots. That's the answer!"

"What is?"

"You remember those connect-the-dot games? When you connect the dots you make a picture of a boat, or a house, or an animal you couldn't even see before."

Mike picked up the torn piece of shirt. "We don't have a pencil or a pen. How do we connect the dots?"

"Rust." He took the message from Mike and dribbled water droplets from a drinking shoe on it, repeating the process several times. "Here." He handed the message to Mike. "Stretch it tight against the rust on the door, and I'll connect the dots with this punch."

Mike stretched it against a particularly rusty section of the door, and Steven moved the punch toward it. Mike pulled the cloth away. "Wait. We have the note facing us so that we can read it. If we form letters on the back, they'll be backwards. The only way you could read it would be to hold it up to a mirror."

"You're right," Steven said. "So we have to turn it over and press on the back so the rust will stick to the front."

Mike turned the cloth so the front stretched flush against the rusty door. Steven moved the punch's blunt end several times over the dots that formed the K, pushing hard. They removed the cloth slowly to reveal a dark orange K that faced the right way. They repeated the process for all the letters and turned the cloth over. The message Squall Baby would carry to headquarters was easy to read.

KADEN MINE. BURLY KILL US.

Steven waved the message to dry it, and Mike picked up the pigeon. "Get ready, Squall Baby." He held her tight, and Steven wrapped the message around her left leg. He then tied a length of leather around the message, double knotted it, and tied another strip below the first one.

Mike checked to make sure the message was secure. "She's never carried a cloth message before. I hope it doesn't fall off."

"Yeah. Well, let's let her go. It'll be dark soon, and it looks like it might rain." Steven pulled himself up to the window ledge. He untied the shirt from the bars and tossed it to the floor. "Well, this is it, Ekim."

"Then let the mission begin, Nevets." Mike handed the pigeon up to Steven, and he placed her between two bars.

"Fly home, Squall Baby! Fly home! Take the message to Ysteb so she can get help." Steven nudged her gently, and she lifted off, leaving the boys alone in the locked shed. She circled once and disappeared.

Mike sat on the floor, pulled his knees up, and encircled them with his arms. "You know, I'm so hungry, I'm not even hungry anymore."

Steven dropped from the window and sat by Mike. "If you'd said that last week, I wouldn't have understood. But I do now."

They quit talking, each consumed with his own thoughts, and soon shadows appeared. Mike nudged his friend to see if he was awake.

"Yeah?" Steven said without moving.

"What do you think Jim's doing now?"

"I don't know. He's pretty tough. Maybe he's not hurt that bad. Maybe he's trying to figure a way out of the pit so he can get help."

"I hope so. You and Jim are my best friends." Mike cocked his head and listened for any sound that might indicate Jim was still alive. He heard none. "Know what?"

"What?"

"I hope someone finds us soon." Both boys continued looking straight ahead.

"Me, too."

"Know what else?"

"What?"

"I hope that someone isn't Burly."

***

Betsy slammed the front door and dried her face and arms with a bathroom towel.

"No sign of her yet?" Donna asked from her chair.

"No, and it's raining. I don't think she'll ever come home." Betsy's chin quivered, and what began as a whimper exploded into an uncontrollable flood of tears.

"Come here, honey." Donna pulled Betsy to her. "It's all right."

"Where are they? What's happened to them?"

"Wish I knew." Donna wiped her own eyes.

"I want to play with them again like I used to."

"I know. I know. I want to see them again, too." Donna rocked her until she fell asleep.

***

The thick cloud cover and light fog made it darker than normal for seven o'clock. A cold front had moved in to break the heat wave, and a brisk north wind blew a cold mist across the Mackey yard.

Squall Baby landed on the coop next to her own. She cooed several times and walked in semicircles on top of the coop. She flapped her wings and half flew and half jumped into her open coop where she nestled into the straw. She preened herself, occasionally stopping to look out of her coop. No one had noticed her arrival.

Chapter 27

THE HAMMER

Nate Simpson parked his 1951 silver Studebaker in front of the Red Dog Pool Hall and walked around to the passenger side. He extended his arms to the man who struggled to get out. "Here, let me help you."

The man pushed him away. "Don't need your help. I can get out by myself."

Nate stepped back, and Burly grunted and stood. White bandages covered much of his face and arms.

The two entered the pool hall, and the dozen or so customers stopped talking and stared at Burly, almost as if cued by an unseen movie director. Burly reached the door that led to his downstairs living quarters and touched the knob. He turned and leaned toward the customers. "Boo!"

The men jumped, and one responded with a high-pitched scream. Burly glared at them. "Word to the wise, men. Unless you want to wear bandages, too, I suggest you stop gawking. I'll take you all on if I have to."

The men quickly turned away. Burly grabbed the doorknob and turned to Nate. "Don't forget—I need your car tomorrow."

Nate leaned against the counter. "Why can't you just see Doc Smith here in Potter instead of driving all the way to Princeton?"

Burly shrugged. "I wasn't given that option."

"I can drive you, Burly. You need to take it easy."

"Don't try to make a sissy out of me, Nate," Burly shouted. "I've always done for myself, and I don't plan to change now."

"Okay, okay." Nate threw his hands up and stepped back. "Just trying to help."

Burly pulled the basement door open and flipped a switch, and light from a bare overhead bulb lit the steps. He walked down, grasping the two-by-four that served as a banister.

The basement, in addition to being Burly's habitat, doubled as a storeroom with soft drinks, food items, and other pool hall supplies stacked high. Things that had nothing to do with the business had also found their way into the basement over the years, including an old lawn mower, a bicycle with no front wheel, and a rusty pogo stick.

He wound his way to his plainly-furnished living quarters at the far end. The kitchen consisted of an old, yellowed refrigerator, a two-burner electric stove, a sink, and a wooden table with two chairs. Opposite the kitchen area sat a couch that was missing its right front leg and an easy chair that was much lower than originally designed. The bedroom area, which took up the wall to the kitchen's left, consisted of a cot next to an upended five-gallon bucket that held a radio and an alarm clock. A toilet and sink hid in a five-foot square room behind all the stored stuff, made private by an unpainted plaster partition.

Burly pulled his shirt over his head and grimaced. He grabbed a flashlight and meandered through the supply and junk maze to the far corner, where the flashlight's beam fell on a yellow bucket. He reached in and pulled out a hammer. He eased slowly into bed, laid the hammer on the floor, and soon fell asleep on his stomach with his head dangling off the cot and his hand resting on the hammer handle.

***

Squall Baby rose early. She drank from her water dish, pecked at the few grains left in her food container, and peered out the open door. An hour passed. No one came with food. She hopped from her cage and briefly stood on the coop below hers. Then she lifted off, circled once, and flew west toward the Morrison Packing Company's open fields.

***

Martha sat on the living room couch and stared straight ahead, oblivious to the big band music that danced from the Philco. Her tears stopped coming two days ago as if the well had suddenly run dry. A new feeling, hopelessness, had replaced shock and denial.

Charles went to work that morning for the first time since the boys disappeared. He and Martha agreed they had to continue as best they could because the bills keep coming even when something terrible happens. The wall clock chime startled her. It was already noon.

Grandpa sat next to her and put his arm around her. "You know what would taste great right now?"

Martha didn't answer.

"One of your delicious pineapple upside-down cakes—that's what. I can taste it now. What do you say?"

"He's dead, Grandpa."

Grandpa removed his arm. "What are you talking about?"

"Mike's dead."

"I don't believe that, Martha, and I don't think you believe it, either. We can't give up hope."

She turned her head slowly toward him. "Grandpa, if they can beat up Burly Thompson and send him to the hospital, what do you think they can do to three eleven-year-old boys?"

"Now, Martha—these aren't just any three eleven-year-old boys. They're Mike, Jim, and Steven. They're all *special* boys."

"I know, but—"

"They'd want us to believe in them."

"I suppose so."

"They wouldn't want us to give up on them, would they?"

She sighed. "I guess they wouldn't."

"If they were to come home today, you know what they'd want?"

"What?"

"A delicious pineapple upside-down cake."

For the first time in days, Martha smiled. "Would that be for them or for you?"

Grandpa winked. "I don't see why we can't all enjoy it."

She pursed her lips. "Well ... I don't have any pineapple slices."

Grandpa stood. "Not a problem. I'll go into town and get a can. Need anything else?"

"That's all. I've got everything else."

"I'll walk. I need the exercise." Grandpa shoved his straw hat onto his head and opened the door to the front porch.

"I know where you're going first."

"Where?"

"To the Mackey's to see if Squall Baby is there."

"Well, maybe," Grandpa said. "Gotta keep the hope, Martha."

The front porch screen door slammed. "Keep the hope. Gotta keep the hope," she whispered. Big band music drowned out her voice.

Grandpa walked briskly toward the Mackey's yard. Betsy waved and ran to him. He lowered to one knee, and she hugged him.

"Is Squall Baby here?"

She released her grip from his neck. "No. Her cage is still empty."

"Let's check again."

He held her hand and accompanied her to the coop. The door stood open and the cage was empty, just as it was the night the boys left. Grandpa gestured toward a black car with Kentucky license plates sitting in the drive. "I see your grandma's still here."

Betsy nodded. "She's helping Mom. She still wants us to move in with her when Jim comes home. He is coming home, isn't he, Grandpa?"

"Why, of course, Betsy." He stroked her hair. "Now, you keep looking for Squall Baby. I have to go to town, but I'll stop by again on the way home."

When Grandpa reached Big John's Market, Burly was leaving the pool hall two blocks away. His face bandage was obvious even at that distance. Grandpa paused by the grocery store's door. Then, he walked briskly toward the man. "Burly. Burly Thompson."

Burly spun around, his hand on Nate Simpson's Studebaker's door handle. "Oh, it's you, Barton. What do you want?"

"I just wanted to tell you how sorry I am about your attack. You feeling better?"

Burly eased his grip on the handle. "Thanks, Barton. I am. Now if you don't mind, I've got to go." He opened the door.

"Where're you going?"

"To the doctor, if you must know."

Grandpa stepped back. "Sorry. Didn't mean to sound nosy. You know, I can drive you there. You look pretty sore."

"Don't need your help." Burly tossed the hammer into the passenger seat and slid into the car.

"What's the hammer for?"

"Hammer?"

"Yeah. That hammer you tossed into the car."

Burly glanced at it, then back at Grandpa. "That's for protection. If those guys attack me again, I want to be ready."

177

"You sure you don't want me to drive you?"

"Nope. I can do it myself." Burly started the car and backed out.

Grandpa left Big John's with a can of sliced pineapples and four Hershey bars. "A special treat for Martha," he had told the checkout man.

Betsy waved to him when he neared the Mackey house. "Still not here?"

She shook her head slowly. "No. I just checked."

"Keep looking. Let me know if you see her."

He was almost home when someone yelled. Betsy ran toward him. "What is it?"

"Squall Baby. She's back."

He ran back to the Mackey house with Betsy. "Where?"

"There." She pointed. "In her cage."

Grandpa dropped the bag, reached in, and pulled out a pigeon. Squall Baby! He stroked her with shaking hands. "Good job, Betsy." He turned the bird, looking for a note. Brown leather strips held a white cloth to her leg.

"Here, hold her, Betsy." He handed her the bird. "These look like the leather strips from the portable cage. . ." He fumbled with the strips, finally untying the first one. "Hold her tight. Don't let her go."

He undid the last strip and removed the message. "Put her in the cage and shut the door, Betsy."

She latched the cage door and ran back. "What does it say, Grandpa?"

He held the message at arm's length. "Let's see. It says 'Kaden mine. Burly kill us.'" Grandpa's eyes remained transfixed on the message. "Kaden mine. Burly kill us." He looked at Betsy. "The hammer!" He ran to the Mackey's house and barged inside without knocking. "Donna. Donna. You here?"

Donna Mackey and her mother ran into the living room where Grandpa and Betsy stood. "What? What is it?"

"Squall Baby brought a note from the boys. They're at the old coal mine, and I think Burly plans to kill them. He left in Nate Simpson's Studebaker a few minutes ago ... with a hammer."

Donna held to her mother for support. "Are they still alive?"

"I hope so. Gotta call Sheriff Conners. Or Marshal Smart. "Do you know their numbers?"

"No." She walked to a green secretary near the stairway. "Just a second. I'll get the phonebook."

"We should call Slim. Princeton is thirteen miles the wrong way. Every second counts."

She grabbed the phonebook from the drawer and flipped through the pages. "Here it is. Slim's number is one-six-three."

Grandpa held the phone to his ear and shouted, "One-six-three, and hurry. This is an emergency."

Hilda answered on the third ring. "Hello?"

"Hello. Hilda? Ted Barton. This is an emergency. Put Slim on."

"He's not here. He went to the Potter Grill to pick up dinner. Should be back soon."

Grandpa paced. "Tell him the boys are at the old Kaden Coal Mine, and Burly's going to kill them. I think he's heading there right now." He slammed the receiver and pointed to the phone book. "We've got to call Sheriff Conners in case Hilda can't get in touch with Slim in time."

Chapter 28

THE DOOR OPENS

Mike and Steven sat facing one another on the dynamite shed's concrete floor. Each wore jeans and shirts, but no undershirt or shoes. Next to them lay two glass shards they'd pried from the broken window pane, each about eight inches long and shaped like a knife. Tightly wound undershirt pieces held by leather strips formed handles to protect their hands from the sharp glass. Every few minutes they glanced at the door. Either the police or Burly would probably open it today, and they'd either be saved or killed.

"Remember, I'm going first." Mike grabbed his knife, slipped it under his shirt, and felt its sharpness against his skin. He took it out and laid it again on the concrete floor. "If Burly gives us a choice, I'm going first."

"No, I will. Why do you want to go first, anyway?"

Mike fiddled with his knife. It made a faint scratching sound against the rough concrete. "I don't know. If he's going kill me, I might as well get it over with. It's like giving a report to the class. If you're first, you're done with it. The last person suffers the most."

Steven made a face. "Why should I be the one to suffer the most?"

Mike put the knife under his shirt again. He placed a hand on the floor and then reached under his shirt with the other and snatched the weapon out as quickly as possible. He sighed and looked up at Steven. "Because you're Steven Culpepper. You're the smart one, and you'd have a better chance of thinking of a way of getting out."

"He won't kill you. We have a plan." Steven held his glass knife high. "We'll stab him with our knives."

Mike slid his knife under his shirt again and saw its form push out

180

his shirt. Would it fool Burly? Or would he see the lump as soon as he opened the door?

Steven sat up. "What's that?"

Mike leaned forward. "What?"

"Sounded like a car door. Shhh."

Steven hid his own knife under his shirt, and both sat motionless, listening. A meadowlark sang not far away. A crow cawed far in the distance. Wait. What was that? Probably just a chattering squirrel.

Steven touched Mike's arm. "Listen."

Mike closed his eyes and tried to blot out the bird and squirrel sounds and listen instead for sounds that didn't belong. Then he heard it, a distant swish, swish, swish, like someone walking through the weeds. He pointed toward the noise, and they stood. Mike clutched his chest again, confirming that the knife was still angled for quick removal. If only he had x-ray vision like Superman, he'd look right through the concrete walls and know if he could relax and get ready to go home, or if he'd need to get into a kill-or-be-killed mode.

The noise stopped. Steel scraped against steel as someone opened the lock hasp. The door creaked open, and a figure appeared in the doorway.

"Hello, boys."

Burly! He repeatedly hit his left palm with a hammer clutched in his right hand. His voice boomed. "Time for one of you to die."

Mike stepped forward and waited for Burly to pull him out and sacrifice him.

"So you're going to be first, huh?"

Mike opened his mouth to answer, but nothing came out.

Burly pulled him from the shed and laughed. "I'm in no hurry. You just stand there and think about what death will be like." He peered inside the shed and pointed the hammer at Steven. "You think about it, too, punk. You're next."

Mike touched his chest. The knife was still there.

"Got an itch, boy? Go ahead and scratch it. We've got a while." Mike pretended to scratch. "I predict that itch'll never bother you again after today." Time passed slowly as Burly rambled on about how the boys deserved to die because they were responsible for Seth's death.

Mike's heart jumped. Something moved in the distance. Marshal Smart! He sneaked behind Nate Simpson's Studebaker. He'd have to make sure Burly kept his back to the marshal.

"It's time to join your friend," Burly said. He grabbed Mike's wrist. "And don't get any bright ideas about trying to escape. You might survive the fall, but you won't survive this." He made a striking motion with the hammer.

Mike didn't struggle. If he wanted to catch Burly off guard, he'd have to lull him into thinking he was in control and then yank the knife from under his shirt and stab him when he least expected it. He had just one chance.

Maybe Marshal Smart would catch him off guard first. He slanted his eyes toward Nate Simpson's car. The marshal, now ten feet in front of the car, held his gun high and took quick, quiet steps. He was a hundred feet from them. Seventy-five. Fifty.

The marshal stepped on something that made a loud snap, and Burly turned and faced him. Marshal Smart aimed the gun at him and shouted. "Let him go, Burly!"

Burly spun Mike around and held him in front of him, squeezing so tight with his left arm that he snapped the hidden glass knife in two. His right hand held the hammer above his head.

"Drop your gun, Marshal, or I'll bash this boy's head in."

Marshal Smart remained frozen.

"This is your last chance, Marshal. Toss that gun over here or this boy will be dead by the time I count to three. One ... Two ... " He raised the hammer a little higher. Marshal Smart's gun landed at Burly's feet.

"That's being smart." He laughed at his unintended pun, tossed the hammer to the ground, and picked up the gun. "But you're not going to be smart for long. No sir, you're going to be the first one to go." He aimed the gun at the marshal. Mike closed his eyes.

Burly's grip loosened. Mike opened his eyes to see the gun slip from his hand and fall to the ground. He stepped back and watched everything happen in slow motion. Burly hunched over and hovered for several seconds, fell to his knees, and his face slammed into the ground. A long, glass shard with a white cloth handle protruded from his back.

Mike turned. Steven stood behind him staring at the glass knife.

Marshal Smart picked up his gun and shoved it back in its holster. "You boys okay?"

"Jim's in that pit," Mike shouted. "You've got to save Jim."

Chapter 29

A HEROES' WELCOME

Mike and Steven spent Monday and Tuesday nights in the hospital. The doctor recommended they rest at home and not return to school at all since only eight school days remained. They ate, visited with family and friends, and answered what seemed like hundreds of questions for the police.

Mike found sleeping difficult. He'd lay awake for hours trying to rid his mind of thoughts of the kidnapping, and when he finally did fall asleep, he always dreamed the same dream.

His back rests against a hard concrete wall in a locked dynamite shed as he stares at the door. Metal sounds against metal, the door opens, and Burly Thompson stands there waving a hammer. Mike realizes he's asleep, and if he can only wake up, he'll be safe in his own bed instead of being mutilated by Burly.

His sleeping mind races against the clock. He has to shake himself awake before Burly can bash his head in. He concentrates on his little fingers first. Move fingers. Now the rest of his fingers. Move fingers, hurry. *Burly steps toward him.* Now the hands. Shake hands. Now the arms. Move arms. *Burly takes another step.* Slam the fists into the mattress. Harder. Harder. Got to wake up. *Burly stands over him with the hammer raised high.* It has to happen now, or it'll be too late. Sit up. Now!

His body shoots up to a sitting position, and he stares in sweat-soaked pajamas at his own bedroom door. He made it. He's safe. Then he falls asleep and dreams the nightmare again.

Over and over the nightmare came. He never mentioned his frightening dreams to his parents or Grandpa. They were happy he was back, and he didn't want to snatch that happiness from them by having them

185

worry about his nightmares.

Every day he felt a little better, and he was adjusting to the reality of being safe at home instead of being locked in a shed and threatened with death. Still, he couldn't shake the feeling that something was missing.

Then Miss Schneider stopped by to see him.

He was sitting on the living room couch staring off into space and thinking of nothing in particular when he heard the knock. Grandpa answered the door. "Why, Miss Schneider. Good to see you. How's Steven?"

She stepped inside. "He's coming along pretty good. Making an eleven-year-old boy rest is nigh to impossible."

Martha entered the room, drying her hands in a towel. "Oh, hi, Miss Schneider. Did you bring homework for Mike?"

"No. I didn't," she said, "but I do want to talk with him about the last day of school."

Martha swung the towel over her shoulder. "Have a seat. Can I fix you some iced tea?"

Miss Schneider sat in the chair across from Mike. "No, thanks. I can only stay a few minutes." She straightened her skirt and leaned forward. "Mike, you may know I haven't been back to school since you boys were kidnapped. Well, the last day of school is the day after tomorrow. I plan to teach that last day, and if I'm going to be there, I expect all my students who are able, to be there, too. You don't have to make up work you missed, but I expect to see you in school on Friday. Do you understand?"

Mike stammered. "But ... but the doctor said I should stay home and rest."

"I know what the doctor said." She stood. "I discussed the situation with him this morning, and he agreed attending school the last day would be the best medicine for you. After all, how can we honor heroes at school Friday if they're not there?"

She opened the door and hesitated. "Oh, one more thing. Bring Squall Baby."

***

Mike waited on the sidewalk in front of the screened-in porch dangling a shopping bag and watching Steven walk toward him. Friday, May 21, 1954, a day that will live in infinity, had finally arrived. For the first time in his life a reason existed for Heidi to like him. He was a hero, or at

186

least Miss Schneider said he was. Everyone likes heroes, don't they?

It had taken some doing, but Mike had convinced his parents he should be allowed to walk to school with Steven on the last day. Mike told Steven his mom's counter proposal involved three armed sharpshooters driving him to school in a tank. The boys did have to promise not to take the secret woods route.

Mike waved at the approaching fellow hero. "Hey, Steven."

"Hey, Mike." He quickened his pace.

"Don't forget. We're supposed to pick up Squall Baby."

"I know. What will we carry her in? The portable cage is busted."

"Not anymore." Mike pulled the cage from the bag he carried and held it up. "Grandpa fixed it, see? It looks just like it did before."

Steven inspected it. "It looks even better."

Mike stuck it back in the bag. "Grandpa said Squall Baby shouldn't be cooped up in a shoebox when she was being honored. He said heroes shouldn't have to spend a single minute in a shoebox."

Squall Baby pranced and cooed when the boys opened her cage. She must have spent extra time preening because her feathers never looked smoother. "This time you get to go inside the school and meet everyone." Mike placed her in the portable cage and shut the door. He folded the bag and tucked it under his belt. "Grandpa said to be sure to put the bag under the cage at school."

Steven held the cage at eye level and gazed into the pigeon's red eyes. "That's right. You're going to be honored as a hero just like we are."

Mike took the cage from Steven. "She's a bigger hero than we are. Without her, we wouldn't even be here today. We'd be in that pit— probably dead."

"True. But if we hadn't figured out a way to write that message, she wouldn't have had it to carry. I guess we're all heroic."

Heroic. Mike liked the sound of that word, and it echoed in his head. Heroic. Heroic. Heroic. Not everyone gets to be called heroic. Not everyone has a special day to have his heroic deeds recognized. He grinned. "I never thought I'd say it, but I'm looking forward to school today."

"Me, too. Aunt Shirley has some surprises planned."

"Yeah? Like what?" Mike shifted the cage to the other hand.

"Can't tell you. If I did, they wouldn't be surprises."

"Come on, Steven." Mike scrunched up his face and stuck out his lower lip in an attempt to look pitiful. "After all we've been through, you can tell me."

"I'm not going to tell." Steven locked his lips with an invisible key and pretended to throw it away.

Mike laughed and shoved him. "I know why you won't tell."

"Why?"

"Because she didn't tell you what they were, either. Did she?"

Steven stuck his nose in the air. "I'm not telling. Maybe she did, and maybe she didn't."

"In other words ... "

"She didn't. She said she didn't want to ruin it for me, either."

Mike peered ahead. Only six blocks separated them from where the Last Day of School Heroes Celebration would take place. "I wish Jim could be with us today."

"Me, too. Do you think he's going to be okay?"

"Sure." Mike forced a smile. "It might take a while, but Jim's going to be just fine."

Steven looked at him with serious eyes. "How do you know?"

"Because he's Jim, that's why. He just has to make it."

They walked a block in silence. "You going to tell her today, Mike?" Steven asked.

"You mean tell Heidi how I feel about her?"

"Yeah. About how you've liked her ever since first grade."

Mike looked straight ahead. "Yeah, I'm going to tell her."

"Bet you'll chicken out again. You're always going to tell her, and you always chicken out."

"Not this time. I know today's the day because if I can't tell her on the day I'm being honored as a hero, I'll never be able to."

"Want to put a little wager on it? If you don't tell her, I win. If you do, you win."

Mike shrugged. "I don't know. Like what?"

"How about a dollar?"

Mike scrunched his nose. "No. That's way too much."

"How about a quarter?"

"That's still too much."

"Okay. How about baseball cards? I'll tell you what. If you tell her, I'll give you my Stan Musial card. If you don't, you give me your Mickey Mantle. Deal?" Steven held out his hand to seal the bet.

"I don't know. I think I might be getting a bad deal."

Steven laughed. "How can you say that? Stan the Man has been a great player for over ten years. Mickey's been playing in the big leagues for only three years. If anyone's getting a bad deal, it's me. I'm just trying to give you a little extra incentive to tell her."

"I don't know—"

"Besides, my Stan the Man is a brand new card with current statistics. Your Mickey Mantle card must be three years old. Not only does it not have current statistics, it has hardly any."

Mike thought for a moment. "Okay. I guess that's fair. If I tell her, I win." They shook hands and walked faster toward the school and the celebration in their honor.

Elaborate decorations hung everywhere in the fifth grade classroom. A huge banner that stretched the full length of the room just above the windows read, "Welcome back Jim, Mike, and Steven." Handwritten signs taped to four different windows honored them individually. "We missed you, Jim." "We missed you, Mike." "We missed you, Steven." "Welcome, Squall Baby."

Miss Schneider had shoved her desk close to the windows to make room for four student desks lined up next to one another. Instead of facing toward the front of the room like the others, they faced toward the back. She'd placed a card with a hero's name printed in careful handwriting on each desk: "Jim," "Mike," "Steven," and "Squall Baby."

Colorful flowers filled the room with sweet smells that mixed with the usual musty book odor. The aroma of freshly baked cookies joined the mix from atop the long table under the windows that usually held encyclopedias and dictionaries. Today they lay heaped on the floor.

Miss Schneider and all the students except Skip were already in the room. He burst through the doors, bumped Mike as he ran toward his seat, and slowed when he saw Miss Schneider. "Sorry. I forgot we were supposed to get here early today."

"Not a problem, Skip," she said. "I'm just glad you got here in time to help sing our special song." As soon as he sat, Miss Schneider motioned for the class to stand. She moved her arms like John Philip Sousa, and they sang a well-rehearsed *For They Are Jolly Good Fellows.*

She motioned for the class to sit and turned to the heroes. "Welcome back. Please notice that I have established a new row of desks in your honor." She pointed to the desk nearest the door with the pigeon's name on the place card. "Put Squall Baby there."

189

Mike placed Squall Baby's cage on the desk, and the students clapped. They clapped again when the boys sat in their designated chairs.

Miss Schneider faced the class. "Jim isn't physically with us today, but he is with us in spirit. Just like Steven, Mike, and Squall Baby, he is also a hero."

She picked up a large, framed picture of Jim she had borrowed from Donna Mackey and placed it on his new desk. "Let's hear it for Jim." Mike and Steven clapped along with the rest of the class.

"The celebration will start at one o'clock. Until then, we'll have school as usual. I've been looking over the math work you've done while I was gone, and for the most part it's not bad." She looked toward the grasshopper row. "I'm especially pleased with your improvement, Skip." He grinned.

Did Heidi just look at me in an adoring way? She's beautiful. She'll always be beautiful. Steven may as well give me that Stan Musial card right now.

***

Miss Schneider raised her voice to be heard above the students coming in from noon recess. "Sit down, everyone. Take your seats so we can begin our special program."

She waited for silence and then motioned for Mr. Jackson, Sheriff Conners, and Marshal Smart to come in from the hallway. They sat in three folding chairs she'd set up in front of the room between the windows and the heroes' desks.

"Class, you of course know Mr. Jackson." He gave a little wave. "And this is Mr. Conners, the county sheriff. He and his deputies worked with Marshal Smart—" she pointed him out—"who coordinated the local police effort to bring the boys home. Well, actually, he was the local police effort."

She waited for the cheering to stop and turned back to the men. "I believe Mr. Jackson wants to say something at this time."

Mr. Jackson rose and stood behind the heroes. "We are here to honor three special boys and one special bird," he said slowly. "I'll not make a long speech. I just want to say these three boys are everything one would hope boys would be. Honest. Resourceful. Determined. Brave. I can use those words to describe Squall Baby, too."

He patted the boys' shoulders. "Boys, today is your day. May you long remember it. Jim is unable to be with us today, but we all look forward to his return next fall." He nodded to the class. "Thank you."

The students gave the three boys and one pigeon a standing ovation even greater than the one they had given Skip when he correctly answered the math question. Miss Schneider held up a hand for silence.

"Children, help yourselves to cookies and punch. Mr. Jackson, Sheriff Conners, Marshal Smart, and I will pour the punch and hand out plates and napkins."

The students drank punch and ate cookies as they moved around. They talked with Mike, Steven, and a cooing Squall Baby. After a while they gathered in groups of three and four throughout the room.

Acting as if he were looking around the room at nothing in particular, Mike allowed his eyes to seek out Heidi. She was talking with Mary, but she glanced up at that moment and motioned for him to sit in the empty desk next to her. Mike swallowed hard, left his special desk, and sat next to her and Mary.

Mary looked around. "Oh, uh, excuse me. I'm going to get some more punch, and I see some people I need to talk to."

Mike and Heidi were all alone in the room full of people. Suddenly, tears streamed down her face. She pulled a handkerchief from her desk and dabbed at her eyes. "I worried about you, Mike. I'm so happy you're back."

"You worried about me?"

"I cried every night."

"You cried? For me?"

"Every night. I prayed for you. I prayed God would bring you and Steven and Jim back. I missed you all so much." She paused. "I missed you the most."

He looked away. "Well, I—your prayers must have helped. Maybe we wouldn't have made it without them. I ... I missed you, too."

A man in uniform came to the doorway and motioned for Sheriff Conners. They stepped into the hall and talked quietly, and the sheriff motioned for Mr. Jackson to join them. The conversation continued.

It's now or never. They call me a hero. Heidi cried for me.

"Heidi ... "

"Yes?" Her voice was soft and beautiful, like a song.

"I have something important to tell you. I've wanted to tell you for a long time."

"Yes?" She looked directly into his eyes.

"Heidi, ever since I saw you in first grade—"

Mr. Jackson walked briskly to the front of the room. "Attention, everyone. May I have your attention please? I have something important to tell you. Please take your seats as quickly and quietly as possible."

Mike watched small groups disappear as students returned to their seats. Mr. Jackson's jaw appeared stiff, like Grandpa's when he had something very important to say.

"Mike?"

He turned back to Heidi.

"What were you going to tell me?"

All the students had moved back to their seats in response to Mr. Jackson's request except Mike and the girl whose desk he had taken. She stood over him, waiting for him to leave. Well, she'd just have to stand there. This was his day, and he was going to tell Heidi about his feelings, no matter what. The girl finally left and sat in Mike's special desk in the front of the room.

He took a breath. "Heidi, ever since I saw you in first grade ... "

Mr. Jackson's voice wavered, and he spoke barely above a whisper. "Jim Mackey died this morning."

Chapter 30

THE GIFT

Less than twenty-four hours had passed since Jim's funeral. Mike, his parents, Grandpa, and Steven sat on the front porch, each lost in thought. Heat and a blast of supersaturated humidity forced sweat to soak their clothing, even though they sat in the shade. The only things moving on the porch were folded sections of *The Evansville Courier* and the arms that moved them, turning them into fans.

Grandpa squinted at someone approaching in the distance. "Say, who is that yonder?"

Martha's knitting needles slowed, and she looked up. "I'll tell you who it is. That's Donna Mackey and Betsy."

A look of recognition crossed Grandpa's face. "Ah. I do believe you're right. I wonder what Donna's carrying and where they're headed."

The needles moved furiously again. "If she's smart, she'll move in with her mother in Louisville. She's already lost one child. If she's not careful she'll lose Betsy, too."

"Martha. That's not a nice thing to say. She's just lost a son."

"You're right, Grandpa. She has lost a son. I know it's hard. I'm just saying if she moves in with her mother, she might not lose her daughter, too."

Grandpa flashed Martha a look. "Shhh. She's coming this way. She'll hear."

Donna and Betsy waved, and their shoe soles clippity-clopped up the red-brick sidewalk. Donna carried Squall Baby's portable cage. The bird bobbed up and down inside to the beat of Donna's steps and occasionally flapped her wings to keep her balance.

Grandpa stood. "Donna and Betsy. Well, I declare. Taking Squall

193

Baby for a walk, I see. How are you two making it?"

"Okay. We're making it okay."

Mike had heard his mother say people looked *haggard* when they were really tired. Donna Mackey certainly looked haggard. The areas below her eyes were dark and her crow's feet were much more noticeable than usual. She appeared to need a long, restful sleep.

"Come on in and sit for a spell."

Donna creaked the door open. She sat in the chair by the swing Mike had vacated and placed the portable cage on her lap. Mike lifted Betsy and placed her on the swing, and Grandpa touched her shoulder. "How about you, young lady? How are you?"

"Sad." She looked at Mike. "There's still no magic rock, is there?"

"No. I'm afraid not, Betsy. I wish there were. I'd use it in a heart-beat to bring Jim back."

Grandpa rubbed Betsy's hair. "It's not easy losing someone you love. But everything's done for a reason. Did you know that, Betsy?"

"What do you mean?"

"Well, God must have needed Jim real bad to call him home when he's so young."

Betsy frowned. "But why would God need Jim, Grandpa? Why would God need anyone when He's God?" She sat quietly, waiting for the answer. Donna's eyes fixed on Grandpa as if she also needed to hear the answer to Betsy's question.

"Well, I don't know, Betsy. There could be a lot of reasons. He's a special boy, you know. Maybe God saw how well he took care of Squall Baby and the rest of his pets and decided He needed him to take care of heaven's animals."

"There are animals in heaven?"

"Sure there are, Betsy. Not a lot, but there are some. Only very special animals go to heaven. Do you remember Doodles?"

"Sure. Is he in heaven, too?"

Grandpa stroked her hair. "Sure he is, and Jim's probably taking care of him right now. You know, giving him food and water and petting him. Years and years from now when you join Jim in heaven, you can help take care of Doodles."

"Really, Grandpa?"

"Really, Betsy. You see Squall Baby there? She's very special, too, isn't she?"

"Yes, she sure is. Jim always said there wasn't another pigeon like her in the whole world."

"Oh, he was right. And one of these days she'll join him and Doodles in heaven, and Jim will take care of her, too."

Betsy fixed her blue eyes on Grandpa and leaned her head against his arm. "What's another reason God needs Jim?"

"Another reason?"

"You said there were lots of reasons. Besides taking care of the animals, what's another reason?"

Donna appeared to want to hear the answer to Betsy's second question, also.

"Well, I don't know. Maybe He needed him to tell all my boyhood friends down at the ol' swimming hole he knows where I am. And that as soon as I get tired of making a fool out of myself here, I'll join them. Jim's probably swimming with them and having a good ol' time right now."

Betsy smiled. "Really, Grandpa?"

"Yep. I think Jim is up in heaven where he's safe and happy."

Betsy reached up and hugged his neck. "Thank you, Grandpa. I love you."

"I love you too, honey."

Donna touched his hand. "I'd like to thank you, too, Grandpa. Thank you for being a special friend to my kids when they needed help."

"I didn't help them, Donna. They helped me."

"Whatever that special relationship was, thank you."

Donna turned to Mike and Steven. "I want to thank you boys, too, for being Jim and Betsy's friends. You're good boys."

Mike and Steven managed to say "thanks." Mike wanted to say a lot more, but that's the only word he could force out.

"Martha and Charles, thank you for sharing Mike and Grandpa with us. I know that was difficult at times, especially for you, Martha. I mean, with your position in the PTA and all."

"It ... it wasn't hard." Martha paused for several seconds and then looked up at Donna. "Really."

"Jim was an adventurous boy, always on the go like Tom Sawyer. He's always been that way, very independent. I loved that in him because that was what made him Jim. Lord, I miss him." She covered her face with her hands and rubbed her eyes. "I'm sorry. I didn't want to cry. I wanted to be strong for Betsy."

195

Mike's mom reached over and hugged Donna. She hardly ever hugged anyone, but she and Donna held a long, sincere hug that ended with pats on the back. "I'm sorry Jim's gone. I know how terrible I would feel if I lost Mike. Jim was a fine boy."

Donna fidgeted with the portable cage. "I'm glad you feel that way, Martha, because I have a huge favor to ask of you."

"You have a favor to ask of. . . *me?*"

"Yes." Donna peered into the cage and watched Squall Baby for several seconds. "Betsy and I are moving."

Grandpa let out a sharp gasp. "You don't say."

"Yes. We're moving to Louisville to live with my mother. She's been after me for a long time to do that, but I didn't because Jim and Betsy loved it here and had you boys for friends." She nodded toward Steven and Mike. "I just didn't have the heart to take that away from them. But after Jim died, I did a lot of thinking. I can get a factory job, and mother can look after Betsy. I'll be able to offer her so much more if we move."

"I don't understand how I can help," Martha said.

"Well, it's this. My mother lives in an apartment, so we can't take Squall Baby with us. She needs a good home, a special home." She held up the portable cage. "Betsy and I would like Mike to keep Squall Baby. I know Jim would have wanted him to keep her, too."

Silence seized the moment and held on. Mike shut his eyes. In situations like this his mom usually embarrassed him by saying something that made those around her feel uncomfortable or hurt. He'd stick his fingers into his ears to blot out her response if he could, but it would be too obvious.

"Mike?"

He opened his eyes. "Yes, Mom?"

"Do you want to keep Squall Baby?"

"Can I? I've watched Jim take care of her. I know I can do a good job." He held his breath and waited for the answer.

Martha reached out, took the portable cage from Donna, and handed it to Mike. "I'd be honored for Mike to have Squall Baby."

Donna's face brightened. "Thank you, Martha. I'll have someone bring her coop over later this evening."

Grandpa held his hand in front of him. "Don't bother with that. You've got too many other things to do, what with getting ready to move and all. Mike and I will get it later."

Donna stood. Betsy, looking sadder than Mike had ever seen her, stood next to her mom. "Thank you, Grandpa," Donna said. "Thank you all for everything. God bless you."

Donna and Betsy left. Mike took Squall Baby from the portable cage and petted her. "I can't believe she's mine now. She means a lot to me because she belonged to Jim."

Grandpa began swinging. "I'm sure Jim's glad you'll be taking care of her. You know, he'd want you both to continue having adventures with Squall Baby."

"He would?" Steven reached over and petted her.

"He certainly would. In fact, I'll bet every time you three have adventures, Jim will watch from heaven. It would be almost like having him with you."

Mike looked up. "It would be, wouldn't it?"

"Mike, you have a very important job. As Squall Baby's new owner, you are now the Keeper of the Bird. That's not an easy job, and a lot of responsibility goes along with it."

"I know."

"You have a very important job, too, Steven."

Steven shook his head. "No I don't, Grandpa. Mike has Squall Baby. I don't have a job."

Grandpa stopped swinging, and his jaw stiffened. "That's where you're wrong. Mike will be very busy taking good care of Squall Baby. That means someone else has to be in charge of planning all of the secret missions. That's your job."

"What about Mike? Won't he plan missions, too?"

"I'm sure he'll have some good ideas now and then to help out, but as The Commander, you'll have the final word."

Steven stared up at Grandpa. "As the what?"

"The Commander. You both have very important jobs."

***

Within a week, all of the neighborhood kids called Steven *The Commander*. The nickname's popularity spread, and within a few months after sixth grade began, all the kids and some of the teachers called him by his nickname. From that point on until he graduated from high school, everyone, even his Aunt Shirley, called him The Commander. After a few years most people didn't even know his real name, nor did they think about it because his nickname seemed so right.

Squall Baby died three years later on June 16, 1957, shortly after Mike and The Commander finished eighth grade. They buried her under the big oak in Mike's backyard. The Commander, in his last official Squall Baby related duty, was in charge of the funeral. He insisted it be exactly like the one they had for Doodles.

Martha attended Squall Baby's funeral and didn't seem to care if someone saw her all dressed up to watch a pigeon being buried. She even joined in when Grandpa led the singing of *Amazing Grace*. When Mike gave the eulogy he said he had lost one of his best friends, and he'd never forget her just as he'd never forget Jim. He pulled a piece of paper from his billfold and read from it the eulogy he had written for Doodles. It seemed as appropriate for Squall Baby as it had for the rooster.

The Commander thanked Squall Baby for saving his life and said when someone dies, something good should come from it. He promised he'd dedicate his life to her memory and become the very best air force officer possible, so he could help defend the United States from enemies everywhere.

Chapter 31

SAYING GOODBYE AND HELLO

M ike pulled into the Weber Funeral Home parking lot and parked in a space next to a car with government license plates. About ten years earlier the new funeral home, which overlooked beautiful Lake Stella not far from the Beemer Baptist Church, replaced the old one that was located downtown. Several tall, white columns graced the red-brick building's long porch, and grass so green it appeared blue stretched from the building to the street. A five-foot-wide strip of crushed red rock with a white brick border surrounded the building. Evergreen bushes painstakingly trimmed like champion poodles lined up like wooden soldiers, standing tall in the crushed rock.

Cars already packed the large parking lot, and vehicles continued pulling in. Many who walked toward the funeral home wore military uniforms with decorations and bars of high-ranking officers.

Mike entered the building behind a group of a dozen or so air force officers and immediately smelled a familiar, yet unidentifiable aroma. Several minutes passed before he could sign the guest book and place a card in a slot next to it. The long line inched its way into a large room. He nodded to strangers.

Most of the pews were already full. At this rate, well-wishers would be forced to stand in the lobby and parking lot when services started. Two well-dressed men flanked an open mahogany casket, and a television and a DVD player rested on a cart behind several dozen floral arrangements. Mike took his place in the line that stretched in snakelike fashion to the casket at the far end of the room. He took occasional baby steps.

Sure, that's what the odor smells like. Miss Schneider's room—that book smell. Probably the hymnals.

About a third of the attendees wore dress military attire and looked important. *Another step.* Mary Murphy sat next to a rather handsome man. Must be her husband. She smiled, and Mike said "Hi" by raising both eyebrows. She whispered something to the man and pointed to Mike. *Another step.*

Then he saw her. Heidi! His eyes stopped. He shouldn't stare, but he couldn't convince his eyes to move. With a single exception— her hair was now white—she looked exactly as she did the last time he saw her a few days after high school graduation—petite, sparkling black eyes, beautiful smile and complexion, deep tan. *She's still beautiful. She'll always be beautiful.*

Another step. His legs felt weak and tingly, and he tried to remember when he'd felt that sensation before. They hadn't felt that way since ... since the last time he saw Heidi.

Maybe they'd talk for a few minutes after the funeral, and he'd tell her he enjoyed seeing her again. No, he couldn't just walk up to her and start a conversation. Why, he'd just end up stammering and spouting gibberish like he did when they were kids.

Another step. He never did tell her of his feelings for her. How many times had he tried? Every time, something got in the way. *Another step.* He almost told her the day he was honored as a hero, but Mr. Jackson told the class Jim had died an instant before he could force his feelings into words. After that he just gave up trying, and they drifted farther and farther apart. She dated Tony steadily in high school and even went to the prom with him their junior and senior years. According to Mary, she married a man she met in college and had a child, a girl who would be in her forties now. *God, she's beautiful.*

Heidi glanced in his direction, and he forced his eyes to stare at the bald spot on the back of the man's head in front of him. *Another step ... another step ... another step.*

Finally, he was at the head of the line. "Susan?"

"Yes?" Although slightly plump, Susan was attractive, about five-foot-six with very light blonde hair.

"I'm Mike. Mike Long."

She embraced him. "Oh Mike, thank you so much for coming." Tears trickled down her face, and she wiped them with a tissue from a box in the pew. "I'm sorry. It's just that your being here meant so much to him. He always talked about you. He considered you his very best friend, even though he hadn't seen you for years. Steven talked about you so much, I feel as if I've known you forever, too. Thanks for agreeing to do the eulogy."

Mike held her hand. "I'm happy to do it. I always thought of him as my best friend, too."

She smiled through her tears. "He said finding you before he died meant more to him than all the medals he'd earned." She blotted her eyes with the tissue. "I hope we'll have a chance to talk more later."

"I'm sure we will." Mike stepped toward the casket.

"Oh, Mike," she called, softly.

He turned. "Yes?"

"I just want to tell you this won't be an ordinary funeral service. Steven said he wanted something good to come from his death. He wouldn't even tell me everything he had in mind. He talked long distance with the preacher several times, and they planned the funeral. Just wanted you to know." She turned and talked with the couple behind him.

Mike stood by the casket and focused on the man it contained. The Commander wore an air force officer's uniform. Although he still looked distinguished, cancer had obviously ravaged his body, making him appear gaunt and tired. The couple behind Mike had finished talking with Susan and walked in his direction. He took one last look to etch the image into his mind and sat in the front pew reserved for family and close friends.

The line became shorter until it ceased to be, and one of the well-dressed men closed the casket. The preacher walked to the pulpit and eyed the huge crowd. She was Louise Cruthers-Wallace, the woman he'd met at the thrift store yesterday.

"Welcome friends," she said. "We have gathered to celebrate the life of Steven Lee Culpepper, whom many remember affectionately as The Commander. There is so much in his life to celebrate. He graduated from Potter High School in 1961 and from the Air Force Academy in 1965. He served in the Vietnam War, the Gulf War, the Iraq War, and various other conflicts around the world and received numerous decorations for his valor. At the time of his retirement in 2005 he had attained the rank of Major General. He married Susan Marie Foster on May 12, 1968.

"They had one child, James Michael, who was born in 1973. James died in 1999 when the air force plane he piloted crashed. Today we pay tribute to Steven Lee Culpepper—patriot, husband, father, and friend. He served his country on the battlefield. Now, he serves the Lord in heaven."

The room was quiet, except for the ceiling fans' whispers.

"I first became acquainted with Steven several weeks ago when he asked if I would officiate at his funeral," she said. "Just as he had planned military maneuvers for over four decades, he had already planned his funeral. After listening to what he wanted, I told him I would be honored to help him achieve it. Many phone conversations and e-mails followed. Although I had not met either of them in person, when Steven died, I lost a friend. When Susan arrived, I consoled a friend."

She looked at Susan and smiled. Susan returned the smile through tears. "I now begin Steven Lee Culpepper's funeral as planned by The Commander himself. Please turn to page 316 in the red hymnal and sing *Amazing Grace*."

Mike stood with the others and sang the familiar song. He could almost hear Grandpa's voice mingling in, like he'd heard it at the funerals for Doodles and Squall Baby. When the song ended, Preacher Louise motioned for the two well-dressed men to come forward. They walked in unison to the cart that held the television and DVD player and pushed it to the front of the altar, its wheels chirping in beat to their steps. After angling the cart so everyone could see the television screen, they walked—almost marched—back to their seats.

Louise thanked the men and looked at Mike. "Mike Long, one of Steven's childhood friends, will now give the eulogy."

Mike proceeded to the podium slowly and grasped it with both hands. He looked out at the sea of somber faces and cleared his throat. "I knew Steven ... " He paused. "I'm sorry, but calling him Steven just doesn't sound right to me. Let me start again. I knew The Commander when we were both young boys. I first met him at the old Star Theater in downtown Potter when we were eleven. He was a bully."

A few people laughed tentatively.

"He sat behind me and put popcorn kernels in my hair. Every time he placed one there, I'd flick it off. I didn't know it at the time, but the last thing he put in my hair wasn't popcorn, but bubble gum. I waited for a while before flicking it off, and when I did, he was apparently buying more treats in the lobby. To make a long story short, the bubble gum landed in his seat, and when he came back, he sat smack-dab on top of it. When he got up at the end of the movie a huge, orange blob of bubble gum was stuck to the back of his pants, and he stormed out of the theater one unhappy lad."

Now, everyone laughed. He waited for silence, looking out over the crowd. "From that questionable beginning developed one of the strongest friendships possible. The Commander and I went through a lot together. That year our best friend died, and we became even closer. I could not have loved him more if he were my brother."

Mike pulled a yellowed piece of paper from his billfold, unfolded it, and smoothed it on the podium. The room was silent.

"When the angels created you, they gave you a heart that contained three times the amount of love as usual. God knew you were special and that you had to be where you could best share all that love. That's why He put you here with us. Nowhere else in the world could you have shared more love. We will cherish your memory forever. Thank you for being you, and thank you for loving us."

Silence, so complete every mourner in the Weber Funeral Home that day could have heard a pin drop on one of the cushioned pews, claimed the room.

Mike looked up. "When we were kids we had a funeral for Doodles, our neighbor's rooster. I just read the eulogy I gave at the rooster's funeral. The Commander told me it was beautiful and said he wanted me to give his eulogy when he died. Three years later I read the same eulogy when our special pigeon, Squall Baby, died. For some unexplainable reason, I've carried this piece of paper in my billfold for over fifty years. I believe it describes The Commander as much as it did Doodles and Squall Baby."

He turned to face the casket with tears flowing from his eyes. "Thank you, Commander, for being you, and thank you for loving us. I love you, and I'm glad we were friends. God bless you."

Mike paused and looked at Susan. "And God bless you, too, Susan." He picked up the creased, yellowed paper and walked to his pew.

Preacher Louise returned to the podium. "Thank you, Mr. Long. I'm sure Steven would have loved it." Then, instead of speaking to the entire crowd that had gathered in Steven's memory as Mike expected her to do, she spoke directly to him.

"You remember when we met at the sale yesterday, Mike? When you introduced yourself I realized you were the person who would give Steven's eulogy, but I didn't say anything in fear I would ruin his surprise. He wanted something good to come from his death."

She turned the television and the DVD player on and pressed "play." A recent image of The Commander, wearing a suit and tie and sitting in a chair on a front porch, appeared. He seemed sickly and haggard. He looked at the camera and started talking.

"I'd like to begin by telling Susan I love her." His voice was raspy and weak. "I'm sorry I had to leave you so soon, but I had no say in the matter. Death, it seems, runs not a democracy, but a dictatorship." He kissed his fingertips and blew her a kiss. "I'll love you, Susan, throughout eternity."

The Commander turned his head slightly and acted as if he were looking out at the mourners for the first time. He feigned surprise. "Wow. Nice turnout." He pointed. "I see Colonel Gilpatrick is here." The colonel waved. "You still owe me eighty dollars from the poker game. You can give it to Preacher Louise on your way out, and she'll put it to good use. If you want, you can give her another twenty for interest."

He peered about again. "I see a lot of my military comrades made it today. Thank you for coming to see me off, so to speak. Many of you may wonder why I chose not to have a military funeral. I love the military. I've always been proud of my role as an air force officer. But one day in Iraq, I began to wonder if my efforts had made a difference at all. That day a roadside bomb killed forty-seven people. The day before that, a bomb killed seventeen. The day before that, thirty-six. It goes on and on. The Vietnam War, the Gulf War, Iraq War, the Afghanistan War. After all these and other conflicts, little has changed. People still kill one another in the name of war, and wars yet unnamed will kill even more. That's when I decided to retire and spend more time with Susan. I had done the best I could, and I had made little difference."

The Commander stood, leaning against his chair back for support. "Three years after I retired I learned I had terminal cancer. I always felt something good should come from a person's death. That's why I decided to be buried in the Good Shepherd Cemetery here in Potter, where my friend Jim Mackey was buried years ago. That's why I decided not to have a military funeral. I believe I can make a bigger difference in this world as a friend returning to his small-town roots than I can as an old general who has faded away."

The Commander took a handkerchief from his pocket and wiped his face. He picked up a glass of ice water from a small table next to his chair and took a long drink. He set the glass down and looked up.

"Oh, hi, Mike. Glad you could make it. Already gave the eulogy, huh? Did you tell them how I used to be a bully? I'll bet you did. I hope you also told them how I was a good friend. I want something good to come from my death, Mike, and I need your help. Come on up here."

Preacher Louise pressed the pause button and motioned for him to come forward. What was going on? He'd already given the eulogy. Why would she want him to come forward again? He pointed to himself like Skip did when Miss Schneider selected him for the part of farmer number two in the fifth grade play and said, "Me?"

Preacher Louise nodded. "Yes, you, Mike. Steven would like you to come up here and stand behind the podium again."

He stood and took unsure steps to the altar. When he gripped the podium, she restarted the video.

"Mike, you remember how I thought it would be great to plan one's own funeral? Well, it isn't. In fact, you were right—it's no fun at all. I would much rather be going about my everyday life and have death blindside me. But since death chose to warn me, I've decided to use that information to my advantage. I know now I can't change the world, but I hope I can change the lives of my two dearest friends."

The Commander took another long drink. "You always wanted to tell a certain girl how you felt about her, but something always got in the way. Mike, she's here today. Did you see her? I realize more than fifty years have passed since you last tried to tell her of those feelings. But it's not too late. Now's your chance. I'm in no hurry. I've got all day. In fact, I've got an eternity. And I'm not going anywhere until you tell Heidi Beck how you feel about her." Preacher Louise paused the video again.

Mike moved his eyes slowly until his gaze found Heidi. It was as if a time machine had transported them back to Miss Schneider's room and placed Heidi in the bee row's front seat, her short, wavy hair glistening in the soft light, and him just inside the classroom door. His knees tingled and weakened. He grasped the podium tighter.

"Heidi, what The Commander is referring to is ... when we were young I liked you a lot. Every time I tried to tell you how I felt, something came up. The last time I tried, Mr. Jackson informed us Jim had died. I just never got up my courage again after that."

Preacher Louise restarted the video. "Well, did you tell her when you started liking her?"

Mike took a deep breath. "Heidi, I've liked you from the time I first saw you in first grade until the day I moved away after graduation."

The Commander spoke again. "Now, ask her out for dinner

tonight. I'll know something good came from my death if you two have a nice little dinner together tonight and discuss old times."

Mike leaned on the podium and spoke softly. "Heidi, may I take you out to dinner tonight? And discuss old times?"

She nodded.

The time machine whisked them back from Miss Schneider's classroom to the Weber Funeral Home, and every person who had come to celebrate Steven Lee Culpepper's life applauded. The applause exploded into a standing ovation that eclipsed the one for Skip when he answered the math question correctly and the one for the heroes Miss Schneider honored in the spring of 1954. When the ovation finally ended, Preacher Louise handed Mike an envelope. "Steven wanted you to have this."

Mike took it from her and walked back to his pew. He opened it and pulled out a folded piece of paper. He unfolded it, to reveal two words The Commander had written. "You win."

He inspected the rest of the envelope's contents—two baseball cards protected in plastic—a 1954 Stan Musial card and a Mickey Mantle rookie card—both in the same condition they were in when two eleven-year-old boys owned them over half a century earlier.

***

Mike shut his car door, walked to the passenger side, and helped Heidi out. The moon darted in and out of the fast moving clouds, disappearing, reappearing, and disappearing again.

Heidi took Mike's hand as she stepped from the car and squeezed it. "Thank you for tonight, Mike. I had a great time. It's so good seeing you after all these years."

"I had a good time, too. I hope you weren't too embarrassed. You know, at the funeral." He shut the car door, and they walked up the sidewalk toward her house.

"Actually, I wasn't. It was like seeing you and The Commander as young boys again." She opened the porch door. It creaked.

Mike paused. "Wow. That's a sound from my past."

"What is? I didn't hear anything."

"The screen door. It creaked when you opened it just like our porch door did when I was a kid."

"I guess I've gotten so used to it, I don't even hear it anymore."

She stepped onto the porch and faced him. "Would you like to come in for dessert? I have some homemade cherry pie."

"Could we sit on the porch? I haven't done that in years."

"Sure. How about some of that pie?"

Mike patted his stomach. "I couldn't eat another thing. A Pepsi sounds good, though."

"Sounds good to me, too. I'll be right out. Make yourself at home."

A wooden swing like the one Grandpa used to love caught his eye. He sat in it and pushed it back and forth. Heidi brought two Pepsis in tall glasses. The ice clinked as she walked toward the swing. She handed him a glass and sat next to him. He took a long drink, and tiny bubbles tickled his nose. He rubbed it with his finger. "Good Pepsi. I always did like Pepsi."

"Me, too."

"It's been great seeing you again, Heidi. I'm glad The Commander suggested we discuss old times. I haven't laughed so hard in years."

"Me neither. We did have some good times, didn't we?"

"We sure did." Mike shook his head. "Kids nowadays miss so much. I doubt if parents would let their eleven-year-olds go all over town playing chalk the rabbit anymore. I'll bet most kids have never even heard of the game."

"You're right. Children don't have adventures like we used to have. They spend more time watching television or playing video games." She looked at Mike. "What are you grinning about?"

Mike's grin became bigger. "Oh, nothing really. Just thinking about how happy Mary seems."

Heidi smiled. "She always says her life is like a fairytale. Her knight in shining armor swept her off her feet, and she's living happily ever after."

"That's exactly what she told me yesterday. What about you, Heidi? How have you been?"

Heidi swirled the ice in her glass. "My life's like a fairytale, too." She held the glass still. "I'm Sleeping Beauty waiting for Prince Charming to wake me up with a kiss and sweep me off my feet."

"You mean your Prince Charming hasn't come yet?" He took a couple more swallows of Pepsi.

"Not until tonight."

Mike swallowed hard. He coughed twice, sat without moving for a few seconds, and then coughed again. "Me? I'm your Prince Charming?"

Heidi set her drink on the floor. "It's always been you, Mike. I've always liked you."

"How is that possible? I was just a klutzy kid."

"No, you weren't. You were a sincere, brave, and intelligent boy who should have been sitting with The Commander and me in Miss Schneider's first row."

"But you were so popular in high school. You went with Tony for a couple of years. There never seemed to be room for me."

She touched his shoulder. "There was always room for you. All you had to do was ask. It was you all along, Mike. You were the only one I ever wanted to be with." She paused and looked into his eyes. "You still are."

He pulled back, and Heidi removed her hand. "I'm sorry things didn't work out between us. If I'd gotten my courage up and asked you to sit with me at that 1954 circus, things may have turned out differently."

"They still can. Mike, I'm retiring at the end of this school year. Mary finally convinced me there's more to life than work. I plan to do a hundred things I always wanted to do but couldn't. You could retire, too, and move back to Potter. We could ... do those hundred things together."

For several seconds the only sound was the faint squeaking of the springs overhead as the swing went slowly back and forth. Mike's brain tried to process conflicting thoughts. "Heidi," he said, finally, "I wish things could be different, but I've got too many responsibilities at work. I'm over-seeing a multimillion-dollar national defense grant that has an onsite evalu-ation in a few days. It's all I've been able to think about for weeks. Fewer than half of the grants will be renewed. Our project is too important to become another statistic of a sagging economy. Besides, I'm too old to be a Prince Charming. I'm too set in my ways."

Heidi sat back in the swing. "So, everything The Commander did and said today was for nothing?"

"Not at all. We can still be friends—special friends. We can e-mail each other every day. It's just—well, I'm no Prince Charming."

He stood and pulled her up. "It's getting late. But before I go, let's exchange information."

They each wrote their phone numbers and e-mail addresses on Post-it notes Heidi got from a desk drawer, and Mike folded the one she gave him and put it in his billfold. She followed him to the front porch.

He hugged her. "Goodnight, Heidi. I've enjoyed seeing you again."

"Special friends," she whispered.

The screen door creaked again when he left. He started the car and looked out the window to see her one last time. She was waving. The yellow porch light that glowed behind her gave the illusion of a dream. "I love you," he said in a voice only he heard. He drove to his Princeton motel. Morning would come early.

***

Much had happened in the nearly three weeks since funeral. The spring semester and another school year had ended. Another school year. How many had there been? Maybe too many. The grant renewal was out of his hands now. He and his staff were well prepared, and the reviewers' comments were encouraging. They'd know the outcome within six weeks.

Mike looked forward to Heidi's daily e-mails and frequent phone calls. Work seemed less important since the funeral. Mike thought about his own mortality. He was sitting at his computer when he looked up, and his reflection in the dresser's mirror startled him. Did he really look that haggard? How much time did *he* have left before he'd be swimming with Grandpa in the ol' swimming hole? Twenty years? Ten? Six months? Three days?

He glanced occasionally at the haggard-looking mirror man as he clicked through the digital pictures he took on his Potter visit. When the Morrison Packing Company pictures flashed by, he stopped. Something was terribly wrong.

He studied the images. Sure. That's the problem. The packing plant in the pictures showed no signs of life. No John Deere tractors chugged in the distance, and no doorless trucks sputtered from barn to barn. Instead, broken windows dotted the vacant buildings, and roofs needed repair. Unless someone rescues it soon, it will resemble ancient ruins, just like the old Kaden Coal Mine, with its forsaken buildings standing alone and useless. What did the barefooted woman say at his old house? *It got old. No one cares anymore.*

He looked at the haggard man in the mirror again. *It got old. No one cares anymore.*

He needed something to make him feel young again, to make life meaningful. Hadacol, the magic tonic once purported to cure practically every ailment known to man, hadn't been available for years. But he did notice an advertisement in the Potter Drugstore window that could be just the prescription he needed, an old-fashioned remedy that's not available anywhere else. He'd call the store tomorrow and make arrangements to have it mailed to him.

***

At ten o'clock at night, five days after the haggard man watched him view the pictures, Mike parked in front of Heidi's house in Potter. The full moon did its best to make the night look bright and cheery. He adjusted his glasses and stared at her house. A faint light shone from the living room window. She was still up.

He gripped the door handle. Everything seemed right. For three years he'd given the national defense grant everything he had and was eloquent, if he did say so himself, in presenting the progress to the re-viewers. It was time for younger minds to take over. It was time to retire. Like Heidi said on the porch after The Commander's funeral, there's more to life than work. He frowned. Where had he heard that before?

Mike stepped from the car and walked toward Heidi's house, patting his shirt pocket just before he reached the porch steps to make sure the drugstore envelope was still there. He rang the doorbell twice, but Heidi didn't answer. He turned and went back down the steps, and was halfway to his car when a flash of light struck him from behind.

"Is someone there?"

He turned. "It's me. Mike."

"Mike?" A barefooted Heidi walked to him. "I'm sorry. I was watching television, and I must have fallen asleep. It's really good to see you, but I'm surprised you're here."

"I'm surprised I'm here, too. All I know is living in Wisconsin just didn't seem quite right any more. Driving four hundred and fifty miles to Potter and standing in front of your house talking with you at ten o'clock at night somehow does."

Dimples appeared on both sides of her smile. "I understand exactly what you mean."

"I'm glad you do because I don't understand it at all. Heidi—I need to clear up something I said at The Commander's funeral. Some-thing that wasn't true."

She looked puzzled. "You said something that ... wasn't true?"

"I did. I said I liked you from the time I first saw you in first grade until the day I moved away after graduation. The truth is I *loved* you from

210

the first time I saw you and I've *never stopped* loving you." He pulled the Potter Drugstore envelope from his shirt pocket, removed two pieces of paper, and held them up. "This is something we should have done over fifty years ago."

"What are those?"

"Tickets for tomorrow afternoon's kids' day circus performance. Will you sit with me?"

She hugged him. "Oh, Mike. I'd love to. I wouldn't want to sit with anyone else."

He put his arms around her and held her tight.

"I love you," she whispered.

He looked into her eyes. "I love you, too, Heidi. Always have."

For the first time they kissed, and their embrace united two shadows in the moonlight.

About the author

Mike McNair

    Retired after thirty-nine years in education as an English teacher and as a high school counselor, Mike McNair now spends most of his time writing. Since May 2005 he has penned "Mike's World," a biweekly humor column for Midwest News (www.mwnews.net) an online newspaper that serves southwest Wisconsin and northeast Iowa. He has written over a hundred editions of the Hooticat Newsletter, a tongue-in-cheek e-publication that he sends out to annoy relatives. Mr. McNair has two adult children and lives in Richland Center, Wisconsin with his wife, Nancy.

LaVergne, TN USA
21 September 2010
197903LV00001B/13/P

9 780982 588680